FORGOTTEN GODS #1

USA TODAY BESTSELLING AUTHOR

TATE JAMES

Feral Magic

Forgotten Gods Book 1

Copyright © 2019 by Katrina Fischer

Cover Art © 2019 Amanda Carroll

Book design by Inkstain Design Studio

All rights reserved.

Feral MAGIc

For Amanda,
Thank you for answering all my questions
about the Yurok tribe!

CHAPTER
ONE

"Could this day seriously get any worse?" I screamed, throwing my phone onto the passenger seat in anger before slamming my forehead on the steering wheel and letting the horn sound a long and angry note.

It'd all begun before the sun was even up on the horizon. My cat of eighteen years, Willow, had finally succumbed to old age and passed away in her sleep. After crying for a solid hour, I'd had to box her up and bury her under the rose bushes at my best friend Meg's house, seeing as my landlords were stuck up bastards who refused to let me plant in the small yard of my rented house.

Next, my boss called to say they would be cutting back my hours because the store wasn't busy enough to support so many staff. And by cutting back, he apparently meant completely. Fired.

I was fired.

Then, in a bid to cheer myself up, I'd gone to the salon to get my pastel purple hair touched up and ended up somehow walking away with a hot pink eyesore. Served me right for accepting an appointment with a trainee.

All things considered, I'd been feeling pretty crappy already when the call came asking for my help. I hadn't even blinked twice before saying yes to a kitten rescue mission in Texas—a full thirty-four hour drive from my home in Portland.

Now, a full six hours into my journey, I regretted my hasty decision to leave.

Growling obscenities under my breath, I leaned over and fished around for where my phone had landed. My fingers gripped the flat-screened device like it was evil incarnate, and I ground my teeth hard as I hit redial.

Remember those pretentious asshole landlords I'd mentioned? They'd just called to say I was being evicted.

"Mom?" I snapped when she answered the phone in her irritatingly sweet voice. "You can't just evict me like I'm some sort of squatter behind on rent. That's *my home!*"

"No, Margaret, it's an investment property for your father and I. We only let you live there while it was a good *investment*." My mother paused, and I could picture her lips pursed as she fiddled with her pearl necklace. Not the fun sort, either.

I rolled my eyes so hard I swear I almost pulled an eye muscle. "Please stop calling me that," I groaned. "My name is Cleo. Has been ever since I was five years old."

Prudence, my straight-laced, blond-haired, blue-eyed, suburban-housewife mother, snorted in disgust. "Because Meg decided all girls from Egypt must be related to Queen Cleopatra? That's both ridiculous and awfully racially insensitive. Margaret is a beautiful name, darling, it suits you."

"Whatever," I muttered, feeling like I was fifteen again. "Point is, you can't just kick me out while I'm not even in the state. There must be laws against that or something."

Prudence hummed a noise under her breath, and I knew I was screwed. "Well, I'm sure there would be if you'd ever signed a lease. But given that we never drew up legal papers, we can *legally* do anything we like." She paused to let that sink in, and I scrambled for words. "Margaret, darling, we aren't just throwing you out into the gutter. You can stay here with me and Dad until you find something else, but unfortunately we won't reconsider on the sale of your house."

"Hah! You just called it *my* house!" I crowed and heard my mom tsk.

"Figure of speech. The offer we received for the house was more than generous, and we'd be mad to turn it down. I'll have all your things packed up and moved over here to your old bedroom so it's all ready when you get back from this ludicrous road trip you're on. Won't that be fun?" The distracted tone of her voice told me I'd already lost this battle; she wasn't even paying attention to me anymore. "Honey, I have to go; my cookies are burning. You stay safe in Tennessee, okay?"

"Texas, Mom," I sighed. "I'm going to Texas."

"Mm-hmm, okay, bye now." She had hung up the phone before I could respond, and I was left looking at my blank screen.

Well, fuck.

Now I had no cat, shitty, neon-pink hair, and nowhere to live.

That last part wasn't totally true, though. I threw a glance over my shoulder at the awesome, retro house-bus that I was driving. It was a vintage, hippie thing that I'd fallen totally in love with when I'd seen it at a junkyard and had spent several years doing it up for the exact purpose I was using it for now.

I'd become a volunteer kitten rescuer a while back, and it'd quickly become obvious I needed some mobile accommodation to keep my costs down when on these long drives across the country, so my bus had become the perfect thing.

"I guess I could live in this for a while," I muttered to myself, my fingers rubbing my necklace pendant over and over in a nervous habit I'd had since childhood. "Not that I have many other choices."

Sighing heavily, I clicked my seat belt back on and turned my ignition key to start the temperamental old bus.

"Come on, Jack," I pleaded as the engine spluttered and died, over and over. "Don't do this to me, not now. Come on, old friend, *start!*"

Seconds later, it became painfully clear that I'd jinxed myself. Yes, Cleo, yes, today *can* get worse, and it just had.

"Fuck!" I screamed, smacking my forehead against the horn

over and over, beeping in time with my curses as I repeated, "Fuck, fuck, fuck, fuck, fuck."

This routine could have gone on and on—given I had no idea what the hell to do next—if not for a knock on my window halfway scaring some pee out of me. Okay, more than halfway. But it was only a little, and that knock had seriously given me a fright!

"What?" I barked, glaring up at the person who'd intruded on my temper tantrum. The late afternoon sun was directly behind them, so all I could see was a shadowy outline as I squinted up.

The person didn't respond, and it took me a moment to realize I needed to open my damn window in order to be heard. As quickly as I could—which was not very quick, given the age of my van—I rolled down the manual window a few inches then repeated my less than polite, "What?"

"Did you need some help, ma'am?" the unnaturally handsome man asked in a gentle, polite voice. "Looks like you've broken down."

I frowned, bringing a hand up to shade my eyes and see him better. "What makes you say that? I could just be taking a nap or checking directions or something."

Okay, yeah. I *was* broken down, but I didn't exactly have smoke pouring out of my engine or anything, so this guy was making assumptions that really only a serial killer or rapist might make.

"Of course," he agreed, giving me a lazy smile with his startlingly attractive mouth. "So you don't need any help then? It's still a long way into town, and there's no public transport out here." His voice was warm and inviting with an Australian accent.

Or was it New Zealand? They sort of sounded the same to me, but apparently they say that about Americans and Canadians.

The instinctual desire to decline his help caught on my tongue as I peered at the empty road ahead of me. It was almost dusk, and staying in my van all night wasn't going to get it fixed. I needed to get it to a mechanic or call a tow truck or... something.

"That's okay," I replied with a tight smile. "I'll just call a tow truck. Thanks, though."

He bobbed his head in a short nod and smiled back. "You can try, but Robbie, the mechanic, broke his foot a week or so back and won't let anyone else drive his truck, so you might be waiting a while."

I squinted at him a moment, trying to decipher if he was messing with me or not. When I said nothing, he shrugged and jerked a thumb in the direction of his car parked behind mine.

"I'll just wait in my car a few minutes while you call to check. I'd hate to leave a lady stranded on the side of the road; my mum would never forgive me." His voice *seemed* sincere, and it was awfully hard to distrust that damn accent. Which was stupid as all shit; even I had heard of Ted Bundy.

"Sure," I agreed, waving my phone. "Thanks."

Rolling my creaking window back up, I waited until he was safely back in his car before Googling the nearest mechanic and hitting dial.

The response I got wasn't even a real person; instead an automated voicemail told me that Robbie's Repairs was closed until further notice and to call Burkee Mechanics in the next town over if it was an emergency.

Not yet willing to accept the help of possible-serial-killer yet super-hot Crocodile Dundee, I called the number provided for Burkee Mechanics.

"Not tonight, sweetheart," the wheezy old man told me when I explained my situation. "That's a solid hour's drive from here, and I'm already three whiskeys deep. Leave your van there and hitch a ride into town; I'll pick it up tomorrow and drop it to Robbie's."

I ground my teeth together hard, but didn't argue. No one should support drunk driving, even if they were stranded on the side of the road with Chris Hemsworth's brunette, tanned cousin who may or may not be a psycho killer who wanted to wear my skin as a coat.

"Okay, thanks," I sighed. "I guess I'll speak to you tomorrow?"

"You got it," the man replied before melting into a series of coughs as he hung up the call.

For a long moment I just sat there drumming my fingertips on the steering wheel and pondering my options. What little options there were. I mean, I *could* just sleep in my van and wait for the Burkee Mechanic to get me in the morning... but it was predicted to storm overnight and without my engine, the heating wouldn't work.

Crap dammit. I really hated being cold, too.

Sucking in a deep breath and pulling up my metaphorical big-girl panties, I unbuckled my seat belt and slung my purse over my shoulder. Just to be on the safe side, I double checked that both my pepper spray and switchblade were where I always kept them before opening my door and stepping out.

Shuffling awkwardly from foot to foot, I tugged the hem of my tight tube skirt down from the inappropriate position it had ended up in after five or so hours of driving. The sexy Australian was indeed back in his car and gave me a small nod of acknowledgement before getting out himself.

"Don't worry, babe; I'm not an axe murderer." He gave me a cheeky grin that—*dear fucking lord*—showed a dimple in his cheek. "Scout's honor." He held three fingers up in what I guessed was meant to be a Boy Scout's salute. Not that I had any clue; it could have been the *Star Trek* hand sign.

"Do you even have Scouts in Australia?" I asked with a suspicious frown as I approached him. As much as I wanted to keep my stranger-danger on high alert, I was being quickly worn down by the combination of his accent, the playful mocking in his words, and that goddamned dimple.

Shit, it had really been too long since I'd gotten laid.

"Sure we do," he replied with that sexy smirk. To my surprise, he came around the car and gallantly held the door open for me. "See, they taught me how to be a gentleman and shit."

I narrowed my eyes at him, hesitating just a moment before getting into the car. It was the icy cold breeze hitting my bare legs that ultimately pushed me to trust him not to chop me up into little pieces and bury me in the woods somewhere.

"Thanks," I murmured as he closed the door for me, then jogged back to the driver's side to slide in. "I called the mechanic in Burkee, but he said he couldn't come until tomorrow. If you can just drop me off at a motel or something, I'd be grateful."

"That, I can do," he replied, clicking his seat belt on then peering at me. "I'm Hunter, by the way."

I gave him a smile. He really did have good manners. "Cleo," I introduced myself and took the hand he offered to shake. "Thank you for stopping to help me, Hunter."

"Don't mention it, Cleo," he replied and almost seemed to purr my name. "My mum would smack me upside the head if she thought I'd left a damsel in distress on the side of the road. That's a pretty awesome van you're driving, by the way."

I grinned, admiring my awesome vehicle as we drove past it and accelerated down the open stretch of road. "Yeah, Jack's something special. Unfortunately, just not the most reliable engine. Not like this thing." I drummed my fingertips against the dash of Hunter's Mustang.

"Ah, true. But temperamental engines just add to the adventure of it all, don't you think?" He threw me another one of those lopsided smirks, and I officially gave up thinking of him as a serial killer. If he was... well fuck it, he was the prettiest damn serial killer I'd met.

Not that I'd met many killers... or any... Ah fuck, now I was rambling inside my own head. At least it wasn't out loud?

"You're still thinking I might be a killer, aren't you?" Hunter's smooth, accented voice cut through my slightly manic thoughts, and I clapped a hand over my mouth. It *had* just been in my head, hadn't it?

He laughed then, and I swear I'd never heard a sexier laugh in my entire freaking life.

"Don't worry, you weren't saying it out loud. You just have a super expressive face." He glanced at me quickly before returning his gaze to the road. "So Jack? That's what you call your van?"

Chewing my lip, I turned my gaze out the window while thanking my Egyptian heritage that I didn't blush easily. "Uh-huh, Candy Jack."

I didn't elaborate, but when I glanced back at my sexy savior, he had a small, knowing smile that said he recognized the name as being a pot reference. What could I say, I grew up in Oregon where stores employed bud-tenders, and I might have been a little bit high when I'd named my candy-turquoise colored van.

"I probably wouldn't count on Gerry actually coming to tow Candy Jack tomorrow," Hunter said after a pause. "He tends to get three sheets to the wind on a Tuesday evening, and is a bit useless until around Thursday. Sorry."

This news was *just* what I fucking needed, and it was only with great effort that I held back my curses in favor of a pained groan instead. "Fantastic," I seethed. "I'm going to need to arrange other transport in that case. Is there a car rental in town?" I'd done a brief stint working for Enterprise Car Rental and knew they had offices freaking *everywhere*. But even they had limits and the town we were approaching was small. Real small.

Hunter confirmed my fears with a shake of his head. "I'm sure someone can help you out, though. There are lots of friendly folk here in Edan. Where are you heading in such a hurry, anyway?"

"Texas," I told him with a grimace. "I volunteer with animal rescues, and there are some kittens due to be killed at the end of the week. I need to get there and pick them up before those bastards gas the poor babies."

As I spoke I shifted in my seat slightly towards Hunter, so I noticed when his jaw clenched and his knuckles tightened on the steering wheel. My mention of the kill shelter in Texas had triggered *something* in him, that was for sure.

"You okay there, Crocodile Hunter?" I attempted humor, but was also considering my options for how to escape a moving car. We were going pretty fast, but the grass beside the road would cushion my fall if I needed to tuck and roll. Wouldn't it?

He barked a laugh, and I saw the tension slip back out of him like it'd never been there in the first place. "Funny," he snickered. "It's been forever since someone has called me that."

It took me a moment to realize his name was Hunter, and I'd just made a Crocodile *Hunter* joke. Wow, I was decently funny without meaning to be.

"Okay, this here is the only accommodation in town. Will you be okay from here?" He slowed his car to a stop outside a dodgy Motel 8. "I actually feel guilty letting you stay here, to be totally honest, Cleo." He peered through the windshield and crinkled his nose in a stupidly sexy sort of way. "I would try and insist you stay at my place, but I know you'd think that was a serial killer move."

I laughed this time, running my fingers through my hot pink hair. "Pretty much. Thanks for the ride, Hunter."

"Anytime, Cleo," he replied, and there was a heated undertone to his voice that made me look back as I opened my door. Had he intended that to sound like a proposition? Maybe it was the accent messing with my head. "There's a bar about two blocks down from here; you can't miss it. They serve pretty decent food, if you're hungry later."

"Was that an invitation?" I blurted out before my mental filter could clamp down on that thought. Could anyone really blame me, though? Hunter was like something straight out of a dirty dream.

A broad grin spread over his face, and I had to pinch my own leg to prevent myself from drooling. "It was a recommendation. But if I happen to be there for a drink around eight, then I'd be offended if you didn't at least say hello."

"Noted." I grinned back and tried to ignore the girlish flutters in my belly. "Thanks again, Crocodile Hunter."

I quickly hopped out of the low car—praying I hadn't just flashed my lace thong to Hunter—then closed the door behind me. Giving him a wave through the window, I turned and made my way into the little reception office.

Somehow, this day had managed to turn itself around in the most unexpected way. Hunter's "recommendation" that I check out the local bar for dinner had me all kinds of excited, so much that I barely even flinched at the dirty room the clerk gave me a key for.

CHAPTER
TWO

Considering I had only grabbed my purse out of Jack and hadn't thought about a change of clothes, I didn't have much getting ready to do before heading out. The short nap I'd taken after watching trashy TV for a couple of hours had left me groggy, so I splashed my face with cold water to try and wake up more.

"Holy fucking cats, you look like a bag of shit, Cleo," I muttered to my reflection in the grimy mirror. Running my fingers through my hot-pink hair, I briefly toyed with the idea of just going back to bed. My mind was made up for me, though, when my stomach rumbled loudly.

Besides, I was only lying to myself if I tried to ignore the flutters of anticipation about seeing Hunter again. Damn sexy man and his adorable dimples...

Rifling through my hippie, fringed handbag, I located the necessary makeup items to look less like a vagrant stranded in the middle of nowhere and more like a sexy, put-together woman.

"Good enough," I told myself when I was finished and used the edge of my pinkie to smear some gloss across my lips. I'd used shimmering gold shadows and inky black liner to highlight what I deemed to be my best feature—my eyes. They were an unusual shade, even for my heritage. Almost cat-like, they were a tawny shade of yellow under some lights. Even more so when I used gold shadows.

Tucking my room key into my bag, I slung the long strap across my body before stuffing my feet back into my beat-up, old combat boots. I was too frugal to take a taxi such a short distance, so I chose to brave the freezing temperatures and power walk my butt down the street. If I was lucky, I'd make it before the impending storm hit.

True to Hunter's directions, the bar was impossible to miss. Two blocks down from the motel, it was possibly the only bar in the entire town. It had flashing neon signs in the window indicating it was open, just in case the loud music and people holding drinks weren't clear enough.

Stepping inside just as the rain started falling, I discovered why the music was so loud. A live rock band was on a small, raised stage, thrashing away on their instruments like they were playing to a stadium. Admittedly, they were damn good, which made me wonder what the hell they were doing in a random, blink-and-you-miss-it town like this.

I made my way across to the bar but couldn't seem to tear my eyes from the band. Or, if I was more specific, from the guitar player. He was, in a word, mesmerizing.

Midnight-black hair fell loose, brushing his broad, strong shoulders, which were covered by a form fitting black top. His skin was bronze, similar to my own, and from where I stood, his eyes seemed almost totally black. He was so tall he would easily dwarf me if I tried to kiss him, considering I was all of five foot four

Why the hell I was picturing myself kissing this total stranger I had no freaking idea. Maybe hunger was making me delirious or something.

"He's pretty good, huh?" A man spoke into my ear, and I jumped, squeaking with fright as I spun around. Hunter stood there, watching me with an amused smirk that made me second guess whether maybe he could read minds.

My gaze flickered back to the band, to the guitar player, before I cleared my throat and gave Hunter my full attention. "Yeah, they're great. How come they're not making it big in LA or somewhere?"

Hunter shrugged, a gesture that was not at all meant to be sexy but managed to draw my attention to his own broad shoulders anyway. What was up with this freaking town? Had I actually died somewhere on my journey and this was heaven?

"They only play for enjoyment; none of them have any interest in making money off it. Besides, they only formed their band a few weeks back." He tipped his head towards the bar. "Have you eaten yet? I was just about to order a burger, if you'd like me to get you one too?"

My belly rumbled its acceptance, which was thankfully drowned out by the loud music. "Sounds great." I nodded.

While Hunter made his way to the bar to order, I snagged a tall table with two bar stools as a middle-aged couple left.

"Good score," Hunter commented as he joined me, carrying a table number and two frosty bottles of beer.

"Beer, huh?" I remarked, taking the offered drink and peering at the label.

Hunter paused with his own drink halfway to his mouth and gave me an uncertain look. "Shit, that was presumptive. Do you even drink?"

As tempted as I was to mess with him and say no, I was genuinely thirsty and not fussy in the least. "It's fine," I assured him with a grin, then took a long sip. "Thanks."

"You're welcome, Cleo," he smiled back, and once again I got the impression he was purring my name. It was the strangest thing, but maybe I'd been spending too much time with cats rather than people.

"Tell me a bit about yourself, Hunter," I prompted after a pause. His gaze on me was just that little bit too intense, like he was reading my mind again, and I needed to break the tension.

"What would you want to know?" he asked, cocking his head

to the side and not taking his eyes off me.

Shifting slightly on my stool, I ran my fingers through my neon hair and averted my gaze back to the band. "I don't know; that's why I'm asking. What is a guy like you doing in a middle-of-nowhere town like this? You're Australian, right?"

I glanced back to him, and he nodded. "Sure am. Sydney boy, born and raised."

"So, how did you end up here?"

Hunter finally took his eyes from me and tipped his head to the stage where the gorgeous, bronzed god was still jamming out on his guitar.

"Came over to visit Raze—that devastatingly handsome bastard on guitar—and just never quite made it home again." There was something off in the way he said this, like the humor had suddenly dropped out of his voice. "Maybe one day I'll make it back."

I raised my eyebrows at him. "Well, that sounds like a story."

He gave me another devastatingly sexy smile and took a long—seriously seductive—sip of his beer. "Story for another day. Why don't you tell me about you, Cleo? You're clearly an animal lover."

"Because I'm on my way to rescue kittens?"

He nodded. "That and all of your tattoos have got animals incorporated somewhere. Or the ones I can see so far do."

I choked a little on the sip of beer I'd just taken, my mind fixating on his suggestion that he might see more of my ink later... with considerably less clothing. Damn, this dude was doing a number on my libido.

"Good call," I replied when I trusted my voice not to sound too sexed up. With my free hand, I rubbed a finger across the foxes on my chest and tried not to think about the big cats woven into the design under my clothes. All that would do was make me picture Hunter taking my shirt off and—

"My best friend, Meg," I explained, "she owns her own tattoo parlor and uses me as a living canvas." I didn't bother explaining that I had been letting her tattoo me in increasingly more obvious places, like my neck or the backs of my hands, because of my intense need to piss off my straight-laced, pearl-clutching mother.

Hunter smiled, his gaze following my finger across my chest ink. "Well, she's a talented artist." He paused then as a waitress arrived and dropped two identical burgers on our table. "Crap, I didn't even ask if you were a meat eater."

With the tip of my finger, I tilted the top bun up on my burger and inspected the heavy meat patty and strips of bacon.

"Quit second-guessing yourself, Hunter," I told him, picking up the whole thing to take a bite. "Love beer and meat. Just 'cause I look like a Portland hipster doesn't mean I'm a vegan."

Hunter snorted a laugh and took a bite of his own burger. For a while, we ate in comfortable silence, listening to the band play and sipping our drinks.

It wasn't until the band took a break that I hopped off my stool and went to grab us more drinks. I'd been nursing an empty bottle for most of the last song but hadn't really wanted to take my eyes off Hunter's friend—Raze.

I paid the bartender for two more beers, then almost dropped the damn things when I arrived back to our table and found the object of my attention casually chatting with the sexy Australian who I was equally as attracted to.

Fucking hell, who knew small towns were the place to meet hot men?

"Cleo, this is Raze," Hunter introduced us. "I was just telling him how I rescued you from the side of the road today."

I dipped my head in a nod, avoiding the stunning man's intense gaze. Up close, his eyes were green but seemed almost backlit, like a wild cat at night.

"Uh, yeah," I mumbled. "I was having a pretty shitty day, so it was a good thing Hunter found me when he did."

There was a bit of an awkward pause, and I could feel Raze staring at me. Or was he glaring? It was really hard to tell without staring back, and for some reason I was too scared to meet his gaze, instead choosing to focus on the ink curling over the back of his hand and up his strong forearm.

"If your day was so shit, why are you drinking this piss water?" he asked me finally, and shock made me glance up. His face was serious, and I couldn't work out if he was joking or not. On closer inspection, I decided he was probably Native American rather than Middle Eastern or North African like me.

"Are you... accusing me of lying?" I spluttered, frowning at the handsome asshole. "I wouldn't make up a day as shitty as I was having. No one could make that crap up."

He shrugged one of those broad, muscular shoulders and quirked a brow. Not once had he blinked that I'd seen. "I'm just saying, you might want something a bit stronger."

Without waiting for my response, he sauntered towards the bar with a sexy swagger, and I caught myself staring at his denim-clad ass the whole way, until Hunter let out a long sigh.

"What?" I feigned innocence, turning back to my new friend.

He rolled his eyes and took a sip of his beer. "You," he replied, "drooling over Raze. Here I was thinking that I might have been in with a chance seeing as I met you first."

This made me choke a little on my own drink again, and I did a bit of a double take to check that he wasn't joking. He was grinning, sure, but did that mean he was kidding? Why was it so damn hard to tell?

"You're kidding, right?" I decided it was easier to just ask rather than assume.

He arched a brow at me. "No, why would I be kidding? That wanker constantly gets the girls. Here I was thinking my accent would work for me, but he has to swoop in all brooding and angry with that gorgeous hair and strong jawline. Ugh. I hate him."

I squinted at Hunter for a moment, feeling like I'd just stepped into an alternate universe or something. Seriously, Allison and her Underland had freaking nothing on the craziness that was Hunter questioning his own attractiveness.

"Okay, now I know you're fucking with me. You look like the

sort of guy who would be a jeans model or an actor or something. Aren't all you Australian men related to the Hemsworths, anyway?" I gave a nervous laugh, grasping at my necklace and rubbing my thumb over the pendant.

Hunter barked a short laugh. "Not quite, but are you saying I'm still in the game here, Cleo?"

"I don't know what *game* you're talking about, but if you're trying to make me say I'm attracted to you, then yeah, I am. You're stupid hot; you both are. Happy?" I tucked my necklace back inside my shirt and picked at the label on my bottle while I desperately searched for a change of subject.

Thankfully, Raze returned then carrying a full bottle of whiskey and four shot glasses, saving me from what was sure to turn into a super awkward conversation. Not that it wasn't already.

"Who's the fourth for?" I asked, curious.

"Boden," Raze replied, then didn't elaborate. He really did have the brooding thing down as he poured out three of the glasses and handed one to me without another word.

Hunter took his and clinked it against mine before downing it in one gulp. "He lives with us," Hunter explained as I drank my own whiskey a little slower. "But I thought he wasn't getting back to town until later tonight?" This question was aimed at Raze who just shrugged.

"So, you three live together?" I asked when it became clear Raze wasn't replying to Hunter about their third friend's whereabouts. It was a dumb question, given Hunter had *just* said as much, but sitting opposite these two was making my brain malfunction.

Again, without really meaning to, my fingers found my necklace and fiddled with the pendant.

"That's an interesting necklace, Cleo," Raze remarked, his voice somewhat sharper than a casual observation required. Hunter must have thought so, too, because the table jerked as he kicked his friend in the leg.

Glancing down at the pendant between my fingers, I nodded. "Thanks. I got it in a junk store when I was a kid. I'd just gotten to the age where I actually understood that I was adopted, and my friend Meg and I went a bit nuts researching my Egyptian heritage. So, when I saw this in a shop, I just... had to have it." I traced the little hieroglyphics carved into the metal disk with my fingertip. "It's probably a bit stupid that I'm still wearing it after all these years, given it was just a cheap knock-off."

"Not stupid at all," Hunter corrected me with a small frown. "It clearly speaks to you, and that's all that matters."

"Do you know what it says?" Raze asked, still in that sharp tone that made me feel a bit on edge.

I shook my head and responded with sarcasm. "No. In case you weren't aware, ancient Egyptian hieroglyphics aren't commonly taught at school in Oregon." His tone had been that perfect blend of snarky and condescending that made my blood boil. Pretty soon we would come to verbal blows. Or I'd just kick him in the balls, one or the other.

He must have come to the same realization because he gave me a tight, insincere smile and poured us all another shot. "Of course. Just wondered if you'd looked it up. No need to get catty about it, Cleo."

My eyes narrowed, and I opened my mouth to bite back at him, but Hunter's hand on my wrist stopped me. He turned my hand over and pushed my sleeve up a bit to reveal my freshest ink—a cute cartoon voodoo doll with a pink bow. Meg and I got them on a trip to New Orleans recently, and it was the only one I had that wasn't done by Meg herself.

"This is cute," Hunter commented, stroking the doll with his fingers.

I wasn't even going to pretend that I didn't shiver at his touch. It felt like he'd just zapped me with electricity or something... except the jolt went all the way to my sex drive. Weird. Not that I was complaining; it had been a long-ass time since any guy had lit me up like that.

"Souvenir," I explained, feeling my heart thundering in my chest and desperately hoping I was pulling off casual-cool and not needy–turned on. "Do you have any tattoos, Hunter?"

His lush lips curved up, and his chocolate-brown gaze captured mine in a way-too-heated moment. "You'll have to wait and see, Cleo."

Ugh, there he goes again, purring my name. So freaking hot.

"Tone it down," Raze snapped, and I jerked out of Hunter's grip. For a moment I'd forgotten we weren't alone and had somehow ended up leaning intimately close to the Australian Adonis.

Clearing my throat uncomfortably, I took a huge gulp of my whiskey and almost missed the irritated glare Hunter shot his friend.

"Don't you have another set to play or something?" he prompted, jerking his head back to the small stage where Raze's bandmates stood chatting but clearly waiting for him to return. "Go on, mate. I'm perfectly capable of entertaining Cleo alone."

The bigger man scowled at his friend, his inky-black lashes framing those glowing green eyes in a way that made my breath catch—in arousal or fear, I couldn't be totally sure.

"That's what I'm afraid of," Raze muttered but placed his glass back on the table and returned to his band anyway.

Alone with Hunter once more, I shifted on my stool and poured another shot of whiskey. The strange feeling of intimacy when he'd touched my skin was making me uncomfortable in retrospect. What the hell had just happened? It was like the whole room had disappeared from around us and all I had been able to focus on was him. Hunter.

"Okay, spill it," I ordered him, sick of asking myself questions I had no answers for.

"Spill what?" he replied, arching a brow at me but not losing the amused tilt to his lips. Did he *know* how badly his innocent touch had affected me?

I narrowed my eyes at him. "There's something weird going on here. It's not normal to break down in the middle of nowhere, only to be rescued by the sexiest import since Hugh Jackman and his drool-worthy bad-boy best friend. So what gives? Why are you two here in this blink-and-you-miss-it town, why do you seem so interested in me, and what the hell just happened when you touched me? This isn't normal, Hunter." Alcohol was loosening my tongue, but really I wasn't all that reserved normally.

His smile spread wider, and I already knew I wasn't getting any straight answers from him. I also knew I wasn't off the mark because he didn't act confused in the least by my questions.

"You think I'm sexy, huh?" He, of course, grabbed onto the compliment and ran with it. Typical man. "Maybe that explains what *happened* when I touched you? You were just overcome by my raw sex appeal?"

I rolled my eyes, but the thought had crossed my mind. Maybe the stress of my day was finally catching up to me and making me space out. "Sure, keep your secrets for now," I conceded. "I think I can get you to fess up by the time this bottle is empty." I tapped the whiskey bottle with my glitter-painted fingernail, and Hunter barked a laugh.

"You think so, Cleo?" he purred my damn name, and I found myself focusing way too hard on his mouth. "Challenge accepted."

Hunter shifted in his seat so that his back was to the band—and Raze—and his focus was locked entirely on me. Almost as though he was taunting me, his fingers brushed against mine as he took the glass I was offering him.

For that brief moment of contact, the same damn thing happened, and when our skin parted, I could feel my heart thundering like I'd been running. Or... some other form of vigorous exercise.

Hunter took my challenge seriously but was dragging me along with him. By the time Raze's set finished, we only had an inch left in the bottle and were both laughing like hyenas over some ridiculous story Hunter had just told.

"Seriously?" the darkly handsome musician snapped as he rejoined us and picked up the almost empty bottle.

A lazy, drunk smile pulled at my lips, and I shrugged. "Don't blame me; I was fine with beer until you bought that."

Raze glared at me a moment, then shifted an exasperated look to Hunter. "This is your idea of entertaining Cleo?"

"Damn Skippy, it is," Hunter slurred slightly as he replied with a grin. "We were just getting to know each other better, and what better way than with a little social lubrication, mate?"

Whatever reprimand Raze was about to dish out was interrupted by the arrival of a third man with equally startling good looks. He was tall, like the other two, but with naturally sun-lightened blond hair. For some reason, my drunken brain decided he must really love nature. Hiking and rock climbing and shit. He just looked like the type, all muscled and tanned and whatnot.

"Hey, Boden!" Hunter greeted the newcomer with a slap on

the back. "You're back early!"

The blond guy frowned slightly at Hunter's inebriated state, then flickered a curious look at me. "Yeah, I had a feeling there might be something going on tonight." His frown smoothed out, and he offered me a hand to shake. "I apologize for my friend's manners, miss. I'm Boden. You are...?"

"Cleo," I replied, taking his hand in mine. "Technically, that's not my name. It's a nickname that Meg gave me when we were kids; my real name is Margaret."

Startled at the little pile of word vomit that had just spewed from my mouth, I clapped my free hand over my lips. The new guy hadn't released me from his grip yet but looked seriously amused by my confession.

"It's nice to meet you, Cleo," he finally said and let go of my fingers.

I sighed in relief that he hadn't decided to use my real name, but a quick glance at Raze's smug face said I would probably be hearing it from him. Dammit.

"Sorry, I don't know why I just told you that," I admitted as Boden dragged a stool over to sit between Hunter and me. "All the whiskey must have loosened up my filter a bit."

"Looks like I missed all the fun," he commented, raising his brows at the bottle still held between Raze's fingers, but the surly rocker just scowled back.

"Hardly," he grunted, flicking a glare between Hunter and myself like we were naughty children. "These two have been drinking like fish and then howling with laughter over something while I was playing with the band. What was so funny, anyway?"

His question brought back the giggles, and I started shaking silently with laughter as Hunter just shook his head and tried to swallow back his own laughter.

After a few breaths, he explained. "I was telling Cleo about our trip to Cancun."

This, of course, set the two of us off again in drunken giggles while Boden grinned and Raze's glare darkened like a toxic storm cloud. Of course he wouldn't have found it funny; the whole story of their trip to Cancun involved how Raze had accidently drugged himself and streaked through a crowded nightclub, evading all the security and eventually needing to be tackled by a drag queen.

With a pissy look on his face, Raze poured the remainder of the whiskey into his glass, then slammed it back in one huge gulp.

"Oh! End of the bottle!" I cried out, pointing to the empty container, then reaching past Boden to whack Hunter on the arm. Even drunk as I was, I was careful to whack him on the shirtsleeve, not his bare skin. As good as it felt when his skin touched mine, it was tripping me the hell out, and I wanted an explanation before giving in to it.

"What does that mean?" Boden asked us, raising just one brow. Such a cool trick.

"It means Hunter has to explain what the hell is going on here," I explained, waving a hand around the table at the three of them.

Raze frowned. "Here? What do you mean, Margaret?"

My jaw clenched, and I ground my teeth in anger. I just freaking *knew* he was going to use my real name. Asshole.

"Cleo thinks there is something suspicious going on, that we don't belong here in Edan and that we shouldn't be so interested in a beautiful, charismatic, magenta-haired pocket rocket like her." Hunter was still slurring a fraction, but I got the feeling he wasn't quite as drunk as he was pretending to be. Just like me. Sneaky fucker. I had freakishly good tolerance for my liquor, and despite the fact that I was a *little* drunk, I was definitely playing it up in the hope that Hunter would let his guard down.

Boden and Raze both looked at me, then back at Hunter as though curious to see how he planned on explaining the weirdness.

"Well?" I prompted, curious myself to hear what he had to say.

Hunter sucked in a deep breath and then leveled me with a direct stare. "You're right. It's no coincidence that you broke down where you did or that we found you. We've actually been here for weeks, waiting for you."

My smile faltered, and uneasiness clenched at my gut. "That's... an odd thing. Why would you be waiting for me?"

Holy mother freaking Cats, they really are serial killers. All of them. They've targeted me!

"Because you are the descendant of Queen Hatshepsut who was chosen by Ra in 1501 BC to bear the Amulet of Light. We are your magically sworn guardians, and it was only a matter of time before fate pulled the four of us together." Hunter delivered this with such a straight face that I *almost* believed him. Almost.

Except for how utterly *insane* he sounded.

After an extended silence, within which the three of them just stared at me, I started laughing.

"Okay sure, good answer. Magic. How silly of me not to think of that." I chuckled as I ran my fingers through my probably messed-up pink hair. "Serves me right for not specifying I wanted the *real* explanation for all this weirdness."

Hunter just blinked at me a couple of times, but Boden laughed a little with me. Raze had a small frown marring his beautiful, bronzed features, though, and when he opened his mouth to say something, Boden shot him a look.

"Yep, that's Hunter for you," Boden agreed, giving me a warm smile. "Always quick to make up wild stories. Can I grab anyone else a drink?" He pushed off his stool and took all our orders before heading to the bar.

Left with Raze and Hunter, I eyed the two of them with resignation. "All right, fine. Keep your secrets. Just don't turn out to be serial killers, or we will have problems, okay?"

For the first time since we'd met, Raze almost cracked a smile. The corners of his mouth lifted just a fraction, and his glowing green eyes seemed to project a little less anger than they had a moment ago. "Not *serial* killers," he assured me.

"Good." I nodded, accepting the margarita that Boden returned with. "Now, I don't suppose any of you know how to fix my van? Hunter suggested that it might be a few days before I can even get it towed into town, let alone fixed."

Boden coughed a laugh. "Hunter didn't tell you? He's a mechanic."

My jaw dropped open, and I glared at the brunette Australian liar.

Hunter just shrugged and looked totally unapologetic. "If I'd just fixed it for you then and there, we never would have had time to hang out. Besides, did you forget the whole part about us being your magical guardians? I didn't want to have to chase your ass halfway across America when we had a chance to just straight up meet you."

"Of course," I deadpanned. "The magical guardian thing. How could I forget?"

Hunter laughed, picking my hand up from where it rested on the table and rubbing small circles across my skin with his thumb. "Tell you what, Cleo. I'll fix your van tomorrow if you do something for us."

His touch was doing that weird thing to me again—my vision was tunneling, and I was losing sense of where we were. All I could focus on was Hunter.

"Hmm?" I murmured. "And what is that?"

"Take us with you," he replied in that sexy, purring voice.

The oddity of his request had me pulling my hand out from under his fingers, and the room rushed back into focus around me. "You want a lift to Texas?" I frowned at him in confusion and glanced at the other two for confirmation.

"Sure, why not?" Hunter shrugged, raising his brows at me in challenge. "If we promise we aren't serial killers, can we tag along with you on your road trip?"

What happened next, I had no explanation for. Blame it on the alcohol or my crappy day or my poor, starved sex life, but for some insane reason... I didn't *want* to say no.

So in a move that I was sure I would come to regret, I nodded. "Okay, deal. You fix my van, and I'll take you to Texas." I stuck my hand out for Hunter to shake to seal our deal, but he hesitated a moment with his hand a fraction from mine.

"Are you sure?" he pressed me with a strangely intense gaze. "If you make a deal with a magical being, you're bound to keep your word."

I smiled at his continued use of this *magical being* story. "Uh-huh, sure. I said I'll take you to Texas, Hunt, it's not a big thing. Just don't turn out to be a psycho." I closed the gap between our hands and shook his before he could fuck around any more. As our palms met, there was a shock of electricity, and I yelped at the same time as Hunter hissed.

"Weird," I muttered, shaking the lingering tingles out of my hand.

Raze made an annoyed sort of sound, which drew my attention, and I wrinkled my nose at him. For dudes who claimed they weren't psychopaths, they definitely acted pretty suspiciously. Like the fact that Raze was glaring at me *even harder*—if that was even possible—like I'd just ruined his life. Or the fact that Boden sagged in his seat and blew out a long breath, like he'd been holding it for a while.

"You guys are so strange," I muttered, taking a long sip of my drink. "I guess we should call it a night if we're leaving tomorrow."

"Nonsense," Hunter scolded. "This is cause for celebration! Dance with me?"

Without waiting for my response, he grabbed me around the waist and whirled me out into the clear piece of space near the stage. No one else was dancing, but the combination of excessive amounts of alcohol, plus the intoxicating brushes of Hunter's hands on my skin—whenever they ventured off my clothing— had me dancing along with him in no time at all.

These guys were strange, for sure. But for some reason, my gut was telling me I'd made the right choice in trusting them. Maybe it was the magic? Hah!

CHAPTER
THREE

When I woke, I was pretty sure someone was taking a mini-jackhammer to my head. My mouth felt like it was stuffed full of cotton, and I was *so freaking hot*.

What the hell had happened last night? The last thing I remembered was dancing with Hunter... and then... I squeezed my eyes closed tighter in a lame attempt to clear the headache thumping through my skull. What had happened after dancing with Hunter?

"Stop thinking so hard; you're giving me a headache," a deep, purring sort of voice muttered into my hair, and I froze.

"Hunter?" I croaked, turning my head slightly and cracking an eye open. "What the hell are you doing in my bed?" A fuzzy memory of doing tequila shots danced across my brain, and I groaned. "Also, I'm pretty sure it's the tequila causing your headache, not my loud thinking."

He mumbled something I couldn't understand, and his arms tightened around me.

For way longer than what was socially acceptable, I just went with it. His frame totally engulfed my own petite form, and the warmth emanating from his skin made me feel like I was wrapped in a huge fur coat. A fur coat that had wandering hands and a rather long, hard length pressed against my backside.

"Hunter," I mumbled. "Did we... ah..." I was both searching my fuzzy brain for any memory of how we'd ended up in bed together and having a hard time focusing on making words. The same sensation was back from touching Hunter's skin, and I couldn't seem to stop myself from arching my back and grinding my ass against his erection.

He let out a low groan, and his wandering hand closed over my breast—*under* my tank top. Where the hell was my bra, anyway?

"We didn't," he sighed. "But if you keep that up, things will change pretty damn fast."

My breath caught, and I toyed with the idea of calling his bluff. Why shouldn't I? We weren't drunk anymore, and as far as I could remember, he didn't have a girlfriend or wife stashed somewhere... What would be so wrong with taking things further?

"Hunter!" someone snapped from the driver's seat of my van. "Tone it down!"

Two things occurred to me simultaneously. One, that was the exact same thing Raze had said last night when I was going all gooey-eyed at Hunter, and two, Boden was driving Candy Jack.

It was probably the second point that saw me shooting out of Hunter's embrace and onto my feet. The second I did so, however, I regretted it. The movement of my van combined with the movement of my hangover saw me stumbling and winding up sprawled across a very unimpressed looking Raze's lap.

"Uh, hi?" I peered up at the angry man as I braced myself with a hand on his rather impressive bicep. He had his shoulder-length hair tied up in a messy manbun-type situation and wore a pair of black-framed reading glasses. The effect was a little bit absurd, like they were fashion statement glasses for a "sexy-serious" photoshoot or some crap.

"Is there a reason why you're half-naked and in my lap, *Margaret?*" he drawled, sounding both bored and annoyed. Fucker. Now that he pointed it out, though, I realized I was dressed in nothing but my tank top and aqua panties.

How the freaking hell did that happen?

"Actually, asshole, there is," I snapped back, feeling my anger rising to combat the fuzziness of my hangover. "Because your lap happens to be sitting on my couch inside my van. What the hell is going on, anyway? Why is Boden driving Jack, and where the fuck are we going? Oh my cats, are you kidnapping me in my own van?"

Suddenly panicked, I scrambled off Raze's lap and backed away from him, which was all of about two feet until my back hit the little kitchenette and my elbow smacked painfully on the edge of the counter.

"Why would we kidnap you in this piece of shit?" Raze snorted and rolled his eyes. Apparently when I'd landed in his lap, I had knocked a book from his hands, which he picked up and resumed reading like I wasn't even there.

Feeling equal levels of panic and anger rising within me, my breath started spiking and I frantically looked for an escape route.

"Cleo, chill," Hunter groaned from the depths of my bed. I had been so proud of myself when I had managed to squeeze a king size mattress into the back of Candy Jack. I'd lost a bunch of storage space to do it, but I did love to starfish in my sleep. Now, though, it had been invaded by the second coming of Ivan Milat—the infamous Australian backpacker murderer—and I was already picturing that beautiful mattress soaked in my blood.

Boden cursed something and braked sharply, pulling Candy Jack over to a stop on the gravel strip along the side of the road. Unfortunately, he had jerked the wheel so hard that I'd been sent flying again. Straight back into Raze's lap.

Fuck!

"Cleo, you need to calm down," the blond man advised me from the front seat as he turned to look at me. "You're going to make me crash with how hard you're projecting your emotions."

"Excuse me?" I spluttered in outrage, trying to scramble out of Raze's lap—again—and finding his huge hands locked to my waist, keeping me where I was. Scowling at him, I smacked his hands off me and stood back up to glare daggers at Boden. "You were driving *my* van while I was passed out half naked under a total freaking stranger! And you're telling me to stop *projecting my emotions?* What crazy-ass planet are you from where this is a situation *not* to freak the fuck out about?"

Raze, who I was fast figuring out was an even bigger douche canoe than I'd given him credit for, snorted and rolled his eyes. "Told you she wasn't taking this seriously."

It took all my willpower to just grind my teeth and not start shrieking for help. Not that it was going to do me much good; a quick glance out the window showed we weren't exactly in a densely populated area.

"Taking *what* seriously?" I hissed at the Native American supermodel with the personality of a porcupine. I was pretty sure he was about to tell me about how I was being held for ransom or being sold into a sex trafficking ring or maybe just being moved into another state so that it would take longer for someone to find my chopped up remains.

So, I didn't really know how to respond when he leveled a stare at me like I had the IQ of a block of cheese and told me in a patronizing voice, "The fact that you made a magically binding agreement to take us with you on your journey. You did this, drunk or not, so don't go crying about it now. Trust me, I wish you hadn't done it, too." This last part was muttered under his breath as he turned his attention back to his book.

For a long moment, I just stared at the top of his head, then flicked my gaze to Hunter—still half asleep in my bed—then finally to Boden in my driver's seat. The three of them had kept up the whole "we're magical creatures" joke all night, from what I could remember, but I'd figured it was just an elaborate metaphor for... uh... life?

"Okay, so that whole thing was entertaining last night, but it's just creepy now. Cut the shit and tell me what the hell is going on!" Anger, or possibly fear, was making me tremble, and I hugged my arms in a lame attempt to hide the shaking from my abductors.

Hunter groaned again from my bed, and his sleep-disheveled head popped up out of the pillows. "Cleo, babe, I explained this to you about sixteen thousand times last night. It's not a metaphor. Magic is real. We are your fated guardians to protect you against Bast and her minions." Hazy memories of him telling me this between shots flashed across my brain, and I cringed.

"Uh-huh." I laughed nervously, still pretty sure they were messing with me. "And I need to be protected because..."

"Because you're the descendant of Queen Hatshepsut, who was—"

"—gifted the Amulet of Light by Ra in 1501 BC," I cut Hunter off and finished his sentence in a horrified whisper. "That's not..." I trailed off and rubbed at my pounding head. This whole trip had been an utter clusterfuck so far, and now I'd drunkenly agreed to pick up three hitchhikers with mental problems.

Rubbing the *amulet* in question, I peered at the three of them one by one, praying someone would start laughing and admit the whole thing was one big joke. When no one spoke, though, my heart sank.

Why were the pretty ones always so crazy?

"Okay, listen," I started, licking my dry lips and keeping my voice as calm as possible, "I can see you're all very invested in this story, but you sound certifiably insane and I'm just not comfortable traveling with you. I'm grateful that you fixed Candy Jack, but I think it's best if you just invoice me for the work and I drop you off at the next bus station, okay?"

"Doesn't work like that, Margaret," Raze sneered, and his cold gaze flicked over me like I was a moron. "Hunter tried to warn you last night, but you went ahead and accepted the deal before he outlined the consequences. So now you're stuck with us like we are with you."

"*Stop* calling me that," I growled, anger making my teeth clench. I was only accustomed to hearing my real name from my mother, and even then it made me want to punch a wall. "And what the hell do you mean? I never signed any contracts in blood nor did I marry anyone—that I'm aware of—so no one is *stuck* with anyone. I changed my mind, end of story."

A cruel smile pulled at Raze's sexy mouth. "Actually, Maggie, you did one better. You bound us in magic, and if you break the deal, then you'll suffer the consequences."

I snorted and rolled my eyes. "Oooh, magical consequences. Of course. Let me guess, I will turn into a toad and need the kiss of a prince to turn me back?"

Boden made a noise that sounded suspiciously like a laugh covered by a cough and ducked his face out of view when I shot him a suspicious glare.

"That's actually a pretty solid guess," Hunter mumbled, then yawned heavily. He had finally surfaced from my bed and was sitting, totally shirtless, on the edge of the mattress as he blinked at me with those sleepy brown eyes of his. "Except I *think* the magic was cued to rodents not amphibians. I don't totally remember because, let's be honest, we were already pretty drunk by that stage." His cheeks took a pink tint, and he ran a hand through his messy brown hair as though embarrassed.

"Huh?" I squinted at him, sick of repeating "what does that mean" every three seconds.

"He means that if you try to break your word to take us with you, then you'll turn into a rat," Raze explained in a painfully dry voice.

Before I could start laughing hysterically, a loud bang sounded from outside the van and the screech of brakes filled the air. Flinching, I covered my ears, but the gesture was pointless when something heavy slammed into the side of Candy Jack and sent me flying back into Raze's lap for the third time.

This was different, though, and his strong arms wrapped around me tightly, shielding my body as my van was hit again. Whatever it was that had slammed into us hit harder this time, and Jack was no match for its superior weight or strength. For a suspended moment, we teetered on two wheels, and then we were falling.

Over and over my van rolled. Shit flew out of cupboards, and the four of us bounced around like popcorn in a microwave for what seemed like an eternity, until it all stopped.

Throughout it all, Raze remained locked around me like a human shield, and when everything fell still, his whole frame remained tense and alert.

Stunned, I didn't try to move. Instead I just lay there underneath the heavy motherfucker while my breathing quickly escalated to the edge of hyperventilation. Thousands of fractured questions zapped across my brain, fighting for supremacy, but only one managed to complete itself.

What the fuck just happened?

"Calm down," Raze ordered me, his chest vibrating against my cheek where my face was smooshed against him. "Maggie, seriously, calm the fuck down, or you're going to pass out."

He was right; of course, he was right. But how the fuck was I supposed to *calm down* when someone had just trashed Candy Jack *with me inside?* For the love of cats, I was lucky to still be alive!

"Cleo, are you hurt?" Boden called out from somewhere nearby, and I considered his question. Was I hurt? I couldn't feel my legs. Holy shit, I couldn't feel my legs!

"I'm paralyzed!" I squeaked in terror. "I can't feel my legs! Oh my god, I'm never going to walk again!"

"She's fine," Raze snapped, peeling himself off me and standing up on what was once Candy Jack's window and was now the floor. "I took the worst of it."

Now that he'd removed his considerable weight from my body, the blood rushed back into my legs, and I was hit with the reassuring pins and needles that proved I *wasn't* paralyzed.

Phew.

"Jesus Christ Supercat, there is a massive chunk of glass in your back, Raze," I exclaimed when he turned slightly and I spotted the easily ten-inch shard protruding from his flesh. Blood was pooling around it and running down his blue T-shirt, causing it to stick to his body in a disturbingly sexy way.

Yeah, okay, I was a little bit fucked up. I could own up to that.

Raze glanced at the glass over his shoulder and grunted his displeasure. He didn't even seem all that concerned by the situation, just *displeased*. More to the point, how the hell were we all alive?

"Guys, what the ever-loving fuck just happened? How are we still alive? Surely bones should be broken or... something. And Jack! My poor van!" I scrambled to my knees and tried to orient myself. From what I could see, Jack was on his side and there was considerable damage to the side above our heads. So much that the back end—where Hunter had been sitting on my bed—was crushed like a tin can. "Hunter!" I blurted out, staring wide-eyed at the remains of my "bedroom".

"I'm fine," the Australian mumbled, crawling out from under a pile of my clothing, which had previously been stacked nicely inside my little wardrobe. "But it's nice to hear your concern, Cleo babe."

I rolled my eyes at Hunter's constant flirtation, but quietly I breathed a sigh of relief. Psychopaths or not, these three were sort of growing on me, and it would have been a shame to see them dead so soon.

"We need to get out of here," Boden said, stating the obvious. "It'll only be a matter of time before those assholes follow us down here to finish the job." Crouched over to avoid the cabinets hanging open and my bar fridge halfway out of its home, Boden made his way to Raze and just wrenched the shard of glass out like it was a flipping toothpick or something.

As I stared—horrified and fascinated—the wound in Raze's back just... *closed*. Like it had never been there. If it wasn't for the residual blood coating his shirt, I would have thought I'd imagined the whole damn thing!

"What the—" My stunned exclamation was cut short by all three men turning their sharp, somewhat glowing gazes on me. Seriously, though, their freaking eyes were freaking glowing!

"Now isn't the time, Cleo," Boden told me firmly, giving me the pretty solid impression he was actually the one in charge of this merry band of nutcases. "We need to get you out of here before they catch up. Let's haul ass, boys."

Without waiting for any further arguments from me, Raze stooped forward and snatched me up in his arms like I was a naughty child. My squirms and protests did me absolutely no good as he carried me out of the wreckage of my beautiful Candy Jack, then deposited me onto the grass below a tree some distance away.

From where he put me, I could see the hill we had just rolled down. More importantly, I could see the big rig parked at the top, which must have been responsible for pushing us off the road. Beside it, several figures stood arguing—if the wild hand gestures were any indication.

"Guys," I murmured, not taking my eyes off the people at the top of the hill for a second. "Are we still in danger here?"

None of the three responded, but Boden's sharp gaze followed my line of sight, and he grimaced.

"Okay, stupid question, huh?" I laughed nervously. "What do we do now?"

"Now we get you the fuck out of here," Hunter replied, wincing as he shook broken glass out of his hair. He was still shirtless, like he had been when he woke up, and only sported a tight pair of boxer briefs on his lower half.

As fucked up as the timing of it all was, I couldn't help checking out his package for a brief moment before focusing on the facts that we'd all almost died and it was looking like it had been pretty damn intentional.

"Take her," Boden ordered Raze, jerking his head toward the dense forest behind us. "Head north, and we'll catch up after we sort this lot out."

Raze's jaw clenched, and he opened his mouth to argue with the blond-haired mountain man. Luckily though, my ears were spared his complaints when the dudes on top of the hill fired something at us and a tree to my left exploded.

Literally. Exploded.

"What the fuck was that?" I screamed for what felt like the

millionth time. I was really starting to sound like a broken record, but who *wouldn't* under the circumstances?

"Shit," Boden cursed, then got no further words out as the next shot fired from above hit him in the shoulder and sent him flying backward three yards.

Raze turned to me with a fierce look on his face, one that left no room for arguments.

"Run," he ordered me, his voice low and underlined with an animalistic growl. "Run now and don't look back."

Even if his words hadn't inspired enough primal fear in me to turn tail and run for my cats-damned life—they had—my mind would have been made up by the barrage of shots raining down on us. Puffs of dirt exploded all around us, and in the distance I saw our would-be killers begin to make their way down the hillside.

Panicked, I scrambled to my feet and took off in the direction both Boden and Raze had pointed me in. Stupidly, though, I did exactly what Raze had told me not to do.

I looked back as I ran.

I looked back just in time to see Hunter leap onto the twisted remains of Candy Jack, his human form distorting and twisting as he flew through the air. When he landed on the side of my van, he was no longer the lean, muscular Aussie who had picked me up on the side of the road.

He was a freaking cat. A huge-ass freaking cat.

CHAPTER
FOUR

I t was only through some miracle of self-preservation that I kept running and didn't pass right the fuck out due to shock. Hunter had just *turned into a cat*. Not a small, cute, and fluffy pussycat either, he had turned into some sort of wild cat with fangs and claws and weighing probably the same amount as an average-sized tiger.

Holy fuck, was he a tiger?

No, that didn't make sense; he hadn't looked anything like the tigers I'd seen at the zoo. His fur, from the brief flash of it I had seen before getting the hell out of Dodge, had been a chocolatey brown, and he had a series of darker stripes across his back. The general shape of him had been more mountain cat—like and less tigery, though.

Ah hell, I had no idea what the fuck I was talking about. The guy I'd been considering fucking had just shifted into the body of a large cat. End of story.

Shit. Would that make it bestiality? Ew. So much ew.

My bare foot snagged on a tree root, and I went crashing to my knees. It was only then that I realized I'd been running blindly through the forest with *zero* idea where I was or where I was going. Add to that the fact that someone had just tried to kill me, probably *had* killed Boden—holy shit—and Hunter had turned into a huge-ass furry animal, and I was on the verge of a mental breakdown.

Or maybe I'd already had a mental breakdown, and this was all in my head? Shit had really gotten bad when the most logical explanation was that I'd lost my sanity and was actually locked in a padded cell somewhere.

"Holy shit," I breathed, panting heavily. I was in shape, sure, but I was no long-distance runner. Sweat coated my body, and now that I was stationary, my legs quivered with exhaustion. How far had I come? Was anyone following me? Had the guys all been killed?

My mind flashed back to Boden flying across the grass, and I couldn't work out if my imagination was adding the blood pooling under him when he landed or if that had really happened.

Before someone had tried to kill us, I had been just about to eject the three of them onto the side of the road. So why did the idea of them being dead make my head spin and my hands shake? Without even noticing what I was doing, I'd pushed myself back out of the dirt and started making my way back the way I'd come. I needed to see if they were okay...

A thud sounded, and I froze.

Slowly, I turned to see what had made the noise, praying it wasn't one of the men who'd run us off the road and then shot at us with weapons I could barely even describe.

Thankfully, it wasn't. Instead, I found a giant, golden-furred cat sitting on its fluffy butt and watching me with obnoxiously intelligent blue eyes. I mean, that in itself was a pretty damn obvious sign that this was no normal cat. What sort of mountain lion had blue eyes, for fuck's sake?

Okay, once again, I had no idea. Maybe mountain lions did have blue eyes, but I was pretty sure they didn't have the *exact* shade of blue that Boden had.

"Seriously?" I laughed nervously, eyeing the enormous creature as his tail swished back and forth. "So this whole *magical creature* thing wasn't bullshit? You're really..." I trailed off as the words stuck in my throat and my vision swam. Maybe I was going to pass out after all?

To make matters worse, the big cat, who I could only assume was Boden, stood its enormous ass up and padded across to me. Up close, he was even bigger than I'd really given him credit for. If I were so inclined, I could ride him like a pony—he was that huge.

Well... that even sounded dirty inside my own head.

The air around him seemed to shimmer, like I was looking at him through a gas leak, then his shape shifted, rearranged, and settled back into human form. Tall, muscular, tanned, and *totally naked* human form.

"So, you're not dead. That's always good," I mumbled, squinting at him as my vision blurred and swam again. "I think I might pass out now, okay?"

"Not okay, Cleo," Boden scolded, deftly catching me in his arms as my knees buckled and I started to swoon. I shit you not. I made like Scarlett O'Hara and *swooned*. "You might have a concussion from the crash. It's not safe to pass out until we can be sure you don't."

"Just a little snooze," I argued, gluing my exhausted eyelids shut and letting him carry my sweaty butt for a bit. "Wait." My eyes flew back open, and I frowned up at his handsome face. "Where the fuck are you taking me?"

His lips pulled up in a grin, and I noticed a few fine lines around his blue eyes. "Are we back onto the serial killer thing, Cleo?"

"Can you blame me?" I scowled up at him. "We are in the middle of goddamn nowhere, someone just tried to murder us all, I'm wearing nothing but a tank top and panties, and you're..." I paused and ran a hand down his body and over his strong ass to double-check my eyes hadn't deceived me. "You're *naked*. So yeah, Boden, we're back on the serial killer thing!"

He sighed but didn't put me down. He also didn't lose the grin, and I was trying real freaking hard not to melt under the force of it. "You just saw me turn from a lynx into a person, and you're worried about whether I have a fetish for knives and pretty, tattooed girls' flesh?"

I frowned, painfully aware of the absurdity now that he'd said it out loud. "I was thinking more like strangulation, but that's interesting that you think I'm pretty."

Oh. My. Cats. Did I seriously just say that?

I was starting to come around to my mother's opinion that I was a bit of a hot mess. Here I was casually discussing murder techniques with a were-lynx, if that was the correct terminology, and all I could latch onto was that he thought I was *pretty*. Fucking what?

"Maybe I do have a concussion," I muttered, rubbing at my forehead. "Put me down, Boden, I can walk."

He peered down at me and raised a brow in a mocking sort of way. "Are you sure? You just swooned like you were in a silent movie and your corset was done up too tight."

I glared back at him, not appreciating that he'd called me on my girly half-faint. To emphasize my point, I wriggled in his grip until he placed me back on my feet.

"Oh wow," I coughed. "You really are naked."

"Quit staring; you'll give me a hard-on in a second," Boden scolded me in a voice that only sounded half teasing. "And of course I'm naked. When is the last time you saw a lynx walking around in a pair of Levi's?"

"Fair point," I agreed, trying *really* hard to do as I was told and quit staring. But seriously, was it really my fault that he was easily the most perfect specimen I'd seen in, well, ever? Aside from Hunter and Raze, that was. But I hadn't seen either of them naked yet.

Yet.

Yep, I was suffering a mental break for sure. My brain had just totally accepted that I'd be seeing the other two beautiful, magical men naked at some stage in the near future and was fully on board.

"You're not going crazy, Cleo," Boden interrupted my rambling brain and dragged me back to the present. He placed his warm palms either side of my face and captured my gaze with his own. "I promise you, you're not going crazy. This is maybe not the way I would have liked to explain things to you, but you can blame Hunter for that."

At his name, panic spiked through me, and I sucked in a sharp breath. "Hunter!" I blurted out. "Is he—?"

"He's fine," Boden assured me, still gripping my face between his hands and stroking my skin with his thumbs.

"And..." I trailed off, not totally sure why I really gave a crap about Raze, considering what a fucker he'd been toward me, yet totally unable *not* to ask.

Boden's lips quirked into a half smile. "Raze's fine too. They're just doing a bit of cleanup and will catch up soon."

His words reassured me way, *way* more than I should have needed for men I barely knew and had suspected of being serial killers until very recently. The depth of crazy emotion I was feeling toward these three was serious cause for concern, if I was totally honest. But it seemed unimportant in that moment, so I shoved it into the back of my mind to deal with later.

"What's going on in your head right now, Cleo?" Boden murmured in a soft voice. "Your emotions are so conflicted I can't get a clear reading on anything. You're either about to kick me in the balls and run, or..."

My breath caught, and I could practically hear my heart beat, it was thundering so loudly. Boden was right; I was equally torn between running for my fucking life and jumping his freaking bones. Call it my fuck or flight reflex, I guess.

"I can't risk you running right now, Cleo. My job is to keep you safe." Boden's voice was low and husky, his gaze steady and unblinking while his strong hands held my face captive.

His words barely had time to compute before his lips were on mine. Lightning zapped between us as he softly pressed against my mouth, tentative for a second, then bolder as he seemed to commit to what he'd just done.

I gasped at the electric sensation, my lips parting in surprise as warmth flooded through my whole body and made me groan. Boden wasted no time, seizing the opportunity and plunging into my mouth with a ferocity that set me reeling. All of a sudden it was like we couldn't get enough of each other. We were all hands and lips, teeth and tongues as I gripped tight to his neck and hoisted myself up.

My legs wrapped around Boden's waist, trapping his hardened length between us with only the thin fabric of my panties separating us. Through my lust-clouded brain, I shot out a quick, silent thanks to Meg for making me keep up my waxing appointments, despite the fact that I'd split from my deadbeat boyfriend months ago.

Boden moved a few steps, not seeming to struggle in the least with me pasted to his front like some sort of lust-drunk spider monkey. He pushed me against a particularly smooth tree trunk and ground his pelvis to mine in a way that made me cry out and rake my nails down his strong, tanned back.

The intensity of the whole situation had made me a little overeager, though, and I gasped when I saw my nails had drawn blood. How freaking sharp had my manicurist left those damn things?

"Shit, sorry," I panted, biting my lip and showing Boden my blood-tipped nails. "I didn't mean to."

A sly smile crept over his face as his hands ran up my sides and fondled my breasts through my thin tank. "Didn't mean to what, Cleo?" he teased. "Mark me?"

My eyes widened, and I sucked in a short gasp. Is that what I'd just done? Was this some... crazy, magical were-cat thing? Had my desperation to get laid just created a cultural faux-pas?

"Don't look so worried," he chuckled as his head dipped low to capture one of the nipples he'd just freed from my pathetic top. "I have every intention of returning the favor."

His teeth closed over my hardened nipple, and I moaned, thrashing against him like... ugh, like a cat in heat. Jesus Christ

Supercat.

The sound of something loud approaching through the trees made us both freeze, but there was no time to correct our compromising position before both Raze and Hunter appeared in the clearing we'd been about to fuck in.

"Fuck you, Boden," Hunter cursed, his eyes wide as he took in his friend's naked ass pinning me to a tree while his lips were glued to my breast.

Raze seemed even more pissed off than usual, which I hadn't thought possible until that moment. "Job is done, General," he snarled. "Safe house has been secured."

Boden, the shithead, took his sweet-ass time separating from me, even going so far as to lay a lingering kiss on my mouth before setting my feet on the ground and turning to look at his companions.

"Good. Let's get moving then. We want to erase our scent trail and be well out of the area before they call in reinforcements." He threw a quick, sultry wink at me over his shoulder that seemed to scream "to be continued" before he accepted the pair of pants Raze was holding.

Come to think of it, both Raze and Hunter wore pants and T-shirts but no shoes, so they had to have changed somewhere. At least I wouldn't be wandering the woods with *three* naked supermodels? There was simply no way I possessed the required self-control not to end up in a four way if the situation presented itself.

Boden headed out of the clearing, seeming confident in where he was going, and Raze stalked off behind him without sparing me a second glance.

Hunter was a different story, though, giving me a cryptic look as I stood there feeling confused as all fuck. Right when I was about to throw my hands up and start raving about needing meds, he grabbed my hand and tugged me closer to him.

"Don't freak out, Cleo-babe," he told me in a calm, soothing voice. "We're sworn to protect you, remember? We won't let anything happen."

"Anything?" I asked in a breathless whisper, my mind still firmly on the *something* that had just almost happened between Boden and me. Had they interrupted deliberately? I had a hard time believing that magical cat-shifters wouldn't have heard each other long before I did.

Hunter grinned then, showing off those damn dimples of his. Without warning, he swooped down and pressed a less than platonic kiss against my flushed lips and let out a small, frustrated groan.

"Anything *bad* that is. Everything else... well, all is fair in love and lust, am I right?" He winked then with the same sexual undertone as Boden had used and tugged on my hand to get me following him. "Come on, babe. It's still a bit of a walk from here to the safe house. Let me tell you a story on the way."

My curiosity peaked. "What sort of story?" I asked, letting the whole matter of him kissing me drop. He'd essentially just announced he was going to make a play for me, regardless of the near-sex situation I'd just been in with his friend.

He grinned playfully at me, knowing his suggestion of a story had caught my attention. "A story of magic, gods, and destiny. Maybe this time you'll be more receptive to the concept, hmm?"

I rolled my eyes and gave him a sarcastic smile. "Yeah, yeah, stupid Cleo thought you were joking. As if anyone would actually take that story at face value. Will you tell me what sort of cat you are? I'm not super well versed on my were-cat species."

Hunter gasped and pulled up short, jerking me to a stop with his hand still wrapped around mine. "You take that back, Cleo Carroll. We are shifters, not were-beasts, and I'm a Tasmanian tiger, *not* a cat." I wrinkled my nose at him, not totally understanding the point he was making. "Tasmanian tigers are technically marsupials, not felines, but you'd be forgiven for the assumption, seeing as we look a bit like a cougar. Except, you know, more badass."

"Of course," I snickered. "Hey, I never told you my last name! How did you know it?"

"Magic," Hunter replied, his face totally serious.

I raised my eyebrows in surprise. "Seriously?"

"No, it was on your van rego. I saw it when I was fixing the engine last night." He chuckled at his own dumb joke and gave my hand another tug to get me walking again. "Now, hush up and listen to my cool story."

CHAPTER
FIVE

A s it turned out, Hunter's "cool story" only served to create more questions than answers. Questions that he hedged and squirmed over until we reached our destination a short time later.

"How did you guys know this was here?" I frowned, peering up at the little hikers' cabin. The lights were already on, and I assumed that Boden and Raze were already inside.

Fuck, I hoped they had some warm clothes in there. Now that the adrenaline from the crash had worn off, the cold had well and truly set in and my teeth were chattering. Admittedly, a tank top and panties weren't exactly suitable clothes for the current weather.

"Magic," Hunter answered again and waggled his brows at me. "Come on, you can harass Raze with your questions after you warm up. It'll be fun for everyone." He paused, tilting his head slightly to the side as though listening for something. "Okay, fun for everyone *except* Raze. But that just makes it more fun for the rest of us." He gave a slightly evil laugh and led the way inside the cabin.

To my delight, a wall of warmth hit me when we stepped through the front door, and my body shuddered in relief.

"Thank the fucking cat gods," I groaned, rubbing my arms with half-frozen fingers.

Boden stepped out of the kitchen then and gave me a smoldering look. "We're not crazy about the cold, so Raze turned the heat up pretty high. Just let us know if it gets too hot."

Why did I get the feeling there was a double meaning to his words? Except it was definitely Boden who'd turned the metaphorical heat up, not Raze.

"I have questions," I blurted out, glaring at the sexy blond man whom I'd just recently played tonsil hockey with. "About... you know..." I waved a hand between him and Hunter, then mimed claws and hissed. Of course that just had to be the moment that Raze walked out of another room and frowned at me.

"Is Maggie having a stroke or something?"

Narrowing my eyes into what I hoped was a withering glare, I sighed. "Asshole. No, I was just... ugh, never mind." I propped my fists on my hips and turned my attention back on Boden, who was clearly the one in charge. "You know what I meant."

His serious face split with a small grin. "I do. But we have a bit of time, if you want to shower and get changed first? There are some spare sweats in the main bedroom, and Raze will get some food ready while you're showering."

"No, I won't." The darkly handsome dickhead muttered, then grunted when Hunter whacked him in the side of the head. "Fine, whatever, I was making food for myself anyway."

He stalked back out of the foyer and into the kitchen, and I shook my head. What the fuck I'd done to piss him off so bad, I had no idea. Boden's suggestion of a shower and sweats sounded freaking heavenly, though, so I took his offer and headed through to the bedroom he'd pointed out.

After spending way longer than I really needed to under the hot spray, I dragged my butt back out and dried off. The sweats that Boden had mentioned were made for a man, so they totally drowned me to the point that the pants wouldn't stay up, no matter how many times I rolled the waistband.

"Fuck it," I muttered to my reflection, giving up on the pants and dropping them altogether. The top was practically a dress on me anyway, so the only thing making me hesitate was my lack of underwear.

I glanced at the scrap of turquoise fabric on the floor and wrinkled my nose. Not only had I been wearing them for two full days now, I'd also been rubbing up all over Boden's hard dick in them and walked for fuck knew how many miles. To say they were dirty was an understatement.

Nope, not putting those back on. No chance. I'd just have to risk it going commando and try not to flash my flaps at any of the guys.

The smell wafting from the kitchen made me haul ass a bit faster, too. My belly felt like it was practically eating itself, and I was starting to get that nauseous-hungry sensation, so here was hoping Raze hadn't spit in my meal.

"Smells good," I said as I entered the kitchen. Maybe if I complimented his cooking, he wouldn't be such an ass-face. The sneer he tossed in my direction before turning back to the stove proved me wrong, though.

"Have a seat, Cleo," Boden suggested, pushing out a chair at the table with his foot. He and Hunter were both already seated with open beers in their hands. "Dinner won't be much longer."

Sitting down, I accepted the beer that Hunter offered me with a smile. Yum.

"I understand Hunter told you a little about our history on the walk here?" The blond man prompted. "You must have lots to ask."

I nodded. "I do. Lots."

Raze dropped a plate onto the table in front of me with a clatter, and I jumped a little in my seat. How had he just snuck up on me so stealthily? Oh, right. Cat.

"Salmon," he informed me. "If you don't eat fish, you're shit out of luck."

Giving him a tight, sarcastic smile as he sat down in his own seat, I picked up my fork and took a huge bite. "I love salmon. Delicious."

His dark lashes tightened around those piercing green eyes as he glared at me but, thankfully, didn't respond. Exhaustion from the day was fast catching up with me, and I got the feeling I'd need all of my wits to win a verbal sparring match with Raze.

"Feel free to ask your questions, Cleo," Boden encouraged. "We can answer anything now that we're bound."

I blinked at him, shoving his broody friend out of my mind. "Huh?"

Boden's lips pursed. "Hunter didn't get that far then?"

"Left that gem for you," the playful Australian told him. "All I filled her in on was the origin story."

Boden sighed and rubbed at his forehead like he had a headache. Actually, now that I thought about it, they all looked a bit the way I felt—totally exhausted.

"Okay, so Hunter told you about how Queen Hatshepsut was selected by Ra—king of the gods in ancient Egypt—to bear his Amulet of Light?" He arched a brow at me to check that this was not new information, and I nodded.

"Yes," I agreed. "But we didn't get much further than that, really."

Boden frowned. "That's it? That's as far as you got?" He turned an incredulous look to the Aussie, who just shrugged.

"Don't blame me," Hunter replied with a grin. "Cleo knew nothing about Egyptian history. I spent the whole time trying to explain how a woman could be pharaoh."

I opened my mouth to give a weak excuse, but all that came out was a heavy yawn. Fuck me, I was going to pass out with my head in my food if I wasn't careful.

"Maybe just give me the CliffsNotes?" I suggested in a weak voice. "It's been a long-ass day."

Boden nodded in agreement. "For all of us. Shifting takes a bit of a toll on our energy."

My eyes widened, and I nodded. "I want to say that I understand, but I really don't. So is that what I am, too? A cat shifter?"

"Not a cat," Hunter interjected, jerking a thumb at himself. "We went over this already."

Boden rolled his eyes, and I hid a smile. Apparently I hadn't been the only one to assume a Tasmanian tiger was a type of cat. "No, Cleo," Boden assured me. "You're not going to suddenly sprout fur and claws if you haven't already. Shifters first discover their nature with puberty, and I'd say you're well past that awkward stage of life."

I cleared my throat and used a bite of food to distract myself from the memory of Boden's hard dick rubbing between my legs. "So, what am I then if not one of you? Why do I have this amulet, and why did those people just try to kill us?"

"You're human," Raze answered my question like it was the dumbest thing he'd ever heard, "obviously."

"Raze is right," Boden agreed. "You're human, but you're descended directly from Queen Hatshepsut, so it is your destiny to carry the Amulet of Light. How it ended up in a junk store in

Portland is a mystery, but the power of Ra is supreme and works in ways we couldn't ever comprehend." His gaze dropped to the golden amulet clutched between my fingers. I'd taken it out of the sweatshirt and had been rubbing it without even noticing. "As for why those people tried to kill you, it's simply the age-old fight for power. You have it, and their mistress wants it."

Raze made a growl under his breath and stabbed a piece of fish like he was picturing my face or something. "Fucking Bastites," he swore. "Brainwashed idiots chasing a myth."

Hunter grunted his agreement, and Boden sighed with a small nod himself.

"We can explain more on that tomorrow," Boden told me. "For now, it's enough to say that those people are the acolytes of Bast. She's had a lady boner to get that amulet since the day it was given to humans; it's why the guardians were created in the first place— to keep you alive and the amulet out of Bast's greedy hands."

I blinked at him a couple of times, my poor, sluggish brain trying to comprehend what he was telling me. "Bast? As in… the ancient Egyptian goddess Bast? She's real?"

"You didn't seriously think that humans were the highest form of evolution, did you?" Raze scoffed, and I glowered at him. Sooner or later, that handsome asshat was going to catch my fist in his face.

"Again, we can get into the history of the immortals another day. I think everyone is a bit exhausted and it's giving some of us a shorter temper than normal." Boden speared Raze with a glare, but the bigger man just shrugged and finished off his dinner with a stubborn look on his face.

"Cleo, babe," Hunter said, tucking a wet, dark-pink strand of hair behind my ear, then trailing his fingertips over my cheek. "Did you have any other questions before you rest, or are you good? Like Boden said, we will answer anything you want to know—not like those dickheads in romance novels who keep secrets from their girl for her own protection, you know?" He gave me a goofy grin, and I bit back a laugh. This wasn't the time to fall for his charms... although I was stupidly turned on by the fact that he read romance novels.

"Uh... I have no idea." I paused and chewed at my lip. "I guess... what does this thing do?" I held up the golden amulet and inspected the ancient writing on it. I'd taken it at face value for so many years it had never crossed my mind that it might be anything but a pretty piece of junk jewelry.

"You mean, what's its power?" Boden tilted his head to the side, and I nodded.

"Yeah, like will it hurt me? Am I better off giving it to someone else more equipped to handle whatever drama comes with it?" I met Boden's gaze head on, but my guts were clenched and churning in anticipation of his response. I didn't *want* to give the amulet away, killer cultists or not.

He gave me a sad sort of smile and shook his head. "You couldn't even if you wanted to—no more than we could give up our positions as your guardians." His gaze flickered to Raze, then he cleared his throat and hurried on. "As for what it can do, well... anything you want it to."

My brows shot up, and my lips parted in shock. "Anything?"

He shrugged. "Anything within reason. Its limitations aren't really known, if it has any. It will just take time for you to bond with the magic and learn how to use it."

I gaped down at the necklace, then wrinkled my nose. "How do I do that?" Because I wasn't a fucking moron. If the amulet could do *anything I wanted,* then surely these cultists working for Bast wouldn't be such an issue and I could just go about my life.

"No idea," Hunter responded, cleaning up our empty plates, then propping his shoulder against the doorframe. "You have to figure it out on your own, Cleo-babe. We're just the muscle to keep you alive."

I nodded dumbly, my brain whirring with so much new information I could practically hear the gears turning. The whole thing was fucking insanity, but there was no denying that magic was real. One didn't watch a grown-ass man turn into a huge cat and back again without accepting that the world wasn't black and white anymore.

"Okay. Cool. I think I need to sleep now." I blinked at Boden, who gave me a sad smile.

Raze grunted a pissed-off sort of noise and scraped his chair back from the table loudly before storming out of the room. Seconds later a door slammed somewhere deeper in the house, and I shot a confused look at Boden and Hunter.

"Who pissed in his kitty litter this morning?" I muttered with a frown, and Hunter grimaced.

"Raze is... in a tough spot," the sexy, Aussie cat-shifter told me reluctantly. "I don't know how much we should say on the matter."

"She's entitled to know, and he's had plenty of opportunities to speak up today," Boden said quietly, flicking a glance at Hunter. "He can't just keep acting like a child without any explanation."

I darted a confused look between the two of them. Clearly Raze was packing some baggage, and as much as it probably *wasn't* Boden's or Hunter's place to tell me, I still wanted to know. Besides, Raze hadn't done much to earn polite consideration from me.

"One of you spit it out," I ordered them.

There was another pause in which the two of them exchanged a loaded look, then Hunter shrugged and shook his head. "This one's on you, boss. I'm heading to bed." With a flirty wink, he too left the kitchen and headed to a bedroom somewhere deeper in the cabin.

"Scaredy cat," Boden muttered after his retreating back. "Okay, I'll keep this brief. If Raze wants to fill in the details, he can." I nodded my understanding and motioned for him to continue. "Raze... has a wife." My jaw dropped. "Which wouldn't actually be that much of a problem, if not for the kids."

Okay. Yep. My jaw just hit the damn floor.

"*What?*" I exclaimed, about to start a panicked freak out before I caught myself.

So what if Raze was married with kids? It wasn't like I'd

fucked him in the back of Candy Jack or anything. I hadn't even *thought* about it. Okay, fine, that was a dirty lie; I had already fantasized about Raze naked and pounding the stuffing out of me about sixteen hundred times in the last twenty-four hours. But, still. Me imagining what it'd be like to fuck him did *not* mean he was thinking the same thing, so what was I really outraged about here?

Checking myself, I collected my dropped jaw and cleared my throat. "I mean, that's cool. Good for him. Does she know he's furry?"

A sly grin crept across Boden's face, and he gave me a moment to squirm in my own awkwardness before replying. "She's not a shifter, but she knows about us. And in case you're wondering, the girls aren't his biological kids. Maeve was his sister-in-law, and when Raze's brother was killed, she and the girls were going to be kicked out of their house. Raze married her to circumvent some bureaucratic shifter bullshit and let them keep the family home."

If anything, this almost shocked me even more. It was such a... *nice* thing for him to do. It didn't match the angry, sarcastic man I'd known for all of a day.

"So, they're not..." I trailed off. What was I asking here? If the path was clear for me to make a move? Jesus Christ Supercats, like it wasn't enough that I'd almost let Boden fuck me in the woods like a wild animal and Hunter was clearly interested, I needed Raze too? He wasn't even remotely interested in me!

Boden smirked. "No, they're not romantic. But he loves those little girls like they're his own. He's angry and frustrated because he knows he won't be around as much to see them grow up or keep them safe. It's misplaced, but he's blaming you."

"No shit," I murmured. "But why? Can't he just... not be a guardian? I didn't ask for you all to tag along, don't forget." Vaguely, Boden's earlier words came back to me, and I answered my own question. "No, it doesn't work like that, does it?" Boden shook his head and sighed.

"Sorry, Cleo. He'll get over it eventually. He's known this would happen for a long-ass time, so he just needs to suck it up." He scraped back his own chair and stood. Placing his hands on my cheeks, he bent down so our faces were level. "It's our sworn duty to protect the descendent, and it's a damn high honor. None of us would trade this for the world, not even Raze."

"I wouldn't be so sure," I whispered, frowning. Raze had really been an asshat the whole time I'd known him, but I guess it sort of made sense in hindsight. I was pretty confident he'd happily give up his calling to be rid of me, though.

Boden gave me a small smile, his eyes running over my face and pausing briefly on my lips like he was thinking about kissing me, but then he released my face and straightened back up. "You don't know him like I do. Just give him time and patience. Or don't... Maybe a good kick in the nuts is exactly what he needs." He made his way to the hall where the others had disappeared. "You can have the master bedroom where you showered. This cabin is protected so the Bastites won't find us here."

"Thanks," I said, trying not to chew a hole in my lip due to anxiety. "Good night."

"Sweet dreams, Cleo," the blond man told me with a wink. Wasn't hard to guess what *sort* of sweet dreams he was wishing me, given that wink was hot enough to set the damn house on fire.

Alone in the kitchen, I groaned and dropped my face onto the table. Maybe I would've been better off with regular old, run-of-the-mill psychopaths and serial killers. I totally could have handled that situation better than all this *magic*.

What in the actual fuck was I going to do?

"Sleep, Cleo. You're going to sleep." I muttered the words to myself under my breath, like it made me less crazy to say it out loud. "In the morning, this won't look so insane. Surely."

As reasonable as that all sounded, I knew damn well it was only going to get more nuts before I adjusted to the whole thing. Call it a hunch.

I still had kittens to rescue, too!

CHAPTER
SIX

When I woke, it was with an odd sense of deja-vu. A hot, hard body was wrapped around me, and I was sweating my damn nipples off.

"Hunter?" I mumbled, trying—and failing—to wriggle out of his anaconda grip. "What are you doing in my bed?"

"Sleeping," he replied with a husky, half-asleep voice. "You started having a nightmare, and it was keeping me awake."

I frowned into the darkness, trying to remember what I might have dreamed but coming up blank. "So you decided to become my personal barnacle? How did that fix anything?"

"You stopped thrashing around when I came in to check on you, so I decided to stay and let us both get some sleep. Besides, you're the perfect little spoon size, did you know?" Hunter yawned heavily and stretched, but dragged me with him so I ended up sprawled across his chest with my legs straddling his waist. Which really wouldn't have been such an issue except that my underwear was still drying from the sink wash I'd given them, and I was still commando.

I froze against Hunter's chest, not wanting to draw attention to my naked pussy pressed against his rapidly hardening cock. He still wore boxers, so maybe he wouldn't notice?

"Maybe this was a bad idea," he murmured with a sleepy grin as his palms slid down my back and encountered the bare skin of my ass. "I'm currently considering all the ways I can take advantage of this situation."

Without conscious thought, I gave a little wriggle, then gasped when his hips bucked softly in response. Dammit. Why couldn't my guardians be crusty old dudes. Or ladies! I never had been into pussy...

Oh wait.

Biting back a laugh at my own mental joke, I pushed up with my hands on Hunter's stupidly chiseled chest to look at him.

"Why would that be such a bad thing?" I was feeling flirty. Or maybe just horny. Whatever, he was the one in my bed, not the other way around. "Unless you also have a wife and kids?"

His lips pulled up at the corners, like he was trying not to laugh at my sarcasm. "I don't, and I hope Boden explained that situation a little better than that."

I rolled my eyes and huffed.

"It would be *bad*," Hunter continued, his hands both now gripping my ass cheeks as his erection rocked against my core in a lazy sort of way, "because technically this is a big old no-no from the powers that be."

Well, that made me pause. "How so?" I asked, my question only a fraction breathy with arousal. I was interested to hear what he meant by that, but to be totally honest, I was *more* interested in learning what it would feel like to lose those pesky boxers of his...

"Our job is to keep you alive, not fuck you stupid. No matter how badly we might want to." He let out a small, frustrated groan but didn't make any moves to stop the torture.

I frowned, then shook my head to try and regain some of my senses. "But earlier, Boden and I—"

"Were about to break the rules in a big way," Hunter finished my sentence for me. "But I can keep a secret if you can." His dirty wink and smile suggested he wasn't just talking about keeping my tryst with *Boden* quiet.

I smirked back, leaning down to kiss him but hesitating just an inch from his lips. "You can, but can Raze?" I sat back up and tried to ignore the urgent throbbing between my legs. "More to the point, *would* he? Loveless marriage and adopted kids aside, he still doesn't seem super inclined to do me a solid, and I can't imagine he'd be thrilled if I slept with both of his buddies."

Hunter wrinkled his nose and pouted in a way that said I had a valid question.

Sighing heavily, I peeled his strong hands off my ass and

scrambled off him. Hot sex with Hunter wasn't going to happen. At least not until I could be sure Raze wouldn't go running off to tattle to whoever was in charge. I had no idea what the punishments for Hunter or Boden would be, but given there were people literally trying to kill us and *magic was a real thing*, I wasn't messing around with the risk.

"I'm going to grab a glass of water," I announced. "You should go back to your room."

"I should," Hunter agreed. "But do you want me to?"

"Fuck no," I groaned, running my hand through my hair, then grimacing when I spotted the hot-pink strands. "But you *should.*"

With that, I stood up and tugged my borrowed sweatshirt over my ass and made my way out into the dark hallway. I never really needed lights on at nighttime, so I just trailed my fingers along the wall until I reached the kitchen.

Once there, the light from the moon lit up enough of the room that I was able to locate a glass and fill it with water from the tap. Leaning on the counter with one hand, I sipped my drink and peered out into the still night. There was something so serene about being in the forest at night. No cars or sirens or other manmade distractions...

"You're going to get us all killed, you know," Raze's angry accusation startled me so hard that I dropped my glass into the sink with a clatter. Miraculously, it didn't break, but the same couldn't be said for my nerves.

Turning to face him, I folded my arms to hide my trembling

hands. He stood so damn close I needed to crane my neck to look at him, and his mere presence was making me sweat. I don't know what it was, but angry, sarcastic men were just such a ridiculous turn-on it wasn't even funny.

"You three seem pretty capable of keeping yourselves alive," I retorted. "The whole claws and fangs thing probably helps with that." I mimed claws and fangs, but he didn't even crack a smile. Stoic bastard.

If anything, his glare just sharpened, and he placed a hand on either side of me on the sink, effectively boxing me in. Damn, that was sexy.

"I didn't mean the three of us. I meant the *world*, Margaret. You're a hot mess. Since the moment you met us, all you can focus on is either sex or serial killers. We showed you that magic is real, and what was the first thing you did?" His accusing sneer scorched me, and I shifted uncomfortably. "You somehow wound up with your legs wrapped around the general of the Shifter Alliance like he's some fuckboy you met in a club. This isn't a game, Margaret. It's the fate of the damn world."

"I'm well aware of that, Raze," I snapped back, feeling defensive as all fuck, even if he did pose some damn good points. "Might I remind you that this is all new information to me? I had no idea magic even existed until I saw Hunter *turn into a huge-ass cat*, so excuse me for requiring a little bit of time to wrap my brain around it all." Gathering up my anger like a security blanket, I jabbed him in the chest with a finger. "As for Boden being in some army... well... that's also news to me. It's not like you've all just been offering this info up on a silver platter."

Raze's dark lashes narrowed around his eyes. "When, exactly, would you have liked us to explain this all to you? When you were drowning in booze last night? When you had Boden's lips wrapped around your perky little tits in the woods? Or maybe just now when you were panting all over Hunter?" His lush lips curved into a cruel smile, and I floundered for a sassy response.

"My tits," I responded in a tart voice, "are *not* little."

This was equally the worst thing to say and the freaking best because as if on reflex, Raze's gaze dropped to the body part in question. The oversized sweatshirt had slipped off one of my shoulders, and the neckline hung dangerously close to exposing one of my *moderate*-sized breasts.

"Fucking hell," the bronze-skinned god of a man muttered. "You really are something."

The way he said that did not sound like a compliment.

"If you'd kindly get the fuck out of my way? It's late, and I'd rather be anywhere but here with you right now, Raze," I lied, swallowing hard and trying not to sound nervous.

His gaze slowly returned to my face from my chest, and a humorless smile touched his lips. "Liar." He called me on my bullshit, leaning in even closer until I could practically feel his body heat radiating off him. "You think I don't see the way you look at me? The way your gaze lingers on my body and your breathing speeds up when I'm close?"

Raze crowded me tighter against the sink, and damn it if my traitorous lungs didn't do exactly what he'd said. What fucking game was he even playing at? He'd made his contempt pretty damn clear.

"You're dreaming," I denied his accusations with a shaking voice. "I'm more turned on by that toaster than you."

This was, apparently, the wrong thing to say. Raze's green eyes glittered with the challenge I'd just presented; I saw his lips curl even tighter in a cruel sort of smirk before his head dipped low and his lips brushed my earlobe.

"You can't lie for shit, Maggie," he informed me, his warm breath tickling my ear and neck in a way that should not have been as erotic as it was. *Ugh, holy fucking cats, I'm in trouble.* "I think we both know that you'd happily let me fuck you over this sink right now." One hand left the countertop, and I gasped as his warm fingers met the skin of my thigh.

Holding his gaze defiantly, I desperately tried to control my breathing and heart rate as his hand caressed my skin, drifting higher underneath my sweatshirt. Lightning shocks of desire zapped through me, despite my better judgement, and it was all I could do to keep my feet under me. Given that I was about three seconds from melting into a puddle of sexually frustrated goo, I needed to end this little standoff ASAP.

Reaching down, I smacked his hand off my thigh, then shoved his chest as hard as I dared.

"You might be hot, Raze, but no amount of rippling abs or

dreamy ink can excuse a bad personality. And for the record, I don't fuck married men. So keep your paws to yourself and stay the fuck out of my way." Thankfully, my words were buoyed with righteous indignation to cover up the trembling arousal he'd set alight in me.

With a disgusted glare, I pushed past him and out of the kitchen.

When I returned to my bedroom and found the bed vacant, I breathed a heavy sigh of relief. After Raze's scorn, I couldn't have handled Hunter's advances. I needed another shower... preferably a cold one this time.

Some time later, after shocking myself with ice-cold water and then mentally berating myself for being such a scatterbrained nitwit, I turned the hot water up and started washing my hair. Again. It was probably pointless, but I kept thinking if I washed it enough, then the color would fade down to something less garish.

The ensuite for the room I'd been using had a really pretty view from the shower, so I took my time soaping up my hair while staring out into the still, dark night.

Something moved between the trees, and I squinted to get a better look. Maybe a deer? Or was it one of the guys in cat form?

Wow, never thought that would be a casual question on my mind. How easily I had just accepted the fact that they turned big and furry and clawed.

No, that wasn't an animal... it was a person. But not one of the guys. This person was too slight in build and was currently running *away* from the cabin as stealthily as possible. As I watched, the shadowy person paused and turned back to the house.

I hadn't bothered to turn a light on in the bathroom, so he probably couldn't see me watching, but I saw him. Clear as day under the moonlight. He was tall but with a leaner sort of build than my cat guardians. His jet-black hair was shaved short on the sides and left longer on top, like he'd done it for a mohawk then couldn't be bothered with the gelling. What was most striking, though, was the silver scar running the length of his face and bisecting his eyebrow. That eye was lighter than the other as well, and I guessed that if I saw him up close, it might be clouded over with blindness.

As I watched, he took something from his pocket and pressed a button.

Throughout the house, explosions detonated, and the darkness was erased by the intense glow of orange flames.

That handsome, scar-faced *motherfucker* had just blown up the cabin!

For a second I stood there, frozen in shock as he stared straight back at me. Apparently the light from the burning house had lit up the night enough that he could now see me. All of me. His gaze flickered down my naked body, then he smirked, gave me a little salute, and disappeared into the forest.

The second he disappeared from sight, it was like the spell had broken.

"Holy fucking cats!" I screamed, leaping out of the shower, grabbing the first towel I could reach, and dashing from the bathroom. The whole damn house was ablaze, and fire was already licking up the bedroom curtains as I ran through into the hallway. The guys must have all heard the explosions, too, on their way *into* my room as I came crashing *out*.

Needless to say, I somehow ended up in a naked tangle of limbs with—ugh, for cat's sake—Raze of all people.

"Come on, we need to move," Boden snapped, lifting me off Raze and throwing me over his shoulder. The three of them moved through the burning house with quiet grace and slipped us out of a broken window at the back of the property.

Once outside, it was clear to see what had happened. Small bombs had been placed around the perimeter of the structure, about three feet from the house itself. The flames produced by the explosions must have grabbed onto any flammable substances.

"Why not inside the house?" I asked with a frown as Boden set me down on my feet under the protection of the trees. "Why only around the outside?"

"Protection spell wouldn't have let them any closer; that's how I know it was Bastites. No one wishing us harm could have got within three feet of the house," Boden replied, coughing a few times before grimacing. The smoke had been getting really thick as we exited, but there was something... not right.

"I don't think they were actually trying to kill us this time," I commented, frowning up at the burning house. "Otherwise wouldn't they have waited around and killed us when we left?"

"She's got a good point," Hunter agreed, ruffling his fingers through his hair and scowling around us, like he thought the Bastites were hiding.

Raze grunted a noise and ran his eyes over me. "Shame she doesn't have any clothes to keep that good point company. Were the towels all on fire too, Mags?"

"Shit!" I yelped, frantically trying to cover all my lady bits with what I now realized was a washcloth, not a towel. Mother. Fucking. Cats. "Well," I huffed, giving up on my boobs and deciding to just cover my taco. "I guess now you can see for yourself. My tits are *not* little."

Raze rolled his eyes, but I swear there was a twitch of amusement in his face before he turned his back on us and stomped into the woods.

"Here," Boden shrugged off his T-shirt and pulled it over my head before glaring at Hunter.

"What?" the flirtatious Aussie grinned broadly, having just torn his attention away from my ass. "I don't wear shirts to bed, otherwise I would have offered. You can have my boxers, though." His hands went to the waistband of his underwear, and Boden smacked him on the arm.

Snorting a laugh at how eager Hunter was to get naked, I shook my head. "I'll be fine, but thanks. What do we do now?"

We'd started following Raze into the woods, leaving the blazing remains of our safe house behind, but I had no idea what the fuck was meant to happen next. I mean, the guys didn't even look that offended about someone literally trying to burn us alive.

"Move to the next safe house, then contact the Council when we're sure we haven't been followed." Boden sounded so matter-of-fact about the whole thing, but I was confused as all fuck.

Jerking to a stop, I turned slightly to look back at the burning house, then frowned at Boden and Hunter. Raze had continued ahead, but I could see him lurking in the distance.

"Hold up." I propped my fists on my hips. "You want to tell me those assholes just wrecked Candy Jack, then shot at us, *then* tried to barbeque us... and we're just going to let them get away with it?"

None of them responded for a moment, and Hunter slid a glance at Boden.

"We have our orders," Boden responded in a no-nonsense tone, "and they don't involve going off half-cocked to chase down killer cultists."

I scowled at him, my inner claws coming out. I may not have been a damn shifter, but those goddess-worshiping psychopaths had just killed my van, blown up a house with me in it, and generally crapped all over my already crappy day. I'd had enough. "You may, but I sure as shit don't. Those fuckers killed Candy Jack, and I intend to see them pay for it!" Without waiting for a response, I started stomping off in the direction that I'd seen the scar-faced man disappear.

"Cleo-babe!" Hunter called after me, "Where are you going? We need to get you to the next safe house!"

"No one kills Candy Jack and lives to tell the tale!" I yelled back, shaking a fist to the sky. "Those Bast-ards will rue the day they messed with Cleo Carroll!"

CHAPTER
SEVEN

The guys didn't let me get super far before catching up and trying to guide me in the direction—I guessed—of the next safe house. Or like, the road? I wasn't listening real hard to whatever the plan was. My total focus was on making those fuckers pay for the death of Candy Jack.

"Guys, seriously," I snapped after Hunter tugged on my arm for the millionth time. "I'm not going to go run and hide or whatever your *orders* are, so just quit it!"

"So what exactly *is* your plan, Maggie?" Raze asked in drawling condescension. Like I would just storm off into a forest with no map, no plan, and no pants.

Shit. That's exactly what I'd just done.

"None of your business, twatwaffle," I bit back, bluffing over my serious lack of a clue. "Just run off to your little safe house and be, like, safe and shit. I'll deal with these assholes myself."

The look on Raze's face seemed half startled and half constipated. What came next, though, shocked me even more than seeing Hunter's sexy ass turn all furry.

He laughed.

Raze whatever-his-last-name-was just *laughed*.

"Holy cats," I breathed, pausing in my stomping to stare at the gorgeous, bronze god before me. "I didn't know you knew how to do that."

He continued to laugh, shaking his head and not seeming to notice that I'd stopped as he continued walking through the thick underbrush. Startled, I flicked a look at Boden and Hunter, who just shrugged at me and looked a bit amused themselves.

Shaking my head, I tried to brush off the jaw dropping image of Raze laughing and hurried to catch up to him. Fucker was casually strolling, and I needed to practically run to keep up... even though I was supposed to lead this expedition.

"Fucking quit taking over," I demanded, hurrying to pass him again. "You're following me, not the other way around."

He made a vexed sound behind me, but I was determined to get back in front and wasn't totally paying attention anymore. So much so, that I ran straight into a black-cloaked stranger crouched behind a tree.

"What the fucking, cat-loving hell?" I exclaimed as my hands slammed into the hard packed earth, barely breaking my fall before my face ate shit. "Who hides in the forest in the middle of the night? And in a black—" I cut off as it clicked. "Ooooh, Bast-ard!"

I scrambled around, springing back to my feet in a smooth and elegant movement. Hah, kidding, I looked like a crab with one leg shorter than the rest.

The fucker who I'd tripped over seemed to have his foot stuck in a broken log, but he pulled it free while I watched, then stood to face me.

"The amulet!" the black-robed man gasped, staring at the gold pendant, which swung free over Boden's T-shirt.

Pumped up on anger and adrenaline, I snarled at the cultist, who totally could have passed as a librarian in another life. You know, without the robes and the ritual dagger tucked into his waistband.

"You want it? Come and get it!" I shouted my challenge with all the confidence of a seasoned fighter. What a shame I sucked at any kind of physical activity... well... any physical activity that would help in *this* situation, anyway.

The cultist took me at my word, though, and charged at me while I flinched and raised my hands to, I don't know, maybe bitch slap him to death? That was all I had in my arsenal, so it was going to have to do the trick!

"For fuck's sake," someone sighed, and I cracked my eyes open just in time to catch Raze snatch the cultist straight out of the air before he reached me. "Seriously, Mags? Come and get it? What exactly was your plan here?" He indicated to my raised slapping hands and arched a brow.

"Leave her alone, Raze," Hunter growled, brushing past his friend and coming to stand in front of me. "Are you okay, Cleo-babe? Did he hurt you?" It was right on the tip of my tongue to tell him I wasn't a porcelain doll, but when his hand stroked my cheek, I leaned into all that delicious, electric warmth instead.

Damn him. I really needed to work out what he was doing to me with all these "innocent" touches.

"I'm fine," I answered him, then raised my voice a little. "I had that handled!"

I definitely did not.

Raze shoved the Bastite down in the middle of a little clearing and said something threatening that was too quiet for me to hear. Probably something growly and broody and badass. Ugh, I hated him.

I folded my arms over my chest and tried really hard not to lean into Hunter, as close as he was to me.

"We should, like, torture him for information or something," I suggested quietly, and Hunter snickered a laugh. Raze and Boden were both searching the area around us—presumably checking if any of his friends were nearby—while the cultist sat in the dirt and looked sad about life.

"Since when did you turn into the serial killer in this relationship, Cleo-babe?" Hunter teased, giving me a lopsided grin that captured way too much of my attention.

I gaped at his accusation. "I didn't suggest *killing* him, just a little light torture and stuff. Besides, we're not in a relationship."

"Oh no?" Hunter huffed, stepping back into my line of sight and drawing my attention away from the Bastite. "Then what would you call this situation we're in? Because it's sure as shit not *friendship*, and I have zero intention of following the rules and keeping my paws off you."

I narrowed my eyes at him, desperately trying not to be charmed by his casual disregard for the rules of his supernatural community. Jesus Christ Supercats, what was it about bad-boy rule breakers that was such a universal turn on?

"Who says I'm even attracted to you, Thor?" I challenged, my fingers creeping to my amulet and rubbing it nervously.

Hunter's grin spread wider. "You did, Cleo-babe. The other night in the bar. You specifically said you were attracted to me."

"Oh." He had a point there. "Well. Uh—*Watch out!*" That last part came out in a strangled shriek as I caught a flash of the cultist's dagger raised in the moonlight as he lunged for Hunter's exposed back.

My whole body jolted with terror as time seemed to slow, and the blade descended in almost comical slow motion. I was frozen in horror, though, unable to do anything but stare as Hunter was about to be skewered on a twisted, ornamental knife.

Right up until the knife, and the cultist, burst out in a bright, hot flare of fire, then instantly turned to ash and dropped to the ground in a pile of... well... ash. I was too fucking stunned to find a better metaphor.

"What the fuck...?" Hunter turned slowly, looking from the remains of our friendly neighborhood murderer and then to me... then to my amulet still clutched between my fingers. "Oh shit."

"Oh shit?" I repeated, turning my wide-eyed stare to the pretty Aussie bloke. "What does that mean, 'oh shit'? How did you do that? Is that a cat shifter power?"

Hunter shook his head slowly, still staring at me with a mixture of awe and something else. Caution? Before he could answer me, Raze and Boden came crashing back into the clearing.

"What happened here?" Boden demanded, spearing Hunter with a sharp look and me with a somewhat softer one. "Where did the Bastite go?"

Hunter and I both just sort of stared at the pile of ash and then glanced at each other. I was getting a really sneaking suspicion that this was *not* a cat shifter power and just maybe had something to do with me.

Maybe.

Probably.

"Well..." I started, tucking the amulet inside my borrowed T-shirt while my cheeks heated with embarrassment. "Funny you should ask."

I'd sort of been thinking someone would cut me off right there, so I paused and licked my lips but didn't continue. After a long, awkward silence, I started to get a clue that these guys weren't big on talking over me when I needed to say something important. That was rare, wasn't it? For a group of hot alpha males to listen to their woman?

Wait, did I just think of myself as *their woman*? A bit presumptive of me. My libido really was starting to take over. That was worrying.

"Cleo," Boden barked—meowed? "You were saying?"

"Oh, uh, yeah, I have no idea. Hunter?" I looked to sexy Steve Irwin for assistance, and he just shrugged. Oh so helpful. Fucker.

Raze took a few steps closer and nudged the pile of ash with his toe, then wrinkled his nose. "I think it's a fair guess to say that someone incinerated the cultist." He arched a brow at me accusingly, and I flushed with heat. "And given that is *not* a power shifters possess, it's not hard to guess who made it happen."

"In my defense," I started, raising my finger to emphasize my point, "he was about to stab Hunter in the back."

Boden and Raze both turned their glares on Hunter who shrugged uncomfortably.

"You try and stay focused while she's standing there all pants-less and shit," Hunter muttered, scuffing his bare foot in the dirt. "But we should—"

"Keep moving," Boden finished for him. Or was he cutting him off? Huh. What had Hunter been about to say, if not that? Ugh, I sounded paranoid, even inside my own head. "Come on, Cleo. We need to get you some more clothes before you catch pneumonia or something." He reached out and took my hand, tugging me away from Hunter and pulling me close to his bare chest. "If you don't already have it. You're freezing."

Now that he mentioned it, I was starting to do my very best impersonation of a popsicle. How the fuck did I keep ending up with so few clothes on? Something about these damn cat shifters...

"We should shift," Raze suggested. "We'll move more quickly through this mess." He kicked at the shrubby shit between trees, and several sticks broke. "Not to mention quieter."

"You're right," Boden agreed. Somehow I'd ended up plastered against his scorching hot chest while he rubbed his palms up and down my goose-fleshed arms. "Raze, you'll need to carry Cleo. Beautiful, can you carry our clothes? We might need them when we shift back."

I nodded my agreement, then sort of registered what he'd just said. "Uh, I can't ride Raze." As soon as the words passed my lips, I mentally snickered and called myself a liar. I could *definitely* ride Raze, but not as a freaking cat!

"Hunter can do it," Raze argued, sounding as happy about the situation as I was.

A low growl rumbled from Boden's chest, and his eyes flickered in a decidedly *nonhuman* sort of way. "Do not question my orders, Raziel. Not now."

Raze ducked his head, dropping all of the arrogant ass-faceness from his posture. "Apologies, sir."

Before I could appropriately voice my objections, Boden had released me and all three guys were tossing their few items of clothing at me and *shifting into huge-ass cats*. Yes, I totally shrieked that in my head. It was that fucking insane. Sadly, the boxers Hunter tossed at me landed on my face, and by the time I'd clawed them off, the guys were all furry. Damn.

Oh well. I'd seen more than enough of Boden's naked ass earlier—yesterday?—to add to my mental spank bank. Don't judge, we all have one.

It was the first time I'd seen all three of them in cat forms up close, though, and the overall result was a little bit terrifying. Suddenly I found myself kind of wishing they *were* serial killers. At least then I'd have a solid chance of escape if I needed to run. Right?

Boden was clearly recognizable as the golden lynx with intelligent blue eyes. Hunter was a scary bastard up close—his fangs were way bigger than I'd first realized, but his striped brown fur was strangely beautiful. Raze... Raze was downright massive.

"What the fucking gods of cats..." I breathed the curse as I eyed him warily. He was pure black and so glossy he looked like he was made of silk, and his green eyes glowed with that unnerving back light all cats seemed to have in the dark.

My inspection of him was interrupted by cat-Boden nudging me with his huge, pale head, and I instinctively scratched behind one of his ears. Like he was a house cat. I paused, waiting for him to get super offended and, like, eat me or something. But he just vibrated with a loud-as-fuck purr and nudged me again to continue.

I laughed nervously and scratched behind his other ear while Hunter prowled closer and sniffed my bare leg. His whiskers tickled my skin, and I reached down to pat him too.

"Pretty kitty," I cooed, tracing my fingers over one of his stripes. He jerked out of my reach and made an annoyed, hissing sound before loping off into the trees.

"I'm sorry!" I yelled after him, trying really hard not to laugh. "Not a kitty! You're not a cat; I didn't forget!" I really hadn't. But he looked a hell of a lot *like* a cat, and "pretty, giant, extinct marsupial" didn't have the same ring to it.

Cat-Boden shook his head with a purring sigh and stepped out of the way for me to approach Raze. The huge black... uh... panther, I think, had crouched down so his belly brushed the ground and I could sort of semi-scramble onto his huge back.

It took a bit of wriggling around to find my balance, and I ended up bunching their clothes up and tucking them under my T-shirt. Eventually I found myself sort of lying down with my knees hugging Raze's strong sides and my fingers tangled in the silken fur at his neck.

As he started running, I hummed country music songs to myself to keep my mind busy. It was that or acknowledge the fact that my naked pussy was rubbing all over a giant pussy. Yeah. Awkward didn't even begin to cover it.

EIGHT

I t probably wasn't long that I rode Raze before we came...
upon a truck stop. I know, I know, but my humor was the
only thing helping me from totally losing my mind. If I
hadn't already. I hadn't totally abandoned the idea that this whole
thing was the creation of my poor, broken, drugged mind as I
rattled around in a padded room somewhere.

"Thank Ra," Raze groaned when he shifted back, and I threw
his T-shirt and boxer shorts at him. I mean, not before I sneaked
just a little peak at his ass. Fucker shifted with his back to me like
he was paranoid I'd check him out—probably justified. "If I had
to listen to you hum Taylor Swift's greatest hits off key for one
more minute, I was going to jump in front of a truck."

Hunter and Boden both grinned broadly as they shifted back

to human and pulled their boxers on. I kept Boden's T-shirt on because otherwise I would be naked and now was not the time for that nonsense.

"All right, let's grab some supplies from the store and then borrow a car," Boden instructed us, nodding to the truck stop just past where we'd stopped inside the tree line.

I raised my hand and crinkled my nose. "Uh, one problem," I pointed out. "We're all pretty much naked. How are we going in unnoticed, let alone how are we paying for supplies?"

The three of them just smiled and shook their heads at me. I lied. Boden and Hunter smiled; Raze just scowled.

"Watch and learn, Cleo-babe," Hunter replied with a wink, then started sauntering across the grass cool as a fucking cucumber in nothing but his boxer-briefs.

I shot a startled look at Boden, who just linked his fingers through mine and started following Hunter. Like... what the actual fuck? We were going to get arrested for public nudity or something! Which begged the question...

"Where are we?" I whispered, fidgeting with his fingers as I shivered. "Like, what police station are we going to end up in when we get arrested? Shit, I don't have my bag anymore, and I don't know Meg's number by heart. That means I would have to call"—I shuddered—"my mother."

Boden shot me a quick look as he hurried us after Hunter and stepped under the bright lights of the store parking lot. "You haven't mentioned your mother before. I bet she's pretty amazing, seeing as she raised you."

A strangled sound somewhere between a laugh and disgust escaped my throat as he led me into the store and straight past Hunter, who was leaning halfway over the cash register and flirting shamelessly with the girl working it. He held her hand in both of his, and the dazed look on her face told me he was working that fucking juju he'd used on me.

Mother. Fucker.

"She's not?" Boden interpreted my noise, and I dragged my jealous gaze away from Hunter and his victim.

"My mother?" I asked, checking that was what he was referring to. "No. Amazing is not how I would describe Prudence Carroll. She's a pearl-clutching Puritan who literally evicted me from my house while I was broken down on the side of the road outside Edan. My mother is a bitch."

Boden hummed an undecipherable sound under his breath, but half my attention was still on Hunter and that girl. "She sounds a lot like Raze's parents," he commented, and *this* drew my focus back.

"How so?"

Boden handed me a pair of sweatpants. "Put these on."

I hesitated a second before doing as I was told. My ass was fucking freezing, and I was getting a bit over my vagina being flashed to half of North America.

"Ask him about it sometime," Boden continued, back to talking about Raze's parents. "It sounds like you guys might actually have some common ground." He raised his brows at me with a small smile, and I gasped dramatically.

"Surely not," I replied with heavy sarcasm. "I somehow doubt mister tall, dark, and broodingly sexy is interested in finding common ground with little old me." As soon as I said it, my cheeks heated with embarrassment. Thank fuck my bronze skin hid the blush from curious gazes. Still, I turned away and grabbed a long sleeve, ladies T-shirt sporting a proud looking bald eagle.

"Hey," I prodded when Boden made no move to turn around for me to change. "You mind giving a girl some privacy?"

A wide grin split his face, and his eyes heated. "You sure? You didn't mind me looking yesterday."

I scowled at him and made the motion for him to spin around—which he did—but he kind of had a point. In fact, I was all for showing Boden my *not small* tits... just not in the middle of a brightly lit truck stop store while Hunter flirted with some other chick.

Once I'd exchanged Boden's thin T-shirt for the long sleeved, bald eagle monstrosity, I handed it back to him and he pulled the fabric over his head.

"Mmm, still warm," he murmured with a teasing smile as he grabbed sweats for himself, then tossed a pair for each of the other guys over his shoulder. "Pick some boots that fit," he told me, pointing to the selection of cowboy boots. "I'll find you a sweatshirt."

Moments later, I looked like Big Jim's 24-Hour Truck Stop

had vomited all over me, but at least I was warm.

"Don't worry," Boden assured me as we wandered over to the hot food cabinet. "We have better clothes stashed at the next safe house, and once we regroup, we can go shopping."

I shrugged, fiddling with the zipper of my new sweatshirt. "No big deal," I replied. "I still fully expect to wake up in a sanitarium soon, so I'm just coasting with this insanity while it lasts." I flashed him a toothy smile and could tell he wasn't totally sure if I was joking or not. Well, that made two of us.

"Here." Boden handed me two hot dogs in buns and indicated for me to sit at one of the plastic tables while he fetched ketchup and mustard. He plunked the condiments down in front of me, then went back for five more hot dogs before sitting down opposite me.

"Uh... got enough?" I nodded to the pile of dogs on his tray, and he grinned.

"Shifting burns a shit ton of energy," he informed me. "Eat up. Raze will be done procuring us a car soon, and he gets a bit antsy if we make him wait."

"You don't say," I murmured with heavy sarcasm, then glanced back to the counter where Hunter seemed to have the cashier under some sort of hypnosis. He was stroking his finger down the side of her cheek while he spoke, and the glazed-over look on her face said she literally couldn't see anyone but him. No wonder our little shopping spree was going unnoticed.

"Ugh," I grunted. "I think I lost my appetite. Is that what he did to me at the bar the other night?"

Boden turned to look in the direction I was scowling, then turned back to me with a shake of his head. "Not even close, beautiful. He wouldn't use that shit on you." Then he paused, considering. "Not deliberately, anyway. Sometimes it can bleed out of him a bit when he's, uh, happy."

It didn't take a genius to read between the lines. "You mean when he's turned on?"

Boden gave a sheepish smile and shrugged. "It's a talent unique to his breed. Kind of an animal magnetism thing that they developed when their kind started dying out. As distasteful as it sounds, when a species starts going extinct, the sole focus becomes reproduction."

I wrinkled my nose, but finished my mouthful of food before replying. "So he has some magic crap that makes chicks want to sleep with him? Explains a lot." I muttered it in kind of a sour way, and Boden coughed a laugh.

"Does it? Hmm, I wonder why so much jealousy is radiating off you, then?" His smirk was way too damn smug, so I ripped off a piece of my hot dog bun and threw it at him.

Damn cat caught it in his mouth.

Why was that instantly sexy? Shit, damn, and cats. I needed to get laid or just like... rub one out or something. My libido had been taking way too much control over my actions lately.

"I'm not jealous," I lied, even as Hunter stroked his fingers through the cashier's hair and my teeth ground together hard.

"Shouldn't we be going? Raze is probably all kinds of pissy out there in the cold."

Boden nodded, scoffing down the last of his food and gathering up the spare clothes. We headed out of the shop, Boden nodding to Hunter on the way past, and straight across the parking lot to where Raze leaned on the hood of... a minivan?

"Interesting choice," I commented as he tugged on the truck-stop branded sweats. "I never would have picked you as a minivan kinda guy, but who am I to judge?"

Raze shot me a withering glare before he yanked open the sliding door open and gestured for me to get in. "Minivans have shitty locks," he informed me as I ducked into the beige interior, "and more space to spread out."

I took the middle row of seats, so he took the back row, where he spread out and got comfortable. I'd deny it if asked, but I was a tiny bit disappointed there would be no opportunity to get all cozy with these big, muscled cat-shifters.

Boden slid behind the steering wheel, and seconds later Hunter came jogging over—still wearing just his boxer shorts. It could have been my imagination, or maybe a trick of the light, but I could swear he was a little bit hard. My jealousy flared.

"No room," I announced, slamming the sliding door shut as he approached.

Confusion crossed his face, but he wordlessly took the passenger seat when Boden popped the door open for him.

Where the fuck did I get off being jealous of some random

truck stop clerk, knowing full damn well he was "flirting" to cover for Boden and I raiding the clothes and food? Ah fuck it, I never pretended to be a saint.

Silence lay thick in the minivan as Boden put us back on the road, and I knew it was my doing. But I was way too deep in my own mixed-up emotions to untangle the mess I'd just made.

"This is the next safe house?" I asked, crinkling my nose and peering out the window at the dodgy looking motel with a flickering neon sign. "Interesting choice."

A heavy yawn pulled at my jaw, and I rubbed my eyes with the back of my tattooed hand. I'd been dozing on and off for the past few hours, mostly just to avoid conversation with Hunter. Good idea? Hell no. As the minutes had ticked past, I'd grown more and more pissed off at the whole situation.

"Not the safe house," Boden responded from the front seat as he pulled into a parking spot outside the little office. "But with the three of you all snoring, I'm about to fall asleep at the wheel."

Raze and Hunter were both snoring quietly, but I huffed with indignation. "I do not snore."

Boden snickered a laugh. "Uh-huh, sure you don't."

He opened his door, getting out, and I scrambled out of the back to join him in the dirty little reception area. There was no one at the desk, despite the old school tube TV being on and playing old episodes of *Sabrina The Teenage Witch*.

We glanced at each other, then Boden reached out and dinged the little bell a couple of times.

"Two seconds!" a guy called from the back room, and there was a clattering that had Boden and I looking at each other with raised brows. What the fuck was going on back there?

Moments later, there was a screaming howl, sort of like—

"Fuck! You shitting stinker!" the same man yelled as a soaking wet pussy*cat* came tearing out from the back room and past us. The front door hadn't closed properly, so in less than a second, the cat was long gone.

"Uh..." I peered into the darkness after the cat, then jolted back around when the motel receptionist appeared with a huff. He was a portly older man in striped pajama pants and a white, coffee-stained tank top over his ample beer gut. His face and arms were a mess of bright red cat scratches, so it wasn't too hard to figure out what we'd just interrupted.

"Sorry to disturb you during... bath time," Boden commented, a smile pulling at his lips. His arm came around my waist, and his hand rested on my hip possessively. It was kinda hot. Who knew I'd be into alpha males? My ex had been submissive as all fuck.

"My girl and I were looking for a room."

The man scowled, but sat down at his ancient computer to check—I guess—for free rooms. Not that I could see this motel being particularly busy, but whatever.

"Room three," he grunted, tossing a key on the counter as he dabbed his bleeding arms with a grimy cloth.

"Actually, could we get an interconnecting room, too?" Boden added with a charming smile. "We have some friends joining us."

The man grunted but threw another key down, and Boden handed over a credit card.

"Have fun," the guy said with a leer as he ran the card, then handed it back. "There're condoms and lube in the vending machine beside the ice machine."

Boden laughed and kissed my neck as we left the office with our two keys, but I cringed and tried really hard not to keep my voice low.

"What kind of motel sells condoms and lube in a vending machine, Boden?" I hissed at him. "Is this like... a rent by the hour kind of place?"

"It's just a place with beds that we can catch a couple hours of sleep in. I don't know about you, beautiful, but I've been in one too many vehicle accidents this week." Boden quirked a brow at me, and I shuddered my agreement. Poor Candy Jack.

"Wait. Hold up. Where did the credit card come from? I thought we lost everything at the cabin?" I scowled at him accusingly, and he gave a slightly guilty smile back.

"The mini-van owner might have left her wallet in the car," he admitted. "I'll make sure she's compensated once we get back to safety."

Oh. Well, yeah, I guess that was preferable to having Hunter work his creepy sex mojo on the motel clerk.

"Should we wake them up?" I asked, pointing to the two sleeping giants in the stolen minivan. "Or like... hide the van or something?"

Boden unlocked the door to room three and held it open for me to enter. "Nah, fuck them. They can keep sleeping in the van for now. Sooner or later they'll wake up and seek out somewhere warmer, but have you ever woken a sleeping cat before? They get scratchy."

I snickered a laugh, thinking of the receptionist's scratched-to-shit arms and face. "Can't be as bad as bathing a cat. Hey, are you guys that adverse to water, too?"

"Wanna take a shower with me and find out?" His heated gaze was all suggestion, and my lady bits all screamed at me to accept. In fact, I was halfway across the room to the bathroom before my better sense barely kicked in.

"Hold up there, fluff-butt. What was it Raze said about you being the general of some-something cat army? And Hunter said it was a crazy big no-no for us to fuck." I propped my hands on my hips and glared at him with suspicion. "Explain."

Boden's shoulders slumped, and his face was almost sad-puppy... if there was a cat equivalent of that? Or was it only dogs who sulked? Anyway, he looked disappointed as shit.

"Commander of the Shifter Alliance," he muttered, *definitely* sulking. "Can I explain more after I shower?"

I nodded, trying super hard not to picture him in the shower. All soaped-up and wet...

"Sure you don't want to join me?" he teased with a cheeky grin, and I almost wavered. Almost. But I needed to know what I was getting into before we went breaking rules. Because holy shit, it was *so* going to happen.

"Go," I sighed. "I'll chill here."

Boden nodded and headed into the bathroom, leaving me alone in the drab brown room. Who the fuck even designed this motel? It looked like someone's grandma's house, mixed with a homeless shelter.

I was exhausted myself. After Candy Jack got wrecked, I'd run for my damn life, the guys had shifted into magical giant cats, the safe house had been set on fire, then I'd had to ride Raze without any pants on... It was no fucking wonder we were all dead on our feet. I never could sleep properly in cars, so I'd only been napping on and off during the drive.

Boden had left the bathroom door open just a crack, and I couldn't seem to stop myself from ogling him in the mirror as he stripped.

Fucking hell, my guardians are stunning.

"Hey." Hunter came through the front door, startling the shit out of me, and I squeaked a seriously attractive sound of shock.

"Boden showering?"

I nodded, wordless. Had he just caught me perving on his friend through the crack in the door?

The grin on Hunter's face said yes.

Whoops!

"So, what's going on, Cleo-babe? You've been avoiding me ever since the safe house. What gives? Was I coming on too strong? If so, just tell me. I can totally back off. Or I mean, I can try. It's not easy around you because you're so..." He trailed off with a helpless shrug, and I scowled.

"So what? Magical? Naïve? Slutty?" I planned to stand up and confront him properly with my hands on my hips and shit, but I was *really* freaking tired, so I settled for scooting up the bed and resting against the headboard. My knees pulled up and I hugged my arms around my truck-stop sweat pants, but my glare... oh boy. My glare was *fierce*.

Hunter frowned and shook his head. "What? No, I was going to say sexy. Maybe intoxicating or just downright incredible. You're irresistible, Cleo-babe." He gave me a lopsided grin that damn near melted my resolve—or my panties. But I caught myself before I cracked.

"No, Hunter. *You're* the irresistible one." The way I said it left no mistake that I was not complimenting him.

With a confused frown, he sat on the edge of the bed near me and reached out to take my hand. When I snatched it out of his reach, his shoulders slumped and a pained look of resignation crossed his face. "Ah, I see."

"Do you?" I snapped back. Because, like, I wasn't totally sure I did. Maybe he could explain me to me.

He nodded slowly. "You think I've been manipulating you."

I watched him warily. "Haven't you? I saw what you did to that girl at the truck stop. She was like a lovestruck teenager meeting her boy-band crush. We could have set off a bomb in the middle of the store, and she wouldn't have noticed, she was so busy batting her eyelashes at you." I spat the words with a little more venom than I had really intended, and Hunter raised his brows at me.

"Wait. Are you pissed because you think I've been using my ability on you? Or because I was flirting with that cashier chick?" He squinted at me, and I squirmed.

"The, uh, the first one." Not even I would have believed me. Damn jealous streak was the width of the Nile.

His gaze sharpened. "Are you sure? You're aware I was doing that because we were all practically naked and had no money to buy clothes, right? Like... I wasn't trying to get a blow job in the back room or anything."

I gaped at him. "I wasn't aware that was a possibility!"

Hunter sighed and rubbed his eyes. "Cleo-babe, I'm so confused what we're even arguing about here. You're clearly upset at me. Why don't you just... tell me why?"

Uh, maybe because I don't really understand it myself, asshole?

But I wasn't admitting that, so I went with the tried and

tested, "Whatever, it doesn't matter. I'm going to nap now."

I tried to scoot down the bed and turn my back on him, but he reached out and placed his hand on my hip. He was probably just trying to stop me from rolling over like a petulant teenager, but I ended up flinching away from his touch so badly that we couldn't actually pretend it hadn't happened.

"So it *is* my ability that you're pissed about," he groaned. "Babe—"

"No!" Whatever lame-ass excuse he was about to give me wasn't gonna fly. Not with Cleo Carroll. Nah-ah. No sir. "I have every right to be pissed, Hunter. I find out that you have an 'ability' that essentially drugs chicks and makes them want to fuck you, but this wasn't something you thought worth mentioning? How many times have you used it on me? Huh? Every time we've touched? Oh my cats, I feel so violated."

I'd scooted farther away from him on the bed, but it wasn't exactly a California king size, so there wasn't *that* far to go.

"Do you really?" he asked me, sounding hurt. "You feel violated?"

His tone of voice gave me pause, and I considered what I'd just said. Truthfully... no. But that would totally blow my argument out of the water if I just went ahead and said that, so instead I went with... "Maybe."

His pretty, golden-brown gaze dropped, and his shoulders slumped.

Shit. *I'm an asshole.*

"Hunter, I just meant—"

"No, I get it. You meant that if I hadn't let my ability bleed over when we touched, then you never would have been interested in me. It was only because of my inherent powers that we ever hooked up. Probably good that you stopped it before we went too far last night; this whole guardian thing could have gotten really awkward otherwise."

He got up off the bed and made to leave the room, and suddenly I felt like the biggest shithead in the entire freaking world. Hadn't he said to me that first night in the bar that chicks were always going for Raze over him? That he didn't think he had a chance at all until I specifically said I was attracted to him? That was way before he'd used that magical mojo on me.

Woman up, Cleo. For the love of cats, you wanted to bang him even when you thought he was a serial killer.

"Hunter, wait," I jumped up and grabbed the sleeve of his truck-stop hoodie before he made it to the door. "I didn't mean that; I was just..." I sucked in a hella deep breath and pulled up my imaginary big-girl panties. "I was just super jealous of that chick rubbing up all over you. I'm sorry; will you explain it to me? I want to understand."

My hand had snaked up to my amulet, and I was rubbing it between my forefinger and thumb—a clear sign that I was anxious as all hell. But I had big enough ovaries to admit when I was being a petty bitch, and this was definitely one of those times.

Hunter gave me a skeptical side-eye. "You want to understand?"

I nodded. "Yes, please. In case you forgot, I kinda thought this whole magical beings thing was just an elaborate metaphor two nights ago."

He hesitated, frowning. "Are you sure? Because I'm not throwing a tantrum; I seriously get it if you're feeling violated. I never intended to use that ability on you, but it's a part of who I am and I know it's leaked out a couple of times... It's bad form on my part, and I can't apologize enough, Cleo-babe."

Hunter looked genuinely embarrassed and ashamed, and I felt like an even bigger asshole. "I'm sure. Please? I swear I don't feel violated." I paused, letting a smirk creep over my lips. "Like... not yet anyway. There's always time to change that."

I intended it to be playful and flirty, but Hunter's frown just deepened. "Cleo... I don't think you appreciate how important consent is to me. Yes, I occasionally use my ability to get us out of trouble, like at the truck stop, but I would never intentionally use it to sleep with chicks. That's rapey and gross."

Grabbing his hand, I tugged him away from the door and sat down on the edge of the bed. "I'm sorry, I didn't mean to make you feel bad. Start over? Please? Hey, how come it didn't happen just now?" I held up our hands, which were quite definitely touching, but my head wasn't going all trippy and the rest of the world wasn't melting away.

Hunter heaved a sigh and peeled his fingers away from mine, creating a noticeable gap between us as he ran that same hand over his head. Now that I'd seen his shifter form, I could see those darker streaks in his hair, matching his pelt as a Tasmanian tiger.

"It doesn't happen all the time; I told you I really do try to turn it off around you. It's just not very easy when I get... uh..." A small blush stained his cheeks, and he suddenly found the pattern on the bedspread super fascinating.

I bit back a smile. "Happy? Boden mentioned something about that."

Hunter gave me a sharp look, then let a small smile though. "Yeah. *Happy*. Anyway, it didn't happen just then because you touched me, not the other way around. If you initiate the contact, then it's sort of"—he shrugged—"unnecessary? I guess? I don't know; I've kind of needed to figure it all out by trial and error. There wasn't exactly a whole shifter reservation to support me like Raze had."

I nodded my understanding. "Boden said your species was becoming extinct, and that's why you have this talent?"

Hunter raised a brow. "Boden sure was chatty. But we're not *becoming* extinct. We are. Or may as well be. As far as the Shifter Alliance can tell, I'm the last of my kind, and seeing as I'm also a guardian to the amulet bearer, I don't exactly see myself running off to start a Tassie Tiger commune with seventy-five wives all knocked up at once to repopulate my species."

My jaw dropped, and it took me a hot second to find some words. "Why not?" I blurted out.

"Uh," he started, shifting on the bed until he was facing me a bit more. Then he gave me a quizzical head tilt. "Well, for starters, guardians historically don't have the easiest time guarding the amulet bearer. You've seen what the last two days have been like... Could you imagine worrying about kids on top of all this?"

I grimaced, instantly washed with guilt and general shittiness as I thought about Raze's kids and wife. "I need to find a way to release Raze from this arrangement. You too, if you want to shack up with seventy-five wives?"

Hunter snickered. "Uh, no thanks. I'm good right where I am."

I shook my head. "You're telling me you *don't* want to live with seventy-five pregnant, hormonal shifter women? I'm shocked." I had no idea if shifters were more hormonal than normal women, but it was a fair guess, right?

Judging by the dramatic shudder Hunter gave, I was probably right.

"Nope, not the life for me. I'll do my part by giving all the DNA samples they could possibly store, but that's it. Anyway, that's about all I know." He shrugged apologetically. "Sorry it's not much."

I reached out and took his hand in mine, proving I wasn't actually afraid to touch him. "I'm sorry for being a little bitch. I was *mostly* jealous, and then I was hurt thinking you'd been working magic juju on me."

Hunter nodded, understanding. "Well, think about it like this. I'm pretty sure the first time I used it—accidentally, I might add—was in the bar when we were already decently drunk. Were you attracted to me before then?"

Easy question. "Fucking cats, yes. Are you kidding? You're..." I waved a hand at all of him, pointing out his strong, surfer physique, his model face, his goddamn perfectly cheeky smile. Ugh. Fucking Hunter was too sexy for words. "Yes."

A small, smug smile crept over his lush lips. "Okay, so... I guess until you're sure I'm not working magical juju on you, you'll have to initiate any contact between us."

My brows shot up, and my insides did a happy dance. "Did you just ask me to make a move on you?"

Hunter just gave me one of those "if you wanted to, then I'd be down for that" kind of faces, and my eyes darted to the bathroom door... which stood open. Steam wafted out, but there was no one inside.

"What the—? Where did—?"

"He snuck out about five minutes ago," Hunter informed me. "Super quiet, like a cat."

I groaned at his terrible joke—because cheesy jokes were *my* job—but shifted closer to him nonetheless. Tentatively, I raised my hand, the one that wasn't gripping his, placed it on his chest, and pushed him back into the pillows.

CHAPTER
TEN

Considering everything I'd learned in the past few days—you know, that magic was a legit thing and not just a figment of authors' imaginations—it was probably a supremely terrible idea to sleep with Hunter.

But, like, since when did I make good choices? I had hot pink hair and throat tattoos, for fuck's sake.

"Wait." I paused right before my lips met Hunter's, and he made a little sound of protest. "Didn't you say we could get in a bucketload of trouble if we fucked?"

"Not we," he corrected, "just me. And a bucketload is totally subjective, so it's a risk I'm willing to run." His smile was pure mischief, and his golden brown eyes danced in challenge.

Jesus Christ Supercats, I could never resist a challenge.

I closed the distance between us, sealing my lips to his and kissing him a little bit more eagerly than anyone would consider smooth, but *fuck me*. Show me a woman who wouldn't be all over Hunter like a cat on chicken, and I'll eat my shoe.

"Wait." This time it was Hunter stopping us, and I gave him a *seriously* look. "I just wanted to double-check, you're initiating this, so it's all free will and has nothing to do with my ability. Right?"

I nodded frantically, and he sighed with relief.

"Okay. Good. In that case, proceed."

I wanted to laugh at his cautiousness, but when I thought about it, it made sense. When his inherent shifter ability essentially let him date rape chicks—not that Hunter would ever do that—it must be something he was constantly worried about.

Guess I would need to set his mind at ease.

"Hunter," I whispered, peppering his lips with little kisses. "My long lost Hemsworth brother. I have wanted to initiate this from the moment you knocked on my window." I kissed him deeper, running my hands down the front of his sexy, truck-stop branded T-shirt and pushing it up to yank over his head.

"No you didn't," he accused me as he tossed the shirt aside and repaid the favor—leaving me with my tits out. Crazy thing how truck stops didn't sell lingerie. "Fuck yes," he groaned, cupping one in each palm and—I think—really appreciating the moderate *but not little* volume I was packing. Fucking Raze.

"What?" I replied, just clicking with what he'd said. I think my slow brain power was understandable given the fact that he had his shirt off, and ho-ly cats. Hunter was just... drool-worthy. "Yes, I did. I almost came the first time you spoke with that deliciously exotic accent."

Hunter chuckled, kissing me again and rolling my hard nipples between his fingers. Oh my claws. Damn that was good.

"You thought I was a serial killer when I knocked on your window. Hell, you still thought I was a serial killer after our crazy night on the booze. Remember?" He was teasing, not actually upset that I'd thought he was an Australian Ted Bundy.

Still.

"Well, I mean, yeah." It was true. I had thought that. "Doesn't mean I also didn't want to fuck you before you murdered me and buried me in a forest somewhere."

We both paused then, hearing that statement out loud.

"That's a bit messed up, babe," Hunter whispered, a bemused smile on his face.

I licked my lips. "Yeah, um, that sounded less creepy in my head. Let's pretend that didn't happen."

Hunter leaned forward, kissing me hard before grinning. "Fine by me."

"Let's get back to, um, you know..." *Oh for the love of cats, Cleo. Shut up!*

Maybe my mouth needed something better to do. Yep, that seemed like a good plan.

Shuffling back a bit, I tugged Hunter's truck-stop sweats down and palmed his huge erection. Wow. Yeah, that would shut me up for a bit.

Licking my lips in both anticipation and lubrication, I wiggled my ass farther down the bed until I was in a good position to suck some pretty awesome cock. My hand-to-hand combat skills might be a little lacking, I would admit, but my blow job skills? Please. Don't even go there. I was practically Jenna Jameson. Or a Hoover.

Hunter let out a low groan and leaned back on the crappy, flat, motel pillows as I took him in my mouth and went to town.

Eager to cover up that super creepy comment I'd just made, I let my very best skills out of the bag. Sucking, twisting, licking, even the occasional scrape of teeth—just lightly, mind. But it couldn't have been more than a couple of minutes before Hunter hissed, moaned, and hauled me back up to kiss my lips.

"Hey," he protested, his hands at the waistband of my sweatpants. "How are you still in pants? This needs to be rectified immediately, Cleo-babe."

A couple of seriously acrobatic moves later, my pants were halfway across the room. Shit yeah. "Wait," I paused as I straddled Hunter, just seconds away from inserting tab A into slot B. "Uh, this is always an awkward convo at this point, but... I don't suppose you have a condom? I mean, I have an IUD, but no offense, we only just met and, uh..." I trailed off before I could dig myself into a more awkward hole.

Hunter arched a brow at me. "And I look like I get around a bit? Harsh, babe."

I shrugged. He was really, stupidly attractive. There was no way he was a virgin. What if he had herpes or something?

"Shifters can't catch diseases, but if it makes you more comfortable, then I can go and buy a condom. There was a vending machine near the ice-maker, I think." He made to shuffle out from under me, and I halted him with a hand on his chest.

"Wait." I squinted at him. "If you can't catch diseases and I can't catch pregnancy, then let's not fuck around." I paused. "Or, I mean, let's *do* fuck, but not fuck around. Are you following?" I was confusing myself.

Hunter grinned. "Are you sure?"

In response, I reached down between us and lined his dick up to my super excited and under-used cunt. "Positive," I groaned, sinking down onto him and gasping with the exquisite fullness. "Oh shit, yes. Yep, I'm sure."

"Thank fuck for that," he replied with a breathy shudder. His hands gripped my hips and shifted my angle slightly. In a really good way.

Wow.

For a while he let me set the pace. I rolled my hips and rode him slowly, savoring the feeling of him inside me. Hunter kept a tight grip on my hips, his fingers digging into the top of my ass in a way that would probably leave bruises, but I sure as shit wasn't going to be sending a letter of complaint.

He leaned forward and captured one of my nipples in his mouth as I bobbed up and down. I groaned, pausing to let him suck on my tits, as I gripped the back of his neck and held him to me.

In the absence of my movement, he took over, thrusting up into me and hitting all the right places.

"Holy fucking cats, Hunter," I grunted when he moved to my other nipple and continued bucking up into me. "This was a good decision." Releasing his neck, I pushed him back into the pillows once more and braced my hands on his chest.

I was really damn close to coming, so I needed him to—

His hand shifted from my hip, and his thumb found my clit like it had a homing beacon. Yeah, that was the shit. Right there.

Something thudded in a weirdly physical way, but I wrote it off as the blood pounding in my brain.

Hunter rubbed and flicked at my clit while I rode his dick hard until I came. A screaming, toe-curling, muscle-clenching climax.

No excuses, I was just downright loud in bed. Hunter groaned his own orgasm a fraction of a second behind me, and a heady sense of satisfaction rolled through me. I collapsed onto Hunter's tanned chest, shuddering with the aftershocks of my orgasm as I clung to him. Not that he seemed to mind. He wrapped his arms around me, pulling me in close and rolling me into his side. Prime cuddle position.

Just then, that noise popped back into my head.

"Hunter?" I murmured into his sweaty neck. He smelled like man and sex and the beach. How the fuck did he smell like the beach?

"Yeah, babe?" he replied with a sleepy yawn. Pressing a kiss to the top of my hot pink hair, he stroked his strong fingers over my naked, ink-covered skin.

"This might have just been, like, I don't know, something popping in my brain because that orgasm was next level insane," I started and could tell without looking that he was smugly smiling. "But did I hear the door slam?"

His hand froze on my hip, and a thread of tension seemed to travel through his hard as fuck, two percent body fat form. Damn, how did he even—

Focus, Cleo!

"Uh, yeah," Hunter mumbled after a small hesitation. "Raze..."

Panicked, I shot up out of his embrace and gathered the sheets to my chest. My gaze darted around every corner of the room, as though I actually thought Raze would be standing there watching or some shit.

"No, babe, he's not here." Hunter sounded like he was really trying not to laugh, which meant I was really trying not to *fucking murder him.* "He came in, and you were, uh, you know, and then he got all pissy and left."

Stunned, I blinked down at him for a long-ass moment. "He came in," I repeated slowly, "and I was... what?"

Hunter gave a little shrug. "You were literally about to come."

I gasped in horror. "And you didn't *say anything?*"

"Gods no. Interrupting a lady who is on the brink of an epic orgasm is terrible manners, Cleo-babe. Awfully, unacceptably rude. You would have killed me! Besides, it's not like he hasn't already seen you butt naked." He spread his hands apologetically, yet also not. Fucker. He had a point, though. If I'd missed out on that orgasm thanks to dickhead Raze walking in, I would have been serial killer level mad.

Still. I buried my face in my hands and tried to scrub away the embarrassment. "Fuck, Hunter. This is really bad! How much did he see?"

Okay, yes, dumb question. We were both naked, and I'd been riding Hunter's dick like I was competing in a rodeo. My back had been to the door, but there would have been *zero* mistaking that act as anything else.

"Yeah... he didn't leave *super* quick, so..." Hunter wrinkled his stupidly perfect nose, and I was torn between wanting to kiss him again or punching him right in the face. Fucking cats, these guys had me all kinds of messed up. The idea that Raze had stood there for a while, watching me fuck Hunter like a starving succubus... damn, that turned me on.

But wait. That wasn't the point here. "Hunter, focus! What about the whole punishment thing?"

He tilted his head to the side and scratched at the dark stubble on his cheek. "I've never done it before, but if you're into it, I'm down to try."

My mind went down a dirty rabbit hole, and I needed to shake my head to keep on track. "What? No, I didn't mean... Okay, keep that discussion for another day. I meant the whole thing with the Cat Army and us not being allowed to do exactly what we just did."

Understanding dawned on Hunter's face, but then he just shrugged again in that slightly infuriating, carefree way. "I wouldn't stress about it," he told me, grabbing the edge of my sheet and using it to pull me closer to him. "Raze has issues, but we've been friends a really long time. He won't go tattling." He paused. "I don't think."

I'd maintained my iron grip on the sheet, so he'd effectively reeled me in like a fish on a hook. I groaned as he snaked his arms back around my waist and started pressing featherlight kisses to the ink on my neck.

"Nope, no, you're not suckering me in again, Crocodile Hunter," I announced, and with *extreme* willpower, I peeled myself out of his embrace and scooted off the bed. "I'm showering, then sleeping." I speared him with a sharp glare as he opened his mouth to say something suggestive. "Alone."

Quickly gathering up my awesome truck-stop outfit, I raced into the bathroom and locked the door behind me.

Holy Cats.

What had I just done?

I picked up the gold amulet from my naked chest and peered down at it accusingly. "This is all your fault," I hissed at the piece of jewelry. "Shit better not get weird with the guys after this, or I'll personally throw you in the ocean like that chick on *Titanic*."

Call it my imagination or fried nerves from all the mind

blowing sex... but did that fucking necklace just zap me?

Either way, I dropped it quickly and cranked the shower. Time to pretend nothing happened! Nope, nothing. No dicks in this pussy. No reason for crazy shifter police to go locking up any of my guardians. None.

Pretend, pretend, pretend.

CHAPTER
ELEVEN

All my pretending flew straight out of the window when I finally emerged, fully dressed, from the bathroom and found Hunter all spread out across the bed. He was still totally naked and didn't seem at all bothered by his lack of blankets as he snored softly. It wasn't obnoxious, dad snoring, more like that content sound cats make when they're deep asleep. Almost a half purr.

"Holy cat shifters," I whispered under my breath, taking a moment—a really long moment—to perve the hell out of him. I'd been so focused on getting his D in my V earlier that I really hadn't appreciated the buffet that was naked Hunter.

I'd briefly skimmed over the ink on his torso with my mouth, but now I could actually see the designs. They were geometric and depicted what I guessed to be a Tasmanian tiger amongst constellations. The tattoo wrapped around his left side, hugging all the tight lines of his muscles and finishing in that deep groove next to his impressive dick.

Wow. Just... freaking wow.

I took a couple of steps closer to the bed—not because I was a creeper who wanted to drool all over Hunter, but because I wanted to sleep somewhere and the floor did *not* appeal.

Trouble was, my Australian fuck buddy was sprawled across the bed in a way that literally had him touching all four corners. My options were a tiny patch on his right between his outstretched arm and leg... or on top of him. And let's not act dumb and pretend that wouldn't turn into more sex.

A pointed throat clearing had me spinning around and clutching my hoodie to my chest in fright.

"Hey, uh, I was just..." I flailed a hand at Hunter's stark naked form, still sound asleep on the bed. "Looking for somewhere to sleep?"

I have no idea why that came out as a question and not a statement. That *was* what I was doing. Mostly. Ugh, I was so busted.

"Come on." Boden indicated to the adjoining room behind him and gave me a small smirk. "Hunter tends to hog the bed."

Ducking my head to avoid eye contact with him, I scurried into the second room and heard him close the door behind us.

Suddenly, it was all awkward as fuck. Had Boden heard me screwing his friend in the next room? Was he jealous? He'd kind of made it pretty clear that he was interested, and I'd made excuses, and then look what happened.

Holy Cats, Cleo, you're a massive hypocrite! Huge!

"Where's Raze?" I blurted out, noticing the lack of brooding, Native American cat shifters in the room. Not that I was anywhere near ready to face him, knowing he'd watched me coming all over his buddy's cock.

Boden made a noncommittal noise, climbing into the mussed bed and getting comfy on one side. "Raze does what Raze wants. He'll be back by the time we need to leave." He eyed me up as I stood there in the middle of the room like the awkward panda I was. "Are you coming to bed? I promise I will let you have a whole half, and I'll even keep my pants on." He arched a brow, and I bit back a smile at his reference to Hunter sleeping totally nude.

Dropping my hoodie on the little table, I crawled into the other side of the motel bed and tried really hard not to roll into Boden. The bed was dipping under his superior weight, though, so it was like trying to balance on a yoga ball. After a few moments of fighting it, I gave up and let gravity take over.

"Sorry," I mumbled, peering up at him. "Not really the most springy mattress, huh?"

He chuckled a warm sound that vibrated his chest and made me all tingly inside. "Sleep, Cleo. There are bad people trying to kill you, remember?"

I grumbled something about "how could I forget" under my breath, but let him shuffle me around until my back was to him and his arms were around me.

"Hunter's right," Boden commented, right as I was about to fall asleep.

My eyelids snapped open. "About what?"

I held my breath.

"You really are the perfect little spoon size," he commented, and all the breath rushed out of me. I was cool with this observation. Little spoon rocked.

Boden only gave us a few hours of sleep before gently waking me up by whispering in my ear, telling me it was time to go.

I was still wrapped up in his warm embrace, and I groaned my protests in incoherent grumbles as he tried to coax me awake.

"Come on, beautiful," he laughed softly. "We need to move on before our stolen van gets spotted here. I promise you can sleep more at the safe house."

"No," I whined, squeezing my eyes tight shut. "I'm still tired. Go away."

Boden seemed to take me at my word and started to slide out of bed behind me until I squeaked in panic. "I take it back! Don't go away! Holy cats, that was like an arctic blast. Never leave me!"

He hugged me again, kissing the side of my neck. "As badly as I want to read way too much into those words, we do need to go. Come on, I'll get you drive-through coffee."

This got my attention, and I cracked one eye open, peering

over my shoulder at the golden-blond god. "What sort of coffee?"

He grinned, knowing he had me. "Caffeinated coffee. And a blueberry bagel."

I groaned again, but this time it bordered on a sexual sort of sound. "Damn you," I hissed, gripping the top of the blanket. "Okay, like a Band-Aid." Gritting my teeth, I whipped the warm quilt off, then practically dove into my hoodie. "Let's roll."

Boden shook his head with a laugh and held out my rocking cowboy boots for me to put on. I stuffed my feet into them and followed him outside to where the minivan was waiting before a thought occurred to me.

"Hey, how did you know I love all forms of coffee and blueberry bagels?" I squinted at him suspiciously as we paused beside the van.

Boden gave me a lopsided smile and stroked a lock of hot pink hair off my face. "I can read emotions, and your level of excitement when I mentioned coffee was enough to turn my dick hard. Blueberry bagel was a logical step from there."

I squinted at him, nodding slowly. "Smart move." It was taking all my willpower to ignore his statement about having a hard dick, and even more effort not to check.

He smirked like he knew where my mind had gone and opened the passenger door. "Wanna ride me today?"

I froze halfway into the car. "Sorry, what?" I blurted, immediately picturing myself riding Hunter some hours earlier.

Boden gave me a quizzical frown. "I said, wanna ride with me today?"

"Oh," I said. "With. Ride *with*. Gotcha."

In an attempt to cover my awkward moment, I hopped into the passenger seat and buckled myself in while Boden came around to the driver's side.

A small smile played at his lips as we waited in silence for Hunter. Seconds later, he came flying out of his room, rubbing sleep from his eyes, and climbed into the back where Raze already waited.

"G'morning," Hunter greeted us with a lazy smile as he got comfy and strapped on his seatbelt. "Everyone sleep well?"

I had no response to that. Or none that wouldn't light up the pink elephant in the room with a fucking neon light. So I said nothing and stared ahead out the window as Boden pulled into traffic.

Raze said something to Hunter, which was too quiet for me to hear, but Hunter's response of "Fuck off, mate," was clear.

Shit. That was totally about me. Of course it was. Oh sweet baby cats, Raze saw Hunter balls deep inside me. This is not good. Not good.

"I mean," Boden said softly, quiet enough that it was for my ears only as he turned into a drive-through Starbucks, "I wouldn't object if you wanted to drop the 'with.'" He shot me a look that was pure sex, and it took me a second to realize he was still referring to riding with him. Or... riding *him*.

Oh wow.

Pressing my hands to my warm cheeks—and clenching my thighs—I stared out the window and acted *super* interested in the menu. "Uh, caramel macchiato, please," I asked him sweetly. "And we can revisit that other offer later."

As soon as I said it, I bit my lip. I really, honestly had *not* intended to say that out loud. Oh cats. It should be illegal to proposition a woman when she was still half asleep and dazzled by all the sexy men in the stolen car with her!

Again I cursed whoever was in charge that they couldn't have just sent me girls to be my guardians. Or even dudes with dad bods! Were all shifters cut like they were made of marble? Or was there a generation of older, portly sort of magical beings? Ones that had let themselves go a bit and weren't going to tempt me into jumping their bones every fucking opportunity I had?

"Hey," I blurted out as the girl at the window handed through our coffees and snacks. "Are there any unattractive shifters? Or are they all walking sex like you three?"

Ah crap, there I went running my mouth again.

Hunter and Boden seemed to find me amusing, but that was apparently the last straw on Raze's restraint.

"Why's that, Margaret?" he sneered at me from the back seat. "Three guardians not enough for you? Looking to add to your little harem of cats?"

I turned in my seat, glaring death at Raze. "So what if I was, huh? You keep banging on and on about not wanting to be here, so why shouldn't I search for a replacement?"

Yep, turning to face him was a bad idea. His flaming green eyes met mine like a bear trap, ensnaring me in their emerald depths and holding me immobile.

"Firstly," he growled—legit growled, "I have never once asked to be released as a guardian, so I certainly haven't been 'banging on' about it."

I huffed. "Yes, well. You've made it clear that's what you want. With, like, uh, body language." Yeah, I could have thought this argument through better before starting it, and I fully blamed Hunter and Boden for scrambling my brain.

"With *body language*," Raze repeated slowly, like he was reinforcing how dumb I sounded.

Biting my lip, I wrenched my eyes away from his mesmerizing gaze. "Whatever."

I was losing this argument fast, so I opted for retreat. Turning my back on him, I sunk into my seat and sipped my hot, sweet coffee. Unnervingly, I could feel him staring a hole into the back of my head for a really long-ass time before Hunter broke the tense silence.

"Hey," he whispered to Raze, "what was 'secondly' going to be?"

"Shut up, Hunter!" Boden and I both snapped at the same time, and I heard a small snicker of laughter from the cheeky tiger. Fucking shit stirrer.

We drove mostly in silence for a while, with just the odd barb traded between Raze and I, until we slowed in front of an ordinary, suburban kind of house.

Or... it would have been at some point.

Now? Now it looked like a crack den or squatter's paradise.

Graffiti covered the walls, the grass in front was overgrown and littered with trash, and all the windows looked to be smashed.

"Shit," Boden murmured as he peered at the house through his window. "That's not good."

"Let me guess," I said with a sigh. "That's the safe house."

"Was," Boden corrected.

The back door slid open, and Raze hopped out. Silently, he prowled toward the house and seemed to just completely disappear into the shadows near the fence line.

"What's he doing?" I whispered. Why I was whispering, I had no idea. It just sort of felt right for the situation.

Hunter was the one who answered me, leaning forward to speak just as quietly. "He's checking for signs of Bast's followers. If it had just been regular vandals, the wards wouldn't have all been disabled. They never should have gotten within three feet of the door."

I frowned, rubbing my forehead. "I thought the wards kept those Bast-ards away, not normal people. I'm confused."

Both Hunter and Boden gave me apologetic smiles.

"It's a lot to wrap your head around in three days," Boden acknowledged. "When we're out of immediate danger, we can try and get you some books to study. For us, this is all second nature. We grew up in the Alliance, so this has been our lives for as long as we can remember."

Raze reappeared right beside the van, and I squeaked with fright.

"I need to put a bell collar on you or something," I grumbled as he climbed back into the car.

Boden didn't wait for Raze's report before pulling back into the street and heading away from the "safe" house.

"Definitely Bast's doing," the sullen brunet informed us as he rebuckled his seat belt. We'd all learned the hard way after Candy Jack's crash, and I hadn't failed to notice everyone was being conscientious about buckling up. "Her symbols were sprayed on the grass around every ward point. They must have thought we were there already to put so much effort into breaking in."

"Huh?" I spun around to look at him, confused. "But that looked like it'd been vandalized weeks ago."

Raze shook his head. "Staged. Could have only happened last night."

I glanced at the clock on the dash to find it was almost dawn. Holy cats, my body clock was all kinds of messed up.

"Good thing we stopped at the motel, then," Hunter commented, then shot me a lust-filled grin. "In more ways than one."

Raze let out a grunt of disgust from the back row of seats and rolled his eyes. "Fucking Ra save me, I know I'm going to regret this..." He drew a long breath in and released it heavily. "We can go to my house. Even Bast isn't brave enough to attack us in the middle of a shifter reservation, and it's only an hour from here."

Boden shot Raze a sharp look in the mirror, frowning a little. "Are you sure? We can just keep going through to the next-closest house."

"Which is another ten hours away," Raze pointed out. "It's

fine." It did not sound fine. "I'm sure Maeve and the girls would love to see you two, anyway."

I didn't miss the emphasis he put on "two" there.

"Uh, am I understanding this right?" I stage-whispered to Hunter. "Did Raze just say—"

"Don't make a thing of it, Maggie," Raze snapped, cutting me off. "We'll stay one night to restock and regroup. If that works for you, boss?" This was aimed at Boden, who nodded.

Nothing I could say was going to improve the conversation, so I sank back into my seat and wished I had more coffee. That first one was long gone, and I was craving more.

Tension lay thick in the car, and I knew it was because of me. Raze was about to introduce me—object of all his troubles—to his wife and kids.

Something told me that, despite the fact that it was a marriage of paperwork and not "love," it still wasn't going to end well.

Not a snowball's chance in hell.

CHAPTER
TWELVE

I had no idea what I expected a shifter reservation to look like. A friend that Meg and I had hung out with as kids had been an eighth Native American and lived with her grandmother on tribe land. But from what I'd seen, it was just a gathering of houses. Not like teepees or anything stereotyped like that.

Other than being a badass basket weaver, Patricia had just been a normal kid like me and Meg. Or... like Meg. It was quickly becoming clear that I was far from normal.

But this was a *shifter* reservation, so I was throwing all expectations out the window. Until we pulled up outside a pretty, craftsman style house with meticulously maintained gardens.

"Um... this is your house?" I blurted out, shooting a baffled look at Raze, who glared back at me.

"What were you expecting, Mags? A teepee tent with people dancing around a fire?" His sneer told me clearly he thought I was making racial stereotypes, and my jaw flapped.

"What? No! That's not—Ugh! That's not what I meant, Raze, you assface! I just meant it's a really pretty house." My cheeks were so hot with indignation that I wouldn't be surprised if it was showing. "I've been on *normal* reservations before, I just haven't been to a *shifter* one."

The suspicious narrowing of his eyes said he wasn't buying my excuses. "Oh, I see. So I'm not allowed to live in a pretty house. Real inclusive, Margaret."

"What the hell?" I exclaimed, "I was complimenting your house, you deranged psychopath!"

"Okay," Boden interjected, "let's just retreat to our corners and save this argument for later. Look." He nodded to the front porch of the house where two dark-haired girls had just spilled out and were running toward our stolen minivan.

Raze shot me one last glare, then hopped out of the van and swept the girls up in a huge hug. The kids squealed their excitement, and I caught a rare flash of genuine happiness on Raze's face before he turned his back on us to head into the house.

"Cute kids," I murmured, trailing behind Boden as he led the way up the flower-lined path to the house.

Hunter snorted a laugh. "If I didn't know better, I'd say you sounded jealous."

I scoffed so hard at that suggestion that I practically choked on my own spit. "Jealous? Not a chance in Egyptian Hell! This Maeve is welcome to him and all his surly bullshit. Ain't nobody got time for that."

"Egyptian Hell?" Hunter repeated, teasing. "Is that a place?"

I rolled my eyes. "I'm sure it is. Wouldn't you guys know?"

We'd reached the front porch, and a dark-haired beauty stood there, leaning on the doorway. Actually, that didn't do her justice. She was cats-damned *stunning*. Like she'd stepped straight off the pages of a women's magazine. Not a trashy one, something classy with thick pages and a satin finish. Homes and Gardens maybe.

"Boden, Hunter, I've missed you troublemakers," she greeted the guys with genuine warmth, hugging each of them and kissing their cheeks before turning her almond eyes to me. "You must be Margaret," she stated, and I cringed.

"Cleo," Boden corrected her, and she gave a small, confused frown.

"Margaret is my legal name, but I haven't used it since I was five," I explained, trying to smooth over the awkward moment.

Hunter made an annoyed sound. "Raze probably left that part out because he's a dick!" he yelled the end of that sentence, probably intending for Raze to hear him, but Maeve scowled and swatted his arm with her hand.

"Language," she admonished. "But anyway, it's lovely to meet you, Cleo." Her gaze traveled over me from my hot pink hair to my many tattoos, my awkward truck-stop outfit, and my chipped glitter nail polish before smiling again, this time with less warmth.

"I look forward to getting to know you. After all, you're going to be a permanent fixture in our lives while my husband remains your guardian."

Me-ow! This non-shifter kitty had *claws*. Neither of the guys seemed to notice the inflection she dropped onto the words *while* and *husband*, but I wasn't fooled. This bitch wanted me gone. Long gone.

Boden laughed easily, following her as she led us through to the kitchen. "Oh, he's your husband now, huh? Last time we saw you, he was any number of names that I won't say in front of your kids." He gave her a teasing smile, and her cheeks pinked in the delicate sort of way *no one* should be allowed.

"Things change, Bo." She turned, folded her arms over her chest, and leaned her butt on the counter. "I guess you're looking for a place to stay while you sort out your trouble?"

Was it my imagination, or did she look at me when she said "trouble"?

"Just one night," Boden assured her. "We've run into some trouble with the Bastites."

She raised her brows in surprise. "So soon? Raze called me the other night to tell me about Margaret but didn't mention cultists."

Okay, the use of my hated given name was *not* an accident. This bitch was testing my patience.

"He lost his phone when they ran us off the road. It's been a rough couple of days," Boden admitted, running a hand through his hair. "We just need twenty-four hours to regroup, check in with the big cats, and then we'll be out of your hair."

Her lips tightened, and I suspected she badly wanted us to be gone... but not if it meant Raze left with us. "Of course," she finally murmured. "My home is yours. I need to get the girls to school and then head to work. You know where everything is?"

"We got this, Maeve," Hunter replied with an easy smile. "Promise not to burn your house down while you're gone."

Both Boden and I cringed at his poor choice of words, but Maeve just gave us a suspicious frown before heading outside to wrangle her kids. They were out on the lawn behind the house, which led down a gentle slope to the shore of a peaceful lake.

"Cleo-babe," Hunter said, nudging me. "I'll show you around. You can sleep with me tonight if you want. I promise not to take up the whole bed again."

"No," Raze snapped, appearing from freaking nowhere again and startling me. "You're not fucking our amulet bearer right under the Alliance's nose. That's asking for trouble, dipshit." He flicked Hunter in the head, but instead of reacting badly, Hunter just sighed and shrugged.

"Worth a try," he told me with a cheeky wink, then headed up the wooden staircase.

"Follow me," Raze ordered me, starting up the stairs himself.

I risked a glance back at Boden, but he just watched me with a totally unreadable expression. Obviously I wasn't dumb enough to think he *didn't* know Hunter and I had fucked. He was awake the whole time, and I don't think I'd been particularly quiet...

Boden met my curious gaze, tilting his head to the side as though questioning what was going on in my head. I was just about to blurt it all out, too, until—

"Maggie!" Raze barked from the top of the staircase. "Quit eye-fucking the boss and hurry up. I have shit to do today."

Cowed, I ducked my head and hurried up the stairs to where he was waiting, then followed him down to a tidy bedroom decorated in grays and blues.

"Bathroom is across the hall. If you need anything else, ask the guys." He delivered the words with absolutely zero emotion, then spun around to leave.

"Hold up," I said, stopping him in the doorway. "Am I some sort of prisoner here? It's, like, breakfast time; you don't seriously expect me to just go to bed?"

He turned back around, stepping toward me in a move that was undoubtedly intended to intimidate me with his size. Hah, joke's on him; that shit was a turn on for me.

Wait.

"Prisoner? Not at all, Mags. You're just not permitted to leave this house until I say so. Clear?" His smile was more predatory than kind.

I glared up at him. Way up. Damn, he was tall.

"That's pretty much the definition of prisoner, dumbass."

He just shrugged. "Whatever you want to call it. Don't leave the house, and whatever you do"—he leaned down close, adding extra oomph to his words—"try not to break any more sacred laws. No matter how greedy your cunt gets."

I gaped in shock, and it took me a few moments to come up with a golden comeback. Sadly, those few moments were all the time Raze needed to storm out of the room and slam the door in my face.

Fucking pussy-ass bitch.

So, despite my bluster with Raze, I was genuinely tired as shit. Shocking, I know. It was crazy what two... or was it three?... days on the run would do to a girl. I could safely say I'd done more physical exercise since meeting the guys than in my entire freaking life.

These thoughts echoed around my head after I woke from an extended nap and took another long shower. I scrubbed my hair with the pretty-smelling shampoo I found on the shelf, but it didn't look like I was getting any more color out. Fucking pink dye.

"Hey," I greeted the guys when I came downstairs and found them out the back, drinking beers. "Uh, any chance I could borrow some of Maeve's clothes?" I directed my awkward question at Raze, who was glaring at me with an intensity that could set shit on fire. "My other outfit is a bit gross."

He didn't answer me for a long time. Like... an uncomfortably long time. Just stared.

"Here," Hunter finally responded instead. "We grabbed you

some fresh stuff from the store. Figured Maeve's stuff would practically drown you." He grabbed me by my hand and tugged me back inside the house, where I spotted a shopping bag sitting on the kitchen island.

"Thanks, Croc." I grinned at him, taking the bag and then casting a look back outside to where Raze and Boden sat talking. "What's his problem?" I asked softly. "I know we argue, but I'm not exactly here by choice either. He's glaring at me like I'm half dog or something."

Hunter looked confused by my question, followed my line of sight, then snorted a laugh. "Raze? Uh, babe... he's not glaring."

I wrinkled my nose. "Are you blind? I asked him a question—politely, I might add—and he couldn't even respond. Just glared like he wanted me to spontaneously combust and solve all his problems."

Hunter really was laughing now, and I was getting a bit ticked off at him.

"Cleo-babe," he chuckled, running his hands down my sides, then lifting me onto the counter so we were *slightly* closer in height. "Sweetheart, he wasn't glaring." Hunter dropped a teasing kiss on my lips, his warm hands still holding my hips and practically burning me through the dark, silken robe I wore.

"Oh no?" I scoffed. "Maybe he just had a stroke and couldn't move his face, then?"

Hunter was still grinning as he nudged my knees open and stepped closer. "Babe, he wasn't glaring, he was *staring*." He paused for dramatic effect, and I waited for the other shoe to drop.

"Because you just came outside all fresh-smelling and damp from the shower, wearing nothing but a robe. *His* robe."

I blinked at Hunter a couple of times, then shook my head. "What? No, this was hanging in the room he—" Realization dawned, and I groaned. "He put me in his room?"

Hunter snickered and leaned in to kiss my neck.

"But why?" I demanded. "Where is he planning on sleeping?"

"Probably on the couch," Hunter murmured. "Or Maeve would happily let him in her room if he gave a flicker of interest."

Hunter had somehow slipped a hand inside my robe and was sneaking it up my inner thigh, and it was taking way too much effort not to jump his bones. It didn't help that I could feel the telltale tingles and the fuzzy focus associated with his ability creeping over me.

"Well, now I feel bad," I sighed. "And I definitely can't fuck you on his kitchen counter. Scat!" I swatted him on the arm, gently, and he reluctantly stepped back to let me down. "I'll get dressed. Grab me a drink, and I'll join you outside. Unless you're talking official business that I'm not privy to?"

I had intended it as a joke, but Hunter took me seriously. "Nah, we're done with that part, you're good to join us."

Cheeky shit that he was, he gave me a playful ass grab as I brushed past him with my bag of clothes. Holy cats, I wanted to change my mind and strip Raze's fucking robe off right then and there...

But that seemed super disrespectful, and as much as we had our issues, I still had some boundaries.

CHAPTER
THIRTEEN

"Okay," I said, flicking the tab on my beer to open it before taking a long sip. We were seated on the lawn in front of the lake, and I was cozy in my new clothes. The sizes had been spot on, right down to the bra and panties—a feat not even I could manage—so I was crediting Hunter with that one.

He had good taste too. Acid-washed skinny jeans with designer rips, a soft, black tank top, and a gunmetal gray cashmere coat. There were other pieces in the bag, too, and it must have cost a small fortune.

Not that I was complaining. They kind of owed me after totaling Candy Jack, right?

"Okay?" Boden repeated, kicking back in his own lawn chair.

"Oh, uh…" I startled, realizing I'd just gotten lost in my own thoughts. "I have questions." I paused, but none of the three guys spoke to stop me. "Firstly, uh…"

I paused again. For reals, I had just expected to say, "I have questions," and then one of them would cut me off with the information they *were* willing to provide. Then we'd go from there. I hadn't actually prepared, well, any questions.

I'd make such a sucky urban fantasy heroine.

"Go on," Boden encouraged, and I huffed. Okay, what questions did I have?

"Umm," I hedged, taking another sip of my cold beer while I thought.

Raze snorted a sarcastic laugh, but when I shot him a glare, he was oh-so-innocently sipping his own drink. Fucker.

"Okay, let's start with this. How come I've never seen or heard of Bast and her little minions in my entire life, and then the second I hook up with you three—boom, there they are, trying to kill us." I directed my question at Boden because, let's face it, he was totally in charge of our merry band of misfits. "Explain that to me."

Boden exchanged a quick look with the other boys. "So, we think they might have been following us. It all seemed really coincidental that they would find you so quickly after we had. There are some assets in the Alliance who set us in the right place at the right time to meet you, so it stands to reason they might have had someone watching us." He spread his hands a bit apologetically. "That's our best theory at the moment."

I gaped at him. "Right. So this is all your fault. Good to know." I was partly joking because, for real, this would have happened at some point. I wasn't going to hold it against them when I could have just as easily fucked up and pulled Bast's attention all on my own.

"We're really sorry, if that counts for anything?" Hunter offered, and I shot him a smile to show I wasn't *totally* serious.

"Question two," I continued. "You guys went all cagey and weird after that thing happened in the woods. You know, with the"—I mimed a stabby dagger—"and the"—I mimed the cultist going up in a poof of flame and crumbling to ash. Go with it; my charades skills were unparalleled.

"We know the *thing* you mean, Maggie," Raze drawled. His boots were up on the wooden table in the middle of our chairs, and his gaze was heavy on me.

I squirmed a little in my seat. Why did the only open seat have to be opposite that twat?

"Yeah, so? Explain." I flicked my fingernail against the can in my hand, trying really freaking hard not to let him intimidate me.

Raze sucked a breath and opened his mouth to speak, but the mean look in his eye said it was going to be something snarky and *not* the answers I was requesting. Luckily for everyone involved, Boden spoke over Raze.

"Okay, let's be brief here. We don't want to be discussing this when Maeve gets back." Boden shot Raze an apologetic look, but the dark-haired devil just shrugged.

"She's human," Hunter explained for my benefit. "While she's allowed some level of knowledge because her girls are likely to be shifters, she's still not... you know... all access."

I nodded my understanding. "Yeah, it sounds like shifters aren't super tolerant of humans?" I shot a quick look at Raze, thinking of how he married Maeve so she wouldn't get kicked out of the reservation when his brother died. It was incredibly selfless but also shitty as all hell that it was necessary.

"Human's haven't exactly been tolerant of shifters throughout history," Hunter said softly, and the edge of pain in his voice spoke to a deeper story there.

"Back to your question, though," Boden continued. "Long story short, you're not supposed to be able to use the amulet. At all. We got all 'cagey and weird,' as you put it, because that should never have been possible."

I was rendered speechless for a minute. "Huh."

"The bearer of the amulet—the descendant of Queen Hatshepsut—is supposed to be human. Totally human, totally unable to use the power of Ra." Raze had lost the sarcasm, but there was a hint of suspicion in his voice. "It's a safeguard against anyone getting ideas of world domination. The powers stored in the amulet are supposed to be guarded by someone who *can't* access them. That person is then guarded by the three most powerful shifters of that generation. So on and so forth. As far as Alliance history shows us, the power of Ra hasn't been accessed in millennia. Certainly never since he gifted it to Hatty back in ancient Egypt."

My lips rounded in an "oh" shape but no sound came out. What he was saying... scared the beans out of me.

"Sort of explains why Bast has such a hard-on for it this cycle," Hunter muttered. "She must know something more about how Cleo is different."

"Wouldn't surprise me," Boden agreed. "Her acolytes are growing stronger."

I shook my head, trying to make sense of the madness. "Surely whoever you work for knows something," I suggested. "You all keep referring to some higher power that will dish out commands and punishments. Don't they know what's going on?"

"They like to act like an omnipotent power, but in reality, they don't know any more than we do," Boden replied with a grimace. "Or if they do, they're not letting on. I called them as soon as we arrived here. One thing they did suggest, though, which might bear some promise, is to go and speak with the last amulet bearer."

Huh. Why hadn't I thought of that?

"We can do that? I mean, like, do we even know who she is? Was it a she? I'm making gender assumptions here." I was also babbling, a clear sign that I was teetering on the edge of a freak out.

Raze raised his brows. Hah, see what I did there? Anyway, he looked at me like I was a moron, and that was less funny than my word play. "Of course we do. The Alliance keeps great records."

"So... can't we just call her? You do know how phones and the internet and shit work,s right? It kind of eliminates the need to physically travel places to ask questions." Yes, I was being sassy. But whatever, I was allowed to be under the current circumstances.

Raze narrowed his eyes. "Would you like to just hand the amulet over to Bast on a silver platter too? They may look like stone-age nutcases, but I promise they're not. They *will* have the modern technology angles covered, so the only safe way to do this shit is face to face. Preferably in a random location where the risk of listening devices is low."

I groaned and scrubbed at my face with my free hand. Then remembered my drink and took another really long sip. Okay, fine. I chugged the rest of it.

When I was finished, and had swallowed an unladylike belch, I sighed. "Okay, so where are we heading? Please say somewhere nearby. I'm really getting sick of the road-tripping shit."

"New Orleans," Boden announced. "Marie-Elizabeth runs a dance club in the French Quarter."

New Orleans. Cool. At least it was a destination I was familiar with. And it would mean passing through Texas. Perfect, I still had kittens to save!

"Could we stop and save the kittens on the way?" I asked, hopeful.

Boden's brows shot up and he exchanged a quick look with Raze. "And bring them with us to New Orleans? With cultists chasing us and running us off the road? It's maybe not the best idea, beautiful."

My shoulders slumped but I knew he had a point.

"Look," Hunter suggested, "I'll make some calls and see if one of my friends can pick them up. Okay?"

It wasn't the same, but I guess if the kitties got saved…

"Thanks," I whispered, giving him a grateful nod.

Whatever else we were going to discuss was cut short by the arrival of Maeve's two squealing daughters, who came tearing across the lawn at top speed and piled on top of Raze, who ended up dropping his beer.

Sucker.

"Daddy!" the bigger one yelled, then proceeded to babble a high-speed report of her day at school, while the smaller one kept trying to talk over her with her own cool story.

"Girls," he interrupted them both, holding his palm up to silence them. "Did you even say hello to your uncles?"

The ankle-biters turned around and squealed greetings at both Boden and Hunter, giving them hugs before returning to Raze's lap.

"Who's the lady?" the littler one asked, eyeing me warily.

The bigger one seemed better informed. "That's the witch momma thinks will steal our dad from us."

I gaped at her in shock.

"Oh," the smaller one said, "I forgot. But didn't she say bi—"

Raze cut her off by clapping a hand over her mouth, but it was *preeeeetty* clear what the kid had been about to call me. I'll give you a hint; it rhymes with witch.

Little shit.

"Okay, girls, how about you show me some of those awesome drawings you've been working on?" Raze suggested, lifting them both off his lap and ushering them inside ahead of him.

"Thanks for nothing, asshat," I grumbled after him. "What kind of mother says 'bitch' in front of her kids, anyway?"

Hunter snickered a laugh and cracked open a fresh drink.

"The kind who is in love with her brother-in-law and terrified to lose him," Boden replied in a soft voice.

At least I wasn't the only one who had noticed that.

"They call him 'Dad,'" I murmured, accepting a fresh drink from Hunter and opening it.

Boden let out a heavy sigh, and Hunter made a sound of frustration.

"They know he's not," Boden told me. "But Maeve isn't helping the situation."

"She's known that Raze is a guardian since they were kids. We get selected pretty much straight after our first shift, and its not the sort of job you can just turn down." Hunter followed my line of sight over to the living area of the house, where Raze was playing some game with the girls that involved flying one of them around the room above his head. "She's just in denial."

I balanced my drink on the arm of my chair and hugged my arms around myself. Maeve herself was in the kitchen, preparing dinner probably, but her attention was totally fixed on the handsome man entertaining her kids.

"That sucks," I commented. I wasn't even being a dick about

it; I genuinely felt bad for Maeve. Seeing how Raze was with her kids, I couldn't blame her for calling me a bitch, either. "I'll figure out a way to let him resign or something."

Boden gave me a weak smile. "It doesn't work like that, beautiful."

"Then I'll fire him." I shrugged. "I'm not super into forced servitude, so like... we can figure it out."

Hunter made a noise that I couldn't make out, and when I frowned at him in confusion, he just wrinkled his nose. "Maybe talk to him about it. You might be surprised by his opinions."

I scoffed. "Yeah, Raze and I have such fantastic, in depth conversations. Okay."

My sarcasm was thicker than a tree trunk, but Hunter didn't bother arguing with me.

Whatever, I'd give it a try. They knew him better than me, after all.

It wasn't until later that night that I had a chance to speak with Raze away from everyone else. The kids had just gone to bed, and Boden was helping Maeve wash up in the kitchen.

Hunter, Raze, and I were back in the lawn chairs, but this time we had a fire burning in the brazier on the low table between us. It wasn't really cold enough to need a fire, but the girls had begged for one because Raze was supposed to be some epic marshmallow roaster.

Not that I'd tasted the proof. My own efforts just came out totally black or not melted at all. Epic fail.

After the three of us had fallen into a comfortable silence for a little while, Hunter had to go and ruin it by standing up abruptly.

"I just remembered," he blurted out. "I need to, uh, do... a thing. Something inside. I'm just gonna... go." He jerked his thumb at the house, then scurried inside before either of us could find a reason for him to stay... leaving Raze and I alone in the darkness.

Fucking Hunter.

Neither of us spoke for a bit, and I attempted to cook another marshmallow. It didn't end well.

"For the love of cats," Raze muttered with a sigh. "Here." He poked his stick across the table at me—not *that* stick, his marshmallow cooking stick—and offered me the perfectly toasted treat on the end.

I couldn't phrase that in any way that would make it sound less like an innuendo, but it seriously was innocent.

"Thanks," I murmured, taking the gooey candy in my fingers and popping it in my mouth. "Wow. You really do cook a good marshmallow."

He just grunted in reply and went about cooking one for himself.

Clearly, Raze wouldn't be making any stimulating conversation, so it fell on me to start. After all, Hunter had made it pretty painfully clear he was leaving us to talk alone.

I sucked in a deep breath, clutching my amulet in an anxious death grip. "So, I just wanted to let you know that I'm firing you." The words all fell out in a rush with my breath. Across the fire, Raze's green gaze flared bright, and I shivered at the intense glare.

"You're... firing me," he repeated, like I'd just spoken Chinese or something.

"Yeah." I shrugged. "Or, like, when I figure out how to, I mean. I just want to be clear that I understand you don't want to be my guardian, and I'm sorry about that. But, you know, I'll fix it. And shit." I trailed off, feeling uncomfortable as he continued staring at me. "Like, I know this whole thing is super inconvenient and you'd rather be here with the girls and *Maeve*. So, just... let's work out how to undo whatever makes you my guardian."

He didn't speak for a long time. A super long, super awkward amount of time.

It wasn't until I shifted around a bit in my chair—thinking about the best way to physically remove myself from the tense silence—that he finally cracked.

"Is that what you want?" he asked, his voice totally devoid of emotion.

That, ah, wasn't what I'd expected. I had sort of been thinking he'd be more excited. Maybe appreciative? I didn't know. Something.

"Uh, does it matter? It's what you want." I frowned at him. "Isn't it?"

"Is it?" he responded, and I glared.

"Stop it."

"Stop what?" His blazing green eyes narrowed at me.

"Stop answering my questions with questions; you're confusing the fuck out of me. I just wanted to let you know that you don't have to feel obligated to me anymore. There's no need to be a douchecanoe about it." I released my necklace and folded my arms with a huff. "I have no idea why Hunter thought it was a good idea to talk to you about this; you're clearly incapable of a rational conversation."

Raze's brows shot up, and he leaned back into his chair. "Is that what we're having here? A rational conversation? Because to me it sounds a whole lot like you're *telling* me what's happening."

I spluttered with indignation. "Yes, but, what? I'm so confused right now. You *don't* want to be fired?"

He shrugged. He fucking *shrugged*. What kind of—

"What the hell does that mean?" I demanded, then mimicked his shrug. "What even is that? Use your words, Raze."

He leaned forward again, bracing his really freaking muscled forearms on his denim-clad knees. "It means that I was chosen as a guardian to the amulet bearer, and no one can take that away from me. Not even you, Maggie."

I parted my lips to reply, then closed them, then tried again. "Huh?"

"You're stuck with me," he said, annunciating every word carefully, then gave me a sarcastic smile. "Until the next amulet bearer is chosen or to death do us part."

I pursed my lips, staring at him. "So... you *don't* want to be fired?"

He just rolled his eyes and sat back. From his armrest he picked up his drink and took a sip, but his gaze never left my face while I puzzled through this change of events.

"Then why are you such an insufferable asshole?" I demanded.

This time the smile he flashed me seemed almost genuine. "Why are you?"

"Fair point," I grumbled, retrieving my own drink from the grass beside my chair to take a sip.

The two of us fell into silence, and I poked at the dying fire with my marshmallow stick. I'd eaten enough of the sticky fuckers to last me a lifetime, but there was something soothing about messing with coals.

"So," I finally said, with a little hesitation and a lot of Dutch courage. I was safely in the tipsy zone, thanks to an evening of beers, and it was just enough to make me say things I shouldn't. "You and Maeve, you're not..."

"Not what?" Raze prompted when I trailed off. Bastard, he knew what I meant.

"Not fucking?" I finished. As soon as the word left my lips, my body flushed with heat, and I knew I was treading on dangerous ground. Despite the fact that Raze *had* seen me naked—accidentally—and also seen me fucking his friend, we hadn't exactly discussed it. There was something strangely... *intense* about this turn of the conversation.

Raze stared across the fire at me for a while, a small half smile tugging at his lush lips. "No," he replied after some time. "She's not my type."

"Oh," I breathed. For some unknown reason, it was like a weight had just been lifted off my shoulders. Yes, unknown. Totally unknown. Don't call me on my bullshit; it won't end well. "What is your type?"

Oops. That definitely hadn't meant to be said aloud.

It was too late, though, as Raze's grin spread wider, and I could fucking swear his gaze flickered over my whole body before he replied.

"I'm more interested in smart-mouthed hipsters with old lady names."

My jaw dropped. For reals. I practically needed to scoop it up off the grass and put it back in position before I could splutter my response.

"I do *not* have an old lady name."

Raze smirked. "Who said I was talking about you? Narcissist."

Shit.

Back-peddling faster than an Olympic cyclist, I stretched my arms above my head and let out a loud and seriously fake yawn. "Gosh, it's getting late," I commented, checking my wrist for a watch I wasn't wearing. "I should go to bed." I jumped up from my seat and scurried my ass back inside... literally running away from my issues.

Yes, I'm aware. I'm very well adjusted.

CHAPTER

FOURTEEN

A fter my speedy escape from Raze and all the awkwardness of our conversation, I made my excuses to everyone and hid in my room. Ugh. Raze's room.

Damn that antagonistic son of a cat. I couldn't escape him anywhere! Even his pillows smelled of his intoxicating mix of spice and jasmine.

I must have fallen asleep at some point, though, because when I woke to pee, it was three thirty-three in the morning. Usually I loved when I looked at the clock and found recurring numbers like that, but this one made me uneasy.

No freaking idea why, it just did.

"Paranoid," I muttered, wrapping myself in Raze's silk gown—yes, I know, shut up—and silently slipping across the hall to the bathroom.

After I peed in the dark, I quickly washed my hands, then felt around for a hand towel. I had a weird thing about not turning lights on when I got up to pee at night. Like, as soon as I turned a light on, I'd wake up fully, but when it was still dark, I could pretend I was still asleep.

Anyway, while hunting for the hand towel, my hand knocked into something that seemed rather glass-like, just seconds before it over-balanced and hit the floor with a smash.

Yep. That was a glass. Whoops!

Fumbling, I reached for the light switched and flicked it.

Nothing.

"Crap," I growled under my breath, squinting up at the light fixture like staring at it would make the bulb work. I didn't want to leave broken glass on the bathroom floor, though, so I'd have to do my best to clean it up in the dark.

Shivering, I tiptoed down the stairs to the kitchen. I'd seen one of the guys grab a dustpan from the pantry earlier, so hopefully that was where I'd find it.

Creeping into the kitchen, I located the light switch inside the walk-in pantry and flicked it on.

Or I tried to. Nothing happened… and that uneasy feeling in my belly tripled.

Something was wrong. Seriously freaking wrong.

A spike of panic shot through me, and I didn't second-guess myself. I raced through to the living room and practically leapt onto Raze where he slept on the couch.

"Raze!" I hissed, shaking his really fucking broad shoulder. He was sleeping shirtless, but the panic zinging through me meant I hardly even noticed. Hardly, but not totally. I was still a red-blooded woman.

"Mags?" he mumbled, squinting at me and rubbing his hand over his face in a slightly adorable, sleepy way. "What's going on?"

"Uh, I'm not sure." I darted my gaze around the room, searching for signs of danger. Maybe an intruder or something? "I think, uh, something's wrong."

"Something's wrong?" he repeated, but at least this time I thought it was sleep confusion and not his usual sass.

"Yeah, I just... I think they're here. The Bast-ards."

He raised one brow at me, but didn't seem anywhere near concerned enough. "Bastites," he corrected, "and they can't be. They're not ballsy enough or strong enough to risk attacking us in the middle of the Yurok Shifter Reservation. That's suicide."

"Yeah, well, pretty sure they're suicidal. I'm telling you, Raze. Something's wrong." My fingers clutched my amulet, and his sleepy eyes seemed to stare at it for a heated moment before he sighed and sat up.

"Okay. Why don't you tell me what started this? Are you sure it wasn't just a bad dream or something?" He ran a hand through his loose hair, ruffling it in a shampoo-commercial kind of way. Gorgeous fucker.

Suddenly I second-guessed myself. Was I totally overreacting?

It was probably just a blown fuse or something. All the running for my life was starting to make me crazy. Or, you know, crazier than normal.

"Mags," Raze said, snapping his fingers in front of my face. "Focus. What happened?"

Fully prepared for him to shoot me down for being a dumbass, I shrugged. "The power is out. It seemed… I don't know, it worried me. But now that I'm more awake, I'm perfectly aware that a blown fuse does not equal Bast-ards invading the house. No need to be an asshole; I'll go back to bed now."

I got up from where I'd been kneeling beside the couch and started to leave, when Raze grabbed me by my wrist.

"The power is out?" he repeated, his face serious, and I nodded. "Why didn't you lead with that, Maggie?" he hissed the words in anger as he yanked me back onto the couch and darted his gaze around the room.

"Uh, well, it seems like a bit of a leap now that I say it out loud," I admitted. "It just freaked me out."

Raze covered my mouth with a huge hand, even though I hadn't exactly been shouting. "Except that my brother was an electrician before he died," he told me. "There's no way this is a blown fuse. This house is wired like a damn spaceship."

I peeled his hand away just far enough to speak. "So… we are being attacked?"

He gave a sharp nod, getting up and tugging me to my feet. His appraisal of the room we were in seemed to satisfy him that we were clear of immediate danger, but that didn't mean it couldn't spring out at any moment.

"Yes," he replied. "Wake the guys. Quick. I'll get Maeve and the girls."

I raced up the stairs after him and burst into the first door he pointed me to. Raze carried on down the hall to wake his family up.

Both Boden and Hunter—who'd been sleeping in twin beds with pretty floral comforters—sat up sharply at my less than subtle entry into the room.

"Bast-ards," I gasped out. It was all I needed to say, and they jumped out of bed and threw clothes on. I left them to get their shit together and hurried back into the hall—just in time to hear an almighty snarl and a window smashing.

"Fuck," I cursed, following the sound into what was clearly the kids' bedroom.

The room was empty.

The picture window had been totally smashed out, and the curtains blew dramatically in the breeze as I stepped closer and peered out.

"Oh shit," Hunter breathed, coming up behind me and looking down to the grass below. Without any further hesitation, he climbed out the broken window and deftly jumped down to the grass like some kind of... uh... cat. Yeah, okay that makes sense.

Boden laid a gentle hand on the small of my back, but his whole frame was tense to the point of shaking as he looked down.

"Stay here, Cleo," he ordered me. "Do *not* come outside; we can handle this."

He didn't wait to extract an agreement from me, just jumped out the window and hit the grass with a soft thud. Like freaking Superman or some shit.

"Fuck that," I growled, racing through the house. I wasn't going to attempt one of those jumps myself because I was around ninety-eight percent sure I would just break both my legs and then probably die, but I sure as shit wasn't going to cower in the house.

The fact that Boden actually thought I would be okay with that while Bast-ards held Raze's kids at knifepoint on the lawn...? Well, that was going to be a very heated argument. Later. When the girls were safe.

"Ah, here she is," one of the cultists announced as I threw open the front door and stormed out. "Nice of you to join us, Descendant."

"Cleo!" Boden snapped in outrage, and I flipped him off.

Yes, I was well aware that I couldn't fight for shit, had no control of magic, and really wasn't even a great hostage negotiator. But it was pretty obvious they were here for one thing. And I *had* that thing.

A quick look around the front lawn of Maeve's property showed the odds were currently stacked in Bast's favor. Or as far as physical numbers went, anyway. There were some twenty-odd cultists scattered around, all robed up in black cloth with those fancy curved daggers at their belts. Two of them held the kids tightly with blades pressed threateningly at their little throats. A third held Maeve, his hand clamped over her mouth to muffle all the obscenities she seemed to be screaming.

So much for the mighty Yurok Shifter Reservation. I couldn't exactly see hordes of big cats descending on these fuckers and biting their heads off any time soon. The whole street looked totally deserted.

On our side, Raze had fully shifted into his big cat form, paws wide on the ground and his head low as he snarled. He looked like he was about two seconds away from pouncing on the cultists and ripping them to shreds, which wouldn't do much to save the kids.

"Descendant," another cultist spoke, stepping out of the shadows and tossing his hood back. It was Scarface! That mother fucker who had tried to torch us alive when I'd been in the shower. Oh, I had a fucking score to settle with this twat-waffle. "Hand over the amulet, and the kittens are free to go."

I scoffed at him. "It's that easy, huh? Just hand it over and we all go on our merry way?" I have no idea why I phrased it like that. I'd never used the word "merry" in my life... except at Christmas.

The scarred Bastite gave me a puzzled frown. "Yes, that's what I just said. Hand over the amulet, and the kids go free. There's nothing else to it. If not..." He gave a little shrugging raise of his hands, and one of the girls let out a squeal of pain as her captor pressed the blade deep enough to draw blood.

Raze snarled a chilling sound, his massive claws digging into the dirt and his shoulders bunching. Shit balls. He was about to snap, and this whole thing would end up with everyone dead. Myself included.

Without considering the potential outcomes, I placed a hand on Raze's fur, right between the coiled muscles of his huge shoulders. Wait, do cats have shoulders? I mean, they have legs, not arms, so can they really have shoulders?

Ugh, focus Cleo!

Raze's snarls subsided a little as I stroked his fur and desperately hunted for another solution to the situation we were in.

"Cleo," Boden snapped, "please let us handle this."

There was an edge of urgency in his voice, and I shot an uncertain glance over at Hunter. The brunet Aussie babe just shook his head at me, silently supporting Boden.

But to what end? These fuckers had come here for one thing. My amulet. Sorry, but there was no way in all Egyptian Hell I would let two kids get killed over a piece of jewelry. Even if they were kinda bratty and their mom was a jealous bitch.

Biting my lip—because this was obviously a dumb-as-fuck move—I lifted the amulet off my neck and held it up in my hand. "Let them go," I ordered Scarface.

He cocked his head to the side, squinting at me in fascination. "That easy, huh?" he murmured, a small smile playing at his lips. For a crazy psychopath in a cult to an ancient goddess, he was kinda hot. His black hair was styled in a messy sort of mohawk, and the shaved sides of his head showed tattoos on his scalp. His scarred eyebrow was pierced twice, and my guess about that eye being clouded was correct. Not that it detracted from his looks, just made them more interesting.

Ah shit. I'd bet he was a shifter, too.

Only shifters were so pretty.

"Come away from the kitty cat," he suggested, giving Raze a wary look. The cultist held his hand out, indicating that I go to him to deliver the amulet.

"Cleo, *no*," Boden growled, giving me a furious scowl.

Even Hunter was shaking his head frantically. "Don't do it, babe. We got this handled."

I glared back at them. "It sure as shit doesn't look like it." I indicated to the girls, who were sobbing and terrified, and to Maeve, who looked like she was about to have a psychotic break any minute now.

Ignoring the protests of my guardians, I took a step away from Raze toward the slightly sexy cultist. Before I could take another step, though, something snagged the back of my sweatpants, and I turned to find Raze's razor sharp fangs in the fabric.

"What? You want me to just let your girls get their throats slit, too?" I demanded, glaring down at his flaming green eyes as he released my pants.

He glared back at me for a second, but then his gaze shot to the kids, rife with indecision. He loved those girls like they were his own babies. I couldn't let him lose them if I could stop it.

"I won't destroy your family, Raze," I said softly. "This is all for this fucking amulet. If it's gone, your kids are safe and you're released from this stupid fated guardianship."

I used his hesitation, backing up a few more steps until I was within arm's reach of Scarface. "Deal's a deal. Let them go," I ordered, indicating to the captives.

Scarface grinned, holding out his palm. "Amulet first. You seem like the type to attempt a double cross."

Anger and indignation bubbled within me, but I was hardly in a position to argue. Both Boden and Hunter kept shouting vague protests at me, but whatever. I held the amulet over Scarface's open palm and released it.

The second it touched his flesh, he nodded to his goons, who released Maeve and the girls. All three of them raced to safety behind Boden and Hunter, sobbing and wailing but *safe*.

Scarface gave me a smug smile, closing his fingers over the amulet. "What a disappointment you would be to your ancestors. The Descendants of Hatshepsut were once feared as smart, cunning, strong women. Until you."

My jaw dropped in outrage. "Excuse me?" I spluttered. "You just got what you wanted; is it really necessary to run your mouth?"

Scarface just shrugged, smiling down at my necklace in his fist. "Just pointing out that you're to blame for what comes next. You're a total, utter, train wreck of an amulet bearer."

Anger flared hot within me at his words. How fucking dare he? How *dare* he stand there and insult me after everything I'd been through thanks to *him* and his stupid, medieval cultists?

"Fuck you, asshole," I snarled, resorting to my baser instincts and punching him clean in the nose. There was a sickening crunch under my fist and blood sprayed, but most of all, *holy fucking cats that hurt!*

I howled with pain, clutching my fist to my chest, positive I'd broken it on Scarface's rock hard skull. He stumbled back a few steps—totally shocked, I was sure—then let out a shriek of pain himself.

Except, not from his bloody nose. He was staring in horror at his hand, and as I watched, his fingers uncoiled and my necklace started to fall to the ground.

Acting on pure instinct, I dove forward, snatching my amulet from midair, and rolled with it until I was a safe distance away from the scarred Bastite.

"What did you do?" he shrieked at me, clutching his wrist and clearly in pain. Not only was blood streaming down his face, the palm of his hand was blistering with a horrible burn... Caused by my amulet? So creepy, but also seriously cool.

I slipped the chain back over my head and scurried backward on my hands and knees like an overgrown crab. Just in time, too. Suddenly the yard burst into action with dozens of huge cats pouncing out of freaking *nowhere* and tearing into the cultists like they were the main dish at a buffet.

"Get the girls inside," Boden shouted to me, and I hurried to do what he said.

Both kids were still clinging to Maeve like barnacles on a

whale's ass, but they didn't protest when I ushered them inside the house and locked the door behind us. No kids needed to see the carnage that was going on out there. Hell, not even I needed to see that!

A deep shudder ran through me, and the clear vision of a huge, black cat tearing a cultist's head from his shoulders seemed to replay on a loop inside my head.

I was never going to look at raw meat the same way again.

"Are you all okay?" I asked Maeve and the kids, but they were crying too hard to give a clear response. "Come to the kitchen," I suggested, clenching my hands into fists to stop the trembling. "I'll get a Band-Aid for that cut." I nodded to the little wound on the older girl's neck, and Maeve whispered some sort of agreement.

The three of us headed into the back of the house, away from whatever was happening on the lawn, but it didn't block out the sounds.

Screams, snarls, and just straight-up tearing flesh. It was a sound I'd be hearing for the rest of my life.

Turned out, they did have it handled after all.

FIFTEEN

The battle on the lawn was over in a matter of minutes, and when the guys returned inside, both Hunter and Boden headed straight for showers.

Raze hesitated near the bottom of the stairs, out of sight of the girls, who were tucked up on the couch with their mom. I was making them hot cocoa—seeing as the power was back on, like magic—and paused when I saw him standing there in the dark.

He raised his head, seeing me—I guess—and indicated that I come closer.

I quickly delivered the mugs to the coffee table, then went to see what he wanted.

"Jesus Christ Supercats," I breathed when I got closer. "That's... uh..." I swallowed heavily to keep the bile down. "You have some... uh... chunks." I indicated to his cheek, and he casually brushed them off with the back of his hand.

Human goo landed on the floor with a wet *splat*, and I stared at it in horror.

"Maggie," Raze rumbled, pulling my attention away from the chunk and back to his blood and gore splattered form. He was totally naked, but for once I wouldn't let my eyes wander from his face. I did *not* need to see his man meat all covered in... meat. "Thank you."

I gaped. "That's, uh, you're welcome. We probably never should have come here, and this trouble is all because of me in the first place, so it sort of seemed like a no brainer to take the trade off, you know?" Yep, I was babbling, but after everything that had just happened, I was also shaking with anxiety.

"Thank you," Raze repeated, "but don't *ever* pull a stupid, airheaded stunt like that again. Boden told you over and over we had it handled. You should have stayed inside like he told you to." His voice had hardened from the soft way he'd just said my name, and it was like a slap in the face. "Unless you learn to *listen* to your guardians and *trust us* to keep you safe, then we're all fucked."

I gaped, speechless, as he stalked his tight, blood-covered ass up the stairs.

That was very definitely not what I'd thought he was going to say, but it was justified nonetheless. Yeah, I had gone against Boden's directive, and yes, that possibly could have ended badly if my amulet hadn't scorched Scarface. But, it'd all worked out, hadn't it?

Still, the way Raze had just scolded me made me feel like total dirt, so instead of rejoining Maeve and the girls, I headed up to get changed and pack my few changes of clothes. I couldn't imagine we were going to hang around, in case any more trouble came to town.

So much for Bast's followers being too scared to follow us here.

I was still sulking when Hunter came outside and found me sitting on the front porch with my bag at my feet.

The front yard was all kinds of messed up, but at least there wasn't a pile of bodies lying around.

"You okay, Cleo-babe?" Hunter murmured, sitting down beside me on the step and wrapping an arm around my shoulders. "That was some scary shit."

I snorted a bitter laugh, but didn't resist when he pulled me in close to his body. In fact, I wrapped my arms around his waist and hugged him back. "I'm fine," I mumbled into his fresh white T-shirt. "I just feel like an asshole for almost messing it all up."

Hunter sighed and rubbed my back. "You didn't almost mess it up, babe. You *did* almost let Bast's pet sorcerer escape with the power of Ra, but it all worked out in the end. Just, maybe listen to us next time?"

I pulled back enough to look up at him. "Next time?"

He gave me a lopsided smile. "You don't seriously think this is the last time those fuckers will come after us, do you?"

I groaned and buried my face back into his T-shirt. "I just

can't figure it out," I muttered. "There was *no one* else here. Like the whole freaking street was empty, and then all of a sudden..."

Hunter's chest vibrated with a small laugh. "That was sort of the point. We couldn't exactly say 'Cleo, chill, there are fifty night panthers creeping up on us, ready to attack the second you get the fuck out of the way,' because then it wouldn't be a surprise."

I huffed. "Yeah, fair point. Lesson learned. What's a night panther?"

"I'm a night panther," Raze replied, stomping past Hunter and I with heavy boots on. He carried a stuffed-full duffle bag over his shoulder and looked stupidly stylish wearing jeans and a gray Henley with a plaid shirt wrapped around his waist.

I peered at Hunter. "I guess that's all the explanation I get?"

He smiled, then shrugged. "For now, I guess. It's a long drive to NOLA from here, though, so maybe you guys can *bond*."

Hunter got up, giving me his hand to help me up too, and I narrowed my eyes at him in suspicion. "Why did you just make that sound dirty, Crocodile Hunter?"

He gasped in mock outrage. "Who me? Never. Come on, babe. I'm calling the back seat with you this morning."

His arm slung over my shoulders again as we headed around the side of the house in the direction Raze had gone. My cheeks still heated slightly, though. "Dirty again," I muttered.

Not that I was complaining.

My hand still hurt, though. Hopefully that would fade.

To my surprise, the drive that day wasn't as tense and horrible as I'd anticipated. Sure, Raze was still a surly bastard, but he seemed less aggressive about his sarcasm. Was that a thing? If not, it was now.

Boden hadn't said anything about my disobedience during the Bastite confrontation, but he'd no doubt overheard either Hunter or Raze telling me off and decided I didn't need it from all three of them.

Or maybe he was just saving it until we arrived in New Orleans, and he'd tear strips off my ass then.

It took some coaxing, but I learned that the inherent talent of a night panther is their ability to blend into shadows. Certainly explained a lot about how Raze kept sneaking up on me, anyway.

I also found out that Scarface had escaped the cat attack. Slippery Bast-ard.

"Do you have any idea what happened with the amulet?" Boden asked me at some stage, turning in his seat to face me. Raze was driving this time, seeing as it was his car. If it could really be called a car. More like a truck. It was this jacked-up, black Ford F-150, which Raze informed me had been kitted out to look like a Raptor. While initially it sounded a bit poseur-ish, he explained that he didn't like the petrol fuel consumption of Raptor's so had opted for a deisel engine and then specced it to look the same.

I still had no idea what a Raptor was.

Either way, it was huge, spacious, and would probably save

our bacon if anyone else tried to run us off the road.

"Er, no?" I wrinkled my nose, toying with the amulet in question. "I was going to ask you guys the same thing. It's not like I was wearing it when it scorched Scarface."

Hunter snickered a laugh. "Scarface."

"That's true," Boden murmured, nodding thoughtfully, "but maybe it was enough that you were in close proximity to it. I imagine you were thinking violent thoughts at the time?"

"Yup." I nodded firmly. Boy, was I ever.

"It's possible that the amulet was reacting to Axle's own magic," Raze commented. "It was never meant to be handled by magic users. Maybe that was a built in defense mechanism."

I squinted at him in the mirror. "Who's Axle?"

He met my gaze for a brief flicker, and I spotted a glimmer of amusement there. "Scarface," he clarified.

"Oh. You guys know his name?"

Hunter grinned. "Yeah, but I like Scarface heaps better. Scar. Hah! Like on *The Lion King*. Oddly appropriate."

They'd totally lost me, but it was pretty obvious they had some prior history with our old friend Scar.

Boden just waved it off. "Story for another day," he said. "Look, we're almost here."

For the next half hour I stared out the window and absorbed all the sights and sounds of New Orleans. I freaking loved this city; it was so totally different from anywhere in the entire world.

Or... as much of the world as I'd seen.

Raze pulled us up in front of a cute, three-story house just outside the French Quarter, and we all piled out. I had kinks all through my back and took a quick second to stretch them all out.

"Ugh, holy cats, that's good," I groaned as my back clicked.

"How are you all knotted up?" Raze asked as he unloaded our bags from the back. "You're the size of a pixie. There was more than enough room in Betty for you to be comfortable."

I arched a brow at him, propping my hands on my hips. "Betty?"

Raze's brow's dropped in a scowl, and his lips tightened. He said nothing in response as he carried both his bag *and mine* up the steps to the front door.

"It's the name of his truck," Hunter whispered to me as we followed him. "You know...'Black Betty'? Like the song?"

I snickered a laugh, instantly knowing what he was talking about.

Boden knocked on the door, and we all waited in silence until an older woman, maybe somewhere in her seventies, answered.

She looked straight past the boys to me. "You're the new one, huh?"

"Uh?" I flicked a glance at the guys, then back to the old woman. "I guess? I'm Cleo." I held my hand out to shake hers. "Are you Marie-Elizabeth?"

The woman shook my hand with surprising strength for her age. "Gods no. Lizzie is at work already; I'm Rita. Come in; I'll show you to the guest rooms."

She bustled up the stairs, all the way to the top, where she pointed the guys to a bunk room and then pointed me to a beautiful guest room with a full king size bed.

"Sorry about the cramped quarters for you three," she apologized to my guardians. "We're a full house at the moment."

The three of them murmured their assurances that they were fine with the bunks, but I was curious who all lived in the big old house. Who was Rita to Marie-Elizabeth?

Just as I opened my mouth to ask some of those questions, Boden cut me off.

"Rita, I hope you don't think me rude, but we'd love a chance to speak with Marie-Elizabeth tonight. Descartes mentioned she owns a bar nearby. Would it be okay for us to drop by and speak with her there?"

I sort of knew what he was thinking. If the cultists found us here, we didn't want to get run out of town without some answers. If she even had any answers to offer us, that was. There were a *whole* lot of ifs going on at the moment.

Rita shrugged. "You can, but you'd better be prepared to dress up. It's prohibition party night. No costume, no entry." She eyed us up, like she was mentally taking our sizes. "You up for that? Otherwise, you're welcome to play gin rummy with me and the other old cats downstairs."

She shot me a mischievous wink, and I bit back a grin.

Raze was the first to respond, clearing his throat and giving Rita a tight smile. "Would you happen to have any costumes we could borrow?"

The old woman beamed. "I might have a few things tucked away. Back in a tick."

She hurried back down the stairs, leaving us alone on the landing.

"Never thought you'd be a fan of costume parties, Raze," I snickered.

Boden smirked, leaning against the doorframe. "I think it was more the old cats that scared him."

I snapped my fingers, just understanding. "Old cats? Like, the old guardians? They live here too?"

All three of them gave me bemused looks.

"Yeah, babe, Rita is one of them." Hunter crinkled his nose at me and shook his head. "You really suck at identifying magical beings."

Slightly offended, I folded my arms over my chest. "How the hell would I know? I didn't even know magic existed a week ago, remember?"

"How could we forget?" Raze commented with heavy sarcasm. "You told us about sixteen times that first night that you thought it was an elaborate metaphor for life."

"Life *or something*," Boden corrected, and I scowled at both of them.

Hunter took pity on me, wrapping me in a hug, then turning me around so my back was tucked into his chest. "Aw, don't be mad, Cleo-babe. I just meant you can't feel the sort of hum around magical beings? For us, we can pick out a magic user just from being in close contact."

"Oh." Okay, that made me feel less stupid. "No, I haven't noticed that. Maybe I should pay more attention?"

Raze snorted. "Probably."

I magnanimously ignored his jab. "So if Marie-Elizabeth's guardians still live here, why don't we ask them about all this shit?" I waggled my necklace at them. "And all the, you know..." I mimed the cultist bursting into flame and crumbling to ash and then the amulet burning Scarface. Roll with it, my charades were on point.

"Is Margaret having a seizure?" Raze murmured to Boden, who looked a bit unsure how to respond to that.

I sighed. "You guys suck."

Thankfully we were saved from any more of my *seizures* by Rita reappearing with an armful of garment bags.

"Here." She handed them out to each of us. "Those should fit. I'm a good judge of size. You'll want to hurry, though. Doors lock at nine o'clock and don't reopen until three am. Part of the authenticity of the party." She gave us another of those playful winks, then left us alone to get changed.

As weird as the whole situation was... I was stupidly excited to get dressed up for a costume party. Hopefully the costume Rita picked for me wasn't horrible.

CHAPTER
SIXTEEN

"**I**s this seat taken?" A sexy, deep voice asked from behind me, and I grinned to myself. He stood so close his breath warmed my bare neck, and it was everything I could do not to shiver with desire.

"Yes, sorry," I replied, spinning on my leather barstool. "It's reserved for one of the three crazy cats who've been stalking me all the way from Oregon. Don't suppose you've seen them?" I took an innocent sip of my brightly colored hurricane, batting my lashes.

Boden grinned back at me. "Crazy cats stalking you? That sounds serious. Maybe I should stick around to keep you safe."

"Oh well, if it's to keep me safe." I gestured dramatically at the open stool beside me. "Be my guest."

His heavy gaze remained locked on me as he slid onto the

seat and spun my own stool so that we were face to face. "Good cocktail?"

I took another long sip and licked my lips. "Delicious. Want some?"

Boden's attention was locked with laser focus on my lips, and a spike of satisfaction hit me when he sucked in a shaky breath. "Gods yes," he said on the exhale. "And I'll try the drink, too."

He reached out and brought my drink to his mouth, taking a sip from my straw while his heavy-lidded gaze returned to my face.

Holy freaking cats. How did he just turn that into an erotic act? Because my panties were officially wet. Wet, wet, wet. Maybe he'd be open to a quickie in the disabled bathroom?

"How many of those have you two had?" Raze demanded, appearing beside us like a fucking storm cloud. Just like that, my panties were dry again. Like magic.

Kidding, they probably got a smidge wetter because, *fuck me*, that asshole looked like something straight out of a sex dream in his twenties style suit, complete with bowtie and tails.

Move aside, Jay Gatsby, my big old pussycats had this era all kinds of stitched up.

Wow.

Just wow.

"Mags," Raze snapped. Literally. Snapped his fingers in front of my face.

That was becoming an annoying habit that I was totally not on board with.

"What?" I replied, peering up at him. It took me a moment to remember his question. "Not many. Why? They're mostly just juice anyway."

Raze looked like he wanted to smack some sense into me... which kind of clued me in before he said, "They're so far from just fruit juice it's not even funny. What's your excuse, boss?" He turned his sharp gaze to Boden, who just smiled and shrugged.

"No excuse, just enjoying Miss Cleo's company."

Raze rolled his eyes and went to run a hand through his hair before remembering it was tied up in a sexy, half-up situation. I'd never been into dudes with long hair before. Ever. But if anyone could make it hot, it was Raze.

And he did. In case you were wondering. Hah, kidding, I know I've said it a zillion times, but I'm likely to say it a zillion more. Raze. Was. Gorgeous.

"For the love of Ra," the bronzed god muttered, "never thought I'd see the day that you'd let your dick do the thinking. Maybe you two should just go fuck in the cloakroom and get it out of your systems."

"Projecting, Raziel?" Boden replied with a slightly challenging smirk, and I awkwardly slipped off my stool. This was *not* a conversation I wanted to be literally sitting in the middle of.

"I'm just gonna... uh... pee." I made my excuse and hurried through the crowded bar to the restrooms. I hadn't needed to actually pee, but after sipping on hurricanes for a solid hour, peeing was probably a good idea.

After I did my thing and washed my hands, I smoothed some water over my fluoro-pink hair while inspecting myself in the mirror. For the first time since my hair disaster, I actually didn't mind the shockingly bright shade of pink.

A lot of that had to do with the gorgeous lilac dress that Rita had found for me to wear. It was a satin shift covered by a heavy, beaded overlay and finished with fringing at the hem, which moved and swayed with my every movement. It was gorgeous and eye catching and probably the prettiest thing I'd ever worn in my life. Somehow—magic, I guess—Rita had even found me a pair of heels that fit and some authentic, thigh-high stockings with seams up the back.

The whole outfit was scorching hot, and it made me wish that we still dressed with the care and beauty of the twenties.

Not that I'd give up jeans and leather jackets for the world, but you know what I meant.

"Cleo-babe!" Hunter called to me when I exited the bathroom and looked around for my guardians. Boden and Raze had gone from the bar area, where I'd left them, and all three were now sitting around a little table in the VIP lounge.

I wove through the tightly packed party-goers to join them and perched awkwardly on the bench seat with my hands under my thighs. Raze's interruption earlier had reminded me that fucking my guardians was still a *no-no*, despite Hunter and I having already broken that rule. Given we were out in public and in a bar owned by the previous amulet bearer, it might be wise to keep my lusty paws to myself.

"Here." Raze handed me another fun-looking drink with umbrellas and fruit all spilling out the top of it.

I accepted it with a small smile. "Thanks." My lips closed over the straw, and I took a long sip. "Mmm, that's really good. What is it?"

"Actual fruit juice," Raze informed me with a small smirk. "Without the alcohol. Sober up, Mags, we're here for work, not play." He shot a glance at Boden. "Can't believe I'm the one reminding everyone of this fact."

Boden just shrugged and took a sip of his drink—which was definitely *not* fruit juice. In fact, it looked like straight spirits, and there was something intensely attractive about a well-dressed man sipping neat spirits from a crystal glass. It was like we were in a time warp, and I never wanted to leave.

"She's a bad influence on you, boss," Raze muttered, checking his watch. "Marie-Elizabeth should be out to chat soon."

"The waitress said she'd be out over half an hour ago," Hunter pointed out. "For now, there's nothing to do but enjoy the party. Doors are locked until three am, remember?"

Just then, another well-dressed man approached our group. He was younger—I think—than my guardians, but decently handsome with neatly combed hair and a clean-shaven face.

"Excuse me," he said giving the guys a cursory glance but speaking to me. "Would you care to dance?"

I gaped at him, caught off guard and not sure how to respond.

"I was watching you and couldn't decide if you were with one of these guys, but then I thought, no man would leave his girl sitting here looking bored when he could be dancing with her, right?"

He gave me a charming smile, but it was the subtle wink that did me in.

"I'd love to," I announced, jumping up and accepting his outstretched hand before any of my companions could object.

As we wove our way through the people to the dance floor, he laid a light—respectful—hand on the small of my back. "I give it five minutes before one of them cuts in," he told me, spinning me around to face him when we found a clear space of floor.

"Five?" I raised my brows. "They'll easily spend longer than that thinking up painful and exotic torture techniques for you. I'll say eight."

The handsome blond grinned and checked his watch. "You're on. Which one?"

I shot a glance back across the bar to where three big cat shifters stared at me. "Uh, Hunter, for sure. The cheeky Australian brunet."

My dance partner laughed a full, rich sound. "No way, you're crazy. It's definitely that delicious looking warrior with the piercing green eyes. He's been looking like he wanted to maul you since the moment y'all stepped foot in here."

I shook my head at him in disbelief, but didn't argue. Deep down, I kinda hoped it would be Raze.

Okay, not that deep. Whatever, we all knew I was hot for him, bad attitude and all.

Brushing off the lingering feeling of three sets of eyes, I let myself go and started grooving with my new friend, who was—I might add—more interested in the men around us than in me. Probably a good thing. I had my plate full enough as it was with Hunter and Boden making sexual innuendos at every possible opportunity.

We only made it through about two, maybe two and a half songs, before a strong pair of hands closed on my waist from behind, and my dance partner—Billy—beamed as he checked his watch.

"I win," he smirked at me, then happily boogied off into the crowd to get down with a man in a flapper dress.

"Maggie," Raze growled in my ear, then spun me around to face him. Or face his chest. Fuck me, he was tall. Or I was short. Or both. "Were you just dancing with that clearly gay man in order to drive Boden and Hunter insane with jealousy? Because it worked. They were trying to one up each other over all the ways they wanted to kill that guy."

"Uh-huh." I craned my neck to peer up at him. "And yet *you're* the one who came over here to chase him off, even though you knew he was gay. So, what does that tell you, smarty-pants?"

I felt real smug, not even going to lie. Right up until Raze leaned down close, so his mouth was right beside my ear and all I could see was his crisp white shirt.

"It tells me that I'm likely to rip the hands off the next guy who touches you, gay or not. It tells me that for all your snark, bluster, and too-stupid-to-live decisions, you've gotten under my skin. Now all I can think about is the vision of you riding Hunter's cock, of all that glorious ink decorating your *whole* fucking body, and of how your perfect little ass clenched when you came. It tells me, Margaret, that you're going to be the gods damned death of us all, but despite that, I still fully intend to fuck you until you're screaming and ruined for everyone else. Hunter and Boden included."

What. The. Fuck.

"Um," I stammered. "I think, maybe, uh, yep I think I need a drink. Is it hot in here? I'm suddenly, uh, really hot."

Raze stepped back just enough for me to see him smirk.

Mother. Fucker.

Had that all been just to mess with me? Was he serious about any of it? Why was it *so hard to tell?*

"I'll join you," he offered, stepping back further to let me pass. "I'm suddenly very *thirsty.*" His smile was pure predator, and I shivered as I sashayed past in my swishy dress. I'm not even going to comment what sort of shiver that was; you can guess.

Shit got awkward after that. Super awkward. I was tripping between being all hot and bothered by the idea of riding Raze like a rodeo bull and being all anxious that he'd been messing with me and would shoot me right the fuck down if I pushed it further.

It had me so confused that I almost couldn't eat the burger that Hunter had ordered for me. Almost. Let's not get too crazy; that baby had bacon *and* peanut butter on it, so no man, no matter how sexy and confusing, was keeping that meat from my mouth.

"Oh my Supercats," I moaned, licking beef juice from my fingers as I swallowed the last bite. Yeah, I was aware how dirty that sounded, but I didn't even care. "This burger is fucking heaven. I need to eat at least seventeen more of these before we leave here, okay?"

I wasn't directing my question at anyone in particular. Maybe just the universe? But it was an older woman with skin the same bronzed shade as mine who responded.

"I'm sure I can arrange that for you, dear." She laughed. "And I'll pass your compliments along to the chef."

She was dressed in theme with a floor-length, red and black beaded gown and black satin opera gloves. A matching beaded band held a delicate collection of feathers at her temple and crossed her forehead, and I was instantly in awe of her elegance.

"Marie-Elizabeth?" Boden took over while I quickly licked all my fingers clean, then dried them off on a napkin. So classy, I know. "I'm Boden. I'm—"

"Commander for the Shifter Alliance. I'm well aware of your position, young man." Marie-Elizabeth shot him a wary look. "But your calling as Guardian supersedes that title; I hope you understand."

Boden ducked his head in a nod and offered her a small smile.

"I was going to say I'm one of Cleo's guardians. But yes, I'm also the Commander."

The older woman huffed, still looking wary, but eventually nodded and sat in the armchair one of her staff had brought over to our table. "And you two." She looked over Raze and Hunter with a critical eye. "Yes, you'll do. Hunter and Raziel, yes?"

They both nodded, and she turned her attention back to me. "Sorry, dear, that was awfully rude of me. I'm Marie-Elizabeth, but you can call me Lizzie."

A little bit dumbfounded, I held out my hand to shake hers. "I'm Cleo."

Lizzie smirked. "How terribly appropriate for our family line."

"Wait," I gasped. "We're related then?"

She gave a casual shrug. "Somewhere along the line, we have to be. Only descendants of Hatshepsut herself can bear the amulet of light, and that's definitely it." She indicated to my gold necklace hanging loose over my lilac beaded dress. "My old dress looks great on you, too, by the way."

"Oh," I said, looking down at the amulet and touching my fingers to it. "I just thought... I was adopted, so..."

"Ah, I see." Lizzie nodded. "I'm sorry, dear. Over the thousands of years since Hatshepsut's time, the bloodline has split countless times. Her descendants could be anywhere across the globe, and there's just no way to guess who the next amulet bearer will be. I myself never had children, which is probably a good thing, considering how long I held that damn thing before it passed to you."

My mouth opened to ask her how long, but then I quickly realized that was the same as asking how old she was. Even I had better manners than that. There was a certain level of wisdom in her eyes, and her accent was everything and nothing all at the same time, suggesting she'd moved around a lot in her *long* lifetime.

"Lizzie," Boden spoke up, "we love your club, but we actually came to ask some sensitive questions pertaining to the amulet. Is there somewhere safe we can speak?"

She gave us a smile. "Of course, Rita called ahead and said you were in a hurry to get some answers. I'm sorry I got caught up dealing with business, or I would have come out sooner." Sweeping her hands over her dress, she stood up and indicated that we follow her. "We can speak privately in my office."

Lizzie led us down the corridor past the restrooms and unlocked a door at the end. She opened it and entered with us all close behind her.

"Take a seat," she offered. "Can I get drinks for you all?"

I was tempted to order another hurricane, just to piss Raze off, but Boden told her that we were fine with water so I kept my trap shut.

"So, what has happened that made you seek me out?" she asked when we were all seated. "I haven't seen hide nor hair from the Alliance in a good fifteen or so years, after they determined I really had no idea where the amulet had gone."

Boden cleared his throat. "I apologize on behalf of the previous Commander. He was a huge asshole, to say the least."

Lizzie barked a laugh. "That he was. So, tell me a story. What brings you all here?"

Boden looked to me, like he was asking my permission to explain. Not that I could, even if I freaking tried, so I waved a hand for him to go for it.

"Cleo found the amulet when she was a kid, in a junk store. She's had it ever since, but we only located her a week ago. Within twelve hours of us finding her, Bast's followers found us and started attacking." Boden paused, and Lizzie murmured a noise of disgust at the mention of Bast.

"That doesn't bode well," she commented, shooting me a sympathetic look.

Boden grimaced. "It's what happened next that we were hoping you could shed some light on. After the Bastites set fire to our safe house, we found one of them in the woods. Or, Cleo tripped over him. Anyway, he tried to attack Hunter and Cleo..." he trailed off, looking lost for how to explain what'd happened.

"Cleo did what?" Lizzie pressed, looking at me expectantly.

For lack of words to explain the situation, I did my super specific mime again to demonstrate how the cultist went up in flames and turned to ash.

Lizzie gaped at me. "You incinerated him?"

The air all rushed out of me in a huge breath. "Thank you! These dickheads keep asking if I'm having a seizure, but I *know* my charades skills are mint."

"Young lady, you're speaking a whole other language right

now, but I got your general meaning. You somehow managed to spontaneously combust the cultist." Lizzie pursed her lips as she stared at me.

"Uh-huh. And then there was this other thing," I continued, "with one of those dickwads. I gave him the amulet—"

"You *what?*" she practically shrieked, rising halfway out of her seat.

"—but then it burned his hand so badly that he dropped it. We wondered if maybe it's a defense mechanism built into the amulet or something?" I gave her my best pleading face, praying she would confirm this theory. "So, ah, did that ever happen to you, maybe?"

The elegant ex-amulet bearer just stared at me in horror for a long moment, then got up and started pacing the small office.

"I think that's a no," Hunter stage-whispered to me, and I whacked him with the back of my hand.

"Shut up, you don't know."

"No," Lizzie exclaimed. "No that most definitely did not happen to me." She paused her pacing, propping both hands on her hips and glaring at me in, like, I think that was anger? Or fear? "You are aware that Hatshepsut and her descendants were chosen to protect the power of Ra *because* we have no ability to use it. You are clear on this part, yes?"

I nodded, sheepish. "Yes, I know."

"So..." She trailed off, throwing her hands up in the air, then proceeding to pace while muttering under her breath.

Raze leaned over so he could whisper. "This isn't going well; we should leave."

Boden nodded his agreement, but Lizzie whipped around again, holding up her gloved hands.

"Stop! No, you're not leaving. Not until I understand how this happened." She stared at the four of us for a long moment, and I could almost see the gears turning in her mind. "Okay, yes, there's only one thing for it."

She sat back down in the chair opposite mine, and tugged off her satin gloves. "Give me your hand, girl."

I did not. "Girl? My name is Cleo, thank you."

Lizzie clicked her tongue in an annoyed way. "Just give me your hand."

I glanced at the guys, seeking guidance. But they mostly seemed curious rather than concerned, so I tentatively stretched my hand out to her.

The old woman snatched it, turning it over to face palm up, and smoothed her own palm over the top of it. Something... weird happened then. Like a static shock jolted from her palm into mine and back again, but straight after, she removed her hand and peered down at mine.

For a long while, an awkwardly long while, she just stared at my palm.

"Um," I started, "are you—"

"Shh!" she silenced me but didn't look up.

I arched a brow at the guys, but Raze and Hunter looked

equally confused.

"She's reading your palm," Boden whispered. "We've heard rumors in the Alliance that after a Descendant passes the amulet along, they develop a certain level of their own powers. Not strong ones, just sort of residue from being in close contact with the power of Ra for so long."

"It's pretty obvious she's reading her palm," Raze commented in a dry tone of voice. "But what is she finding?"

Just then, Lizzie released my hand with a gasp, turning her eyes up to me in shock. "Holy Mother of Egypt," she breathed. "You're not a Descendant at all."

"What?" I exclaimed in unison with all three of the guys voicing their own confusion. "How do you mean? Of course I am, how else do I have this?" I held up the amulet and waggled it in front of her face. You know, just in case she hadn't seen it.

"Look, I don't know how it happened or how you came to be in possession of the amulet, but you're not human. You should never have had it." Lizzie was turning a bit pale—as pale as our skin allowed—and her hands were trembling as she pulled her gloves back on. "It's no wonder the Bastites have been so relentless; they must know you're not the true Descendant." She shot Boden a severe glance. "You need to remove it from her and return it to the Alliance. They're the only ones who can locate the true bearer."

"Hold up!" I snapped, jumping up from my seat to confront the old woman, who was hurrying over to her desk. "No one is taking shit from me. I've had this necklace most of my life, and I'm not just giving it away on the word of some hack fortune teller. You clearly have no idea what you're talking about because I *am* human."

I folded my arms over my chest, raising my chin with a stubborn tilt.

Lizzie paused with her phone in her hand, possibly about to call that mysterious shifter police I kept hearing about.

"Cleo, you don't understand. The true Descendant has an inherent ability that allows her to evade Bast's followers. All this drama, all these attacks, they didn't happen to me. Or nowhere near as frequently as they have to you. I think I can count maybe ten run-ins with Bast and her acolytes in the entire hundred and fifty years I protected the amulet." Lizzie's hand shook where she clutched the phone, and her mouth was a tight slash across her face.

I didn't totally know what to say in response, though. "Maybe, uh, maybe they got lucky." That didn't sound convincing even to me. "Whatever. Point is that I'm not just going to hand over a potentially world-destroying magical amulet on the word of an elderly palm reader. How do we know *you're* not working for Bast, huh?"

Lizzie gasped in horror. "What a revolting accusation. I'm calling the Alliance; they can come and deal with you. Whatever you are."

Boden stood up then, reaching over to take the phone from Lizzie's hand. "That's not necessary, ma'am. We can deal with this ourselves, and you've been most helpful."

She was suspicious, for sure, but somewhat mollified. "You can't stay at my home," she snapped. "I won't have those loonies turning up on my doorstep. We're all far too old to deal with them again."

Boden shot a look to Hunter and Raze, who seemed to be discussing something silently. Shit. Did they have telepathy? Could they read minds? Holy *cats*.

"We understand entirely, Marie-Elizabeth," Hunter said, standing up and walking over to her. As I watched, horrified, he placed his hand on her arm—just above where her glove ended and bare skin began. "We would just like to stay until morning, if you'd be agreeable to that? Just long enough that I can arrange transport for us all back to Alliance headquarters. Would that be okay?"

Lizzie blinked slowly, staring straight into Hunter's eyes like no one else in the room existed. Ah, man. I knew what that was like. She didn't stand a freaking chance.

"Of course," she murmured in a sleepy sort of voice. "Anything you want."

"Yikes," I hissed under my breath. "That's strong shit."

"Needs to be," Raze murmured back. "We can't risk her reporting everything we've said back to the Alliance. Not until we're well clear of this city, anyway."

Hunter continued speaking to Lizzie in a low and soothing tone, and I frowned at Raze. "Doesn't Boden work for the Alliance?"

"Yeah, he does." Raze nodded, his eyes curious. "So?"

"So... shouldn't they be on our side?" I was totally missing something here.

Raze grimaced. "Considering how many sacred laws you've already broken, I wouldn't be running to them for help. They're more likely to lock you in a cage or torture you for answers than help. The Alliance is integral to maintaining order in shifter communities, but they're also cruel, power hungry and totally antiquated. The only reason they haven't claimed the power of the amulet for themselves is that they haven't had an opportunity." He gave me a pointed look, and a sick feeling rippled through me.

"I'm that opportunity," I whispered with understanding.

Raze just gave me a lopsided smile, and for once there didn't seem to be any snark behind it. "Good thing you have us, isn't it?"

I sighed, feeling like a bag of shit, but somehow his words did make me feel a tiny bit better. I did have them, and they weren't handing me over to be tortured.

At least... not yet.

CHAPTER
SEVENTEEN

Hunter—apparently—was really freaking cashed up. He spent the rest of the night back at Marie-Elizabeth's house on the phone arranging things, and by midmorning we were boarding a private plane at an exclusive airstrip just outside New Orleans.

We hadn't encountered any issues with Marie-Elizabeth's elderly guardians at all, which Hunter explained was due to something Boden had done that prevented her from sharing what we'd told her.

What it was, I didn't ask. My brain was already fried with her suggestion—okay, fine, accusation—that I wasn't human. Or at least not totally.

Yes, I had seen my three attractive travel companions turn into huge-ass cats on several occasions, as well as a bad dude turn to ash, but the idea that I wasn't human was blowing my freaking mind.

Maybe I really was crazy, after all. I'd sort of given up on that idea when I hadn't woken up in a mental hospital already, but it was starting to sound like the most logical explanation, right? That this was all one huge, extended delusion.

Damn, how pissed would you be if that's what this all turned out to be.

Fortunately for you, and unfortunately for me, I didn't see myself snapping out of it anytime soon, and so my journey continued.

"Why Boston?" I asked when we were all strapped into our comfy recliner chairs on the eight-seater jet. I'd overheard Hunter speaking with the pilot when we were getting loaded up just minutes before. "And more to the point, why the hell did you make me drive the entire length of the freaking country when Hunter had a private plane tucked up his sleeve?"

"You didn't drive," Raze pointed out, and I flipped him off. Sarcastic, sexy asshole.

"Because," Hunter responded, ignoring Raze, "I lost my wallet back when Candy Jack crashed, and my finance people make me jump through sixteen thousand hoops to regain access to my accounts. It's a safeguard feature, but it requires more time with phone and internet than we've really had up until now."

I frowned at that blatant lie. "We had a full day at Raze's house."

Hunter looked a little embarrassed and dodged my gaze,

looking out the window at something *fascinating*.

"He was more focused on buying you clothes than sorting out transport. By the time he remembered, the local airstrip was already closed for the day. Disadvantage of the reservation being really far away from any major cities," Boden explained. "And we're heading to Boston to visit a friend of mine. He works in the genetics laboratory at Harvard."

I hummed my understanding. "You want him to test my DNA to see if Lizzie was telling the truth." It was a statement, not a question.

"Are you okay with that?" Boden asked, tilting his head to the side. He was sitting opposite me, with Raze across the small aisle and Hunter facing Raze.

I chewed my lip for a minute, rubbing my amulet between thumb and forefinger. Was I okay with that? Getting some sort of scientific proof that I was or wasn't human? "I suppose so," I murmured, sighing. "But can genetic tests really show that kind of thing?"

Boden nodded. "These ones can. Technically, Sean works for the Alliance, but he's been my friend for long enough that I think we can trust him."

Raze snorted a sarcastic laugh. "Or at least buy his silence."

I raised my brows, asking what the story was there, and Boden shrugged. "Sean's a gambler. Money always helps keep his mouth shut."

"I see," I murmured. "Okay cool. Boston it is, then."

The plane had already taken off while we were talking, and cotton wool clouds danced past the window as I stared out. The whole thing was a lot to take in, but I still held onto the belief that Sean's tests would come back negative for anything except 100% human. I should know, right? I'd never turned furry or shot lightening from my fingertips, nor had I ever turned anyone into a frog. For the love of cats, I couldn't even feel that magical hum that Hunter talked about surrounding other magical beings.

No. I was human, there was no doubt about it. But if the guys needed some sort of scientific evidence to convince the Alliance, then so be it.

Fuck knew I wasn't afraid of needles!

"This might sting a little," Sean told me, positioning the needle over my inner elbow. Was that the right name for it? Inner elbow? The part in the middle of your arm where they draw blood from. Inner elbow. Sure, that works.

"Is it called an inner elbow?" I asked Hunter, while Sean drew several vials of blood from my veins. "I always ponder this when I'm having my blood drawn but then forget before I get a chance to look it up."

"Cubital fossa," Sean answered, still focused on the blood pouring from my arm into the... was that the *seventh* vial? Damn, this dude was draining me dry!

"I call it an inbow," Hunter told me, and I snickered.

"That works too." I peered at the tray of already full blood vials beside Sean as he clicked another one into the needle. "Hey Sean, are you a shifter too? I figure you must be, if you work for the Alliance."

"No," he replied with total deadpan seriousness. "I'm a vampire."

He said this right as he finished the last tube of blood and withdrew the needle from my arm. A small bead of bright red collected in my inbow—thanks Hunter—and I held my breath. Holy shit. Should a vampire really be drawing blood? That seemed really irresponsible!

A fraction of a second later, he dabbed my puncture wound with a cotton ball, then stuck one of those little dot Band-Aids on top.

"Kidding," he told me with a grin. "I'm a wolf."

It took me a hot second to recover from that little prank, but when I did, I was fascinated. "You're a werewolf? That's so cool. Is it like how TV and movies make you out to be? Going all furry and feral on the full moon?"

Sean sat back on his wheelie chair and gaped at me in utter disgust.

"Did you just call me a *were*?" he gasped, glancing at Boden who was shaking with silent laughter. "Please tell me you explained to the poor girl what the difference is!"

Boden still shook with laughter. "No, we haven't had a chance," he finally managed to say. "But the look on your face is priceless."

I was confused as all fuck but didn't care enough to press the issue. Instead, I made a mental note that shifters and weres were different beasts—hah—so to speak, and it was insulting to mix them up.

"Dickhead," Sean muttered, rolling his chair over to a table loaded with high-tech equipment. His lab was *huge* with every fandangled gadget a scientist could ever hope for. I think. I mean, I was totally guessing, seeing as I had no freaking clue what any of the stuff did.

The door opened, and two college-aged kids came in, then paused when they saw us all there.

"Oh, Daniel, Elise, come in," Sean called out to them. "These are some friends of mine from the Alliance."

"Um." I gaped at Sean, baffled. So much for secrecy?

He shook his head at me. "Don't worry, Daniel and Elise are my research assistants. They're bound by nondisclosure agreements. Both legal and magical. They'll help me get these samples processed for you quickly." He arched a brow at Boden. "I'm assuming you need them done quickly? I get the general impression you're in some kind of trouble."

"Fast would be great," Boden replied with a tight, secretive smile.

Sean nodded, fishing out a pair of glasses from his pocket and putting them on. "Very good. I'll get started then."

He turned back to the desk in front of him and started labelling the vials of my blood with stickers and a ball point pen.

"Do shifters get bad eyesight?" I whispered, fascinated.

"No," Daniel, the lab assistant, replied. "He just thinks they make him look the part. He also doesn't need a white coat."

I grinned because I totally got it. The glasses and coat *did* make him look the part. "Okay, I'm hungry and don't totally want to lurk around here for hours while Sean the not-vampire plays with my blood. Can we go somewhere?"

"Yep, I'm up for coffee," Hunter agreed.

Raze nodded, pushing off the bench he'd been leaning against. "Let's see if that coffee shop is still around the corner. The one with the awesome cake."

"Bernie's Books?" Elise the lab assistant asked. "He's still there. Today's cake is hummingbird."

I raised my brows as Hunter and Raze started heading for the door. "I don't know what hummingbird cake is, but if it makes Raze less of a painful douche, then I'm all in. You coming, Boden?"

My blond guardian shook his head. "I'll stay and chat with Sean while he works. Just bring me back a slice of cake."

"You got it, boss," I saluted him and followed the other two out of the lab.

The café they'd been talking about was actually a bookshop which also sold coffee, cakes, and sandwiches. It was cute as shit and totally something that I would have expected to see at home in Portland. The owner was totally fine with customers grabbing a book to read while they were there, too, which was pretty awesome of him. College kids weren't always the most cashed-up individuals.

I soon discovered that hummingbird cake was a type of banana and pineapple situation with spices. Totally delicious, I couldn't believe I'd gone my whole life without trying it.

The three of us had found a hidden-away corner of the shop with vacant armchairs, so we'd parked for the afternoon and eaten more cake than anyone should really eat in one sitting. Kidding, there is no limit; cake is life.

"We should head back," Hunter said at some point, jolting me from the pages of the book I was reading.

I scowled at him. "No." I was halfway through an incredible story about a girl and her dragon lovers. Wait. Were dragons real too? I was just about to ask, when Raze snatched the book out of my hands and stalked away with it.

"What the shit?" I demanded of Hunter, seeing as Raze was gone. "I was reading that!"

He smiled. "We know. You've been reading that for the last hour and a half solid. You didn't even notice when the waitress brought back more cake."

I gasped, looked to the table, and found an empty plate dotted with crumbs. "You monsters."

Hunter just grinned. Smug fuck. "Anyway, Sean should almost be done now, so we need to head back to the lab. Find out what variety of monster *you* are."

I shuddered, remembering why we were in Boston to begin with. "What if I am one?" I asked him in a small voice. "What if

Lizzie was right and not actually a nutso, wannabe fortune teller? What then?"

Hunter got out of his seat, coming around to perch his ass on the table and take my hands in his. I hadn't even noticed that my fingers had crept back to my amulet again, but he peeled them free gently.

"Firstly, monsters are defined by the actions and choices they've made in their lives, not by their genetic code. Secondly, whatever those tests say you are, we're still you're guardians. We're still here for you, no matter what. Even if..." His gaze dropped to our entwined hands, and his thumb rubbed my wrist. "Even if the other night was just a once off, I'm not going anywhere. Neither are those other two assholes. We know beyond a shadow of doubt that *you* are the one we were chosen to protect."

His words were really touching, and I needed to swallow a couple of times to clear my throat of all the emotions. So many emotions! These guys were definitely changing me.

"Even if I'm a were?" I asked, my voice a husky whisper.

Hunter laughed. "Wow, we really need to explain weres to you, Cleo-babe. For starters, you'd have to be bitten by another were. But even if you were a were, I'd still think you're pretty awesome." He stood up and pulled me out of my seat. "Come on. Let's take Boden his cake before he gets hangry."

Hunter slung his arm over my shoulders and walked with me back to the front of the café-slash-bookstore where Raze was waiting for us.

"Here." Raze handed me a plastic bag with "Bertie's Books" printed on the side of it. He didn't say anything more, just stalked ahead of us, but when I peered inside, I found he'd purchased the book I was reading. Along with the two sequels. At the bottom there was a plastic box containing two more slices of cake for Boden, but... Raze had bought me books. That was really fucking sweet of him, and I had no idea how to handle sweet Raze.

Shooting a quick glance at Hunter, who was *zero* help whatsoever, I went with the only thing I could think of.

I.

Hugged him.

Raze.

I hugged Raze.

Yes, I'm aware I took my own life in my hands by doing this. Trust me. The second my stupid arms closed around his waist, I mentally screamed, *What the actual fuck are you doing, Cleo? Step away! Now! Quick, before he notices.*

Of course, it was already too late.

Raze stopped walking immediately—which was a good thing because have you ever hugged someone who was walking? It's awkward and uncomfortable.

Like I was.

"Margaret?" he asked, peering down at me, where I was attached around his waist like a big old human belt. "What are you doing?"

"Uh," I replied, peering up at him. For some totally unknown reason, my arms were *still* around his waist, despite how intensely awkward things had become. "Hugging you?"

Raze scowled down at me. "Why are you hugging me?"

"Um, because you bought me books, and that kind of seems like the nicest thing you've ever done—ever, in your life, or at least in the life I've known you for, which I'm aware is only a week, but... you know. Nice." Oh wow, there I went with the babble again. How had I never noticed how often I did that until I met these guys?

"So, uh," I continued when he said nothing, "I wanted to say thank you."

Raze carefully peeled my spider monkey arms off himself, then took my bag of books and cake from my hand and passed it to Hunter—who was watching us on the edge of laughter. Traitor.

"You wanted to thank me for the books?" Raze asked, and I nodded. "That's not how you do it, Maggie."

This felt like a trap. I was definitely walking into a trap here.

"How... how do you do it?" Oops, there I went. Headfirst into a big old trap.

Raze reached out, and his big hands grabbed me, lifting me up and forcing my legs to instinctively hitch around his waist. "Like this," he informed me, then *kissed the ever-loving crap out of me.*

Yes, that was screamed. Mentally. I mentally screamed that.

His lips crushed into mine with an intensity that left me totally breathless, gasping as he forced his way into my mouth and just fucking dominated me like... I have no idea what an appropriate analogy was for the way Raze kissed me. He had officially short-circuited my brain. I was brain-dead because Raze kissed me.

Thanks a lot, you overgrown pussycat; now I won't be able to do stuff anymore.

Who was I kidding? No stuff was more important than getting more of his hands—and other parts—all over and in me.

When he released me about a year and one pair of panties later, my knees were weak and my head was spinning.

"Well." I cleared my throat, running a shaking hand through my hair. "Good to know." I smoothed a hand down the front of my top, for lack of any better ideas what to do next. "I will... keep that in mind."

When I finally plucked up the courage to look up at Raze, there was a lazy, smug smile on those seriously kissable—I had proof—lips. It was almost enough to clear the fog from my brain. Almost. Until I met his eyes and found a promise of all kinds of dirty things there.

Holy mother of cats.

"Well shit," Hunter said, slinging his arm over my shoulder and directing us back toward the labs. "Looks like I need to start doing things to get thanks for."

EIGHTEEN

S omething was wrong. That much was evident the second we stepped back into the lab and saw Boden, Daniel, and Elise all huddled around Sean as he looked through a microscope.

If we had any doubts, the guilty way they all looked at us—at me—when we approached them was a dead giveaway.

"What?" I demanded, folding my arms over my chest and bracing myself for the worst. "What did you find? What am I?" Suddenly another thought popped into my head. "Oh cats. I don't have some kind of disease, do I?"

"No, no diseases." Sean shook his head, pushing back from his workstation and taking his fake spectacles off. "Ah, this is all a bit baffling, to be honest, Cleo. Take a seat."

"Uh-uh." I shook my head. "No, I'm okay standing. Thanks."

I glanced at Boden, who just gave me a seriously puzzled sort of look back. Very encouraging. We'd have words on that later.

"So, what did you find?" I pressed when Sean didn't immediately info dump all over the floor at my feet.

He cleared his throat and rubbed the bridge of his nose. "Well, we discovered that Marie-Elizabeth was not totally correct in her summation. You *are* human—"

"Oh, thank the gods of cats everywhere," I exclaimed, releasing my pent up breath in a huge sigh. "Wow, you had me worried—"

"—but you're also something else," Sean continued, talking over me like I had just done to him.

I blinked a few times, then sat down in one of the vacant wheelie chairs. "Come again?"

"You're human *and* something else." He summarized.

I gave a tight nod. "Yes, I heard that. But what else? What is the *something*?"

It seemed like they were withholding something major here, and I'd really love if they spat it out before I passed out.

Sean exchanged a glance with Elise, and it was her that responded.

"By our best guess, you're half human and half *god*." She gave me an awkward sort of smile. "How cool is that? Right?" She didn't sound anywhere near as enthusiastic as I was sure she'd been aiming for and quickly continued. "I mean, it's not totally conclusive because we don't have a whole lot of genetic material to compare against. Record-keeping and DNA testing weren't super popular back in ancient Egyptian times, you know?" She tried to laugh at her weak joke, and it fell flat.

Really flat.

"Wait, ancient Egypt? Why do you say from there? Surely there are thousands of other gods; why are we leaping straight there? Is it because of how I look?" I scowled at them but not like... super seriously. I sincerely doubted that was their reasoning; I was just trying to make light of the whole fucked-up mess.

Because they'd just said I was half *god* and that... hurt my brain.

"Oh, well that leads us to the most confusing part of what we found," Sean took over again, and this time he looked really excited. "Your DNA holds certain genetic markers which are, in short, extinct. But all of them indicate both parts of your makeup originate in Egypt."

"What... I'm lost. What are you saying, exactly?" I leaned forward, like physical proximity might make the information clearer.

"I'm saying that if these results came to me on paper and I hadn't personally drawn your blood, I'd say that I was looking at the DNA of a woman who'd lived in Egypt around the Eighteenth Dynasty." He paused, and I said nothing. I was too busy trying to figure out what year that was. "Around 1450 BC."

"Um." I blinked a few times. "What?"

Sean drew a breath and was probably about to repeat everything he'd just said, so I waved a hand in the air to stop him. "No, I heard you. I just don't understand... What the fuck? Can someone less science-y please explain? In Cleo language?"

Boden started to speak, but Elise shushed him.

"I got this one," she announced, then turned to me. "Okay, so my other major is in classical history, so I kind of have a wild guess on what—or who—you are." She grinned widely. "There was a rumor going around back in the day. You know, back in Queen Hatty's day."

I squinted at her. "You mean three and a half thousand years ago? There was a rumor…? Okay sure, I'll bite. What was the rumor that somehow survived three and a half millennia and traveled halfway around the world translated from a dead language?"

Elise totally missed my sarcasm. Or ignored it. Whatever. "Right, so the rumor was that Hatty and Ra were actually lovers. The 'records' say he gave her his power hidden inside an amulet during a war between the gods, in order to keep it safe. But then he never returned for it and was never seen—physically—again. Everyone still believed in him as a 'god' in, like, the spiritual sense of the word, but we magical beings know that the gods existed in a far more physical way. Physical enough to conceive a baby with the pharaoh, whom he trusted enough to guard his power?" She shrugged but looked smug. "You tell me."

I squinted at her harder. "Girl, you are putting cheese with cardboard and calling it cake. You want to tell me that an ancient Egyptian queen… and a *god*… did the nasty and had a love child." She nodded excitedly. "And that *somehow*… that child is me?"

She nodded again, like, *Hey, you're finally getting it!*

I was not. I was not at all getting it.

"Does anyone else see the glaring issue here?" I arched a brow at freaking *everyone else* in the room. "No one? No one at all. I'm the only one wondering where the four thousand years in between went?"

Elise leveled me with an impatient glare. "Three and a half thousand, and geez, it's like you don't believe in magic or something." She threw her hands up and stalked away, muttering under her breath.

I let Sean have the rest of my *what the fuck* face. "Are you buying this? You're a scientist, for the love of cats."

He nodded. "I also turn into a wolf with close to three times my current body mass. Some things can't be explained through logic and science, my dear."

"So we're all just meant to run with this idea that my parents were a pharaoh and a god and somehow baby me got lost in time for thousands of years until popping up in Oregon... just waiting to be adopted by Prudence and Hank Carroll? That's... that's the best theory we're working from?"

Sean nodded, and I rubbed both hands over my face.

Just when I thought shit couldn't get any more insane...

"I think I need some air," I announced, pushing up from my wheelie chair and hurrying through the lab. One of the guys called after me, but I just *really* needed air.

Holy fuck, I couldn't breathe.

I was suffocating. Someone was suffocating me. Was the room full of gas? No, everyone else seemed fine. Fuck. No. I still couldn't breathe; I needed to get outside.

Now.

I shoved the doors open, hurried up the short staircase to the foyer, and then burst out into the late afternoon sunlight, gasping for air.

I was so fucking focused on getting air into my lungs—because I don't care what one half of me was, the other half was human and humans need air to live—that I ran straight into the back of a tall man wearing black.

"Sorry," I gasped, "I wasn't—"

My apology cut short when the man turned around and smiled down at me... with only one good eye.

Ah, *fuck*.

"Cleo!" Boden burst out of the building behind me, then pulled up short when Scarface spun me around and pressed a knife to my neck with scary speed and dexterity. "Axle. How did you find us here?"

"That would be giving away trade secrets, Bo," the man holding me captive replied with a throaty chuckle. "Besides, what does it matter? I'm here, and your little cat just fell right into my lap."

Raze and Hunter had emerged from the building now, too, and warily watched as Scarface used the tip of his knife to fish my amulet out of my top. My captor seemed totally uncaring that we were in public, in daylight, and he was holding me at knifepoint.

In fairness, we were some of the few people left as everyone else was focused on heading home for the day. Gods damn mobile phones, *no one* was looking in our direction at all.

"This is what I came for, but seeing as I can't touch it myself, I'll have to take you with me." He braced his arms around me, like he was preparing to drag me somewhere, and I just...

Panicked.

Fear spiked through me. I had no idea where he planned to take me or how he planned to get me there. What if he knocked me out? But then he hit me too hard and gave me a brain bleed, and then I ended up paralyzed. What then? Nope, no way, I couldn't let him take me freaking *anywhere*.

So, like I said, I panicked.

Blinding light flared from my amulet, quickly erasing everything from sight until the entire world was bright, white light and then...

Poof.

Okay, it was less of a "poof" and more of a "pop," like the weird sensation of air pressure being suddenly displaced. Yeah, I don't really know how better to describe it and "poof" sounded magical and dramatic, so just roll with it.

The light cleared, and I found myself, uh, exactly where I was a second ago.

Scarface was still holding me captive, and we were still facing the science building. The only difference was... the guys were gone.

Just like that.

Poof.

CHAPTER

NINETEEN

"**W**hat the fuck?" Scarface exclaimed, loosening his hold on me as he looked around.

Yes! That was my chance!

Swinging my leg back, I slammed my heel into his nuts as hard as I possibly could.

Then ran like hell.

All the way back into the science building and down the stairs to Sean's lab... which was locked. Light off, no one home.

What in the cat-loving fuck? He had just been here a minute ago. Him, Elise, and Daniel... they couldn't have packed up and gone home that quickly.

The sound of the doors above me banging open made me jump in fright, then frantically hunt for a hiding place. Stupid

Sean's stupid lab was on the basement level, and the only way out was back up. As in, past Scarface.

Out of time and out of ideas, I ducked down behind the hazardous materials waste bin and crossed my fingers. Surely the shadows were deep enough and I was small enough that he wouldn't see me?

Heavy footsteps clomped down the stairs one at a time, totally unhurried. Ugh, what a prick. He must have known he had me cornered. What kind of sick fuck drags out the anticipation like that, anyway? Just get it over with!

"Miss?" a voice that was definitely *not* Scarface's said. "Are you okay? Do you need help?"

Cracking my eyes open and uncurling my arms from over my head, I peeked up at the... uh... the janitor.

Not one to let my guard down so easily, I peered past him, checking for hidden cultists using the janitor as a smoke screen. I wouldn't have put it past him, either, deranged psychopath that he was.

Scarface, I meant. Not the janitor. He seemed like a nice gentleman.

"Uh, yeah," I replied, climbing up off the floor and dusting the back of my jeans off. "Just, ah, thought you were someone else."

I gave him a tight smile and awkwardly edged past him to the stairs. If Scarface hadn't followed me—yet—I should get the fuck out of there. No one liked to be a sitting duck.

At the top of the stairs, I looked out the window and spotted a black-clad figure striding across the grass in quite the opposite direction to where I was. And by striding, I did mean limping somewhat because I had nailed him *hard*. Heh.

"Well shit," I muttered to myself. "That was easier than anticipated."

Or was it?

Where had the guys gone? Why was the lab all locked up and closed? Maybe I should have asked the janitor.

"Cake," I whispered. "Maybe they went for cake."

Because that *totally* made sense. Oh hey, Cleo is being held at knifepoint by a crazy cultist; let's all run to Bertie's Books for more cake! Maybe Scarface will be swayed by the delicious smell of baked goods.

Right. I'm aware how dumb that theory was. But for lack of any better ideas, I headed to Bertie's Books, hoping to find my guardians there with a plate of fresh cake.

When I arrived, the store was empty and the waitress from earlier was just... unlocking? Why would she be unlocking? Why had they been *locked*?

"Good morning," she greeted me with a smile. "I'm still opening up for the day, but you're welcome to take a seat and I'll bring over coffee shortly."

"Uh..." I blinked at her in confusion. Opening up for the day? But I'd just spent most of the afternoon here.

She nodded to the counter where an older man was laying out fresh cakes. "Would you like me to bring you a slice? Today's flavor is mocha swirl."

I rubbed the bridge of my nose and looked around. Had I somehow entered a parallel dimension?

"Uh," I started, nervously biting my lip. "I thought it was hummingbird?"

The girl just cocked her head to the side, confused. "Mmm, nope, we just had hummingbird cake three days ago. Bertie likes to mix it up, so that flavor won't be back for at least a week. Did you want to try the mocha swirl? It's really good, I promise."

I sat down at the table she directed me to in the window of the quirky little store, and a sneaking suspicion crept up on me.

"This is going to sound a bit, um, odd," I said, giving her an apologetic smile, "but could you tell me what day it is?"

She looked a little confused—rightly so—but still replied. "It's Saturday, the twenty-third." She paused, giving me a more concerned look. "Are you okay, hun? Do you need help?" Her eyes darted around, like she might find someone coming to hurt me—which was kind of adorable seeing as I had just been held at knifepoint.

"Yeah, yes, sorry, I'm fine. Just had a hard night out," I lied with a fake laugh. "Totally lost track of my days."

Fuck. Me. Saturday? It had been Wednesday when we'd arrived at the lab... Where the fuck did three days just go?

Oh shit. The light and the poofing! No wonder the guys weren't still outside the science building; me and Scarface would have disappeared three freaking days ago. But now what? How the fuck did I find them? Based on the dark and locked-up nature of the lab, and the fact that it was the weekend, I didn't think Sean would be coming back to work any time soon. I had no mobile phone and no idea how to contact my guardians. Holy shit. I had no money.

"Wait," I put my hand out to pause the waitress as she was about to pour me a coffee. "I'm so sorry, I just realized I don't have my wallet." I started to get up from my seat, and she waved me back down.

"Don't stress, hun, we've all been there." She proceeded to fill the mug with coffee. "Take a minute; drink some coffee. It's on the house."

Her smile was totally genuine, and I was a bit speechless. So much so that I didn't find any words at all until she returned and dropped a plate of rich, brown cake in front of me.

"Thank you," I whispered. "That's—"

"Don't even stress," she cut me off. "We all have off days, and it never hurts to deal out a little kindness. Now, try the cake. Bertie wants to know what you think." She jerked her thumb over her shoulder to where the older man was leaning on the counter eagerly.

A bit embarrassed but not knowing what else to do, I took a forkful of the cake and popped it in my mouth.

"Oh my cats," I groaned around the food. "That's really good." I leaned past the waitress to tell Bertie directly, "Bertie, your cakes are amazing!"

He beamed and gave me a nod of appreciation before ducking back into the little kitchen. I licked my fork clean, then dug it in for another bite while the waitress laughed.

"Try it with a sip of coffee," she suggested as she wandered away to continue setting up. "Totally changes the flavors."

"Wow," I muttered to myself, trying what she advised and being so freaking glad I did. Amazing. So tasty.

It wasn't until I'd totally finished my coffee and cake that I started thinking about what the hell I would do next. I had no money, no way of contacting the guys, nowhere to stay... Holy crap. I was homeless. How the fuck had I become homeless and not even realized it?

This was bad. Really freaking bad.

As was my nervous habit, my fingers rubbed at the amulet hanging around my neck. If only I knew how to use the fucking thing, maybe it could help me out of shit creek.

With slightly comical timing, the amulet zapped me.

"Are you kidding me?" I hissed down at the jewelry, shaking my hand to clear the zap from my fingers. It was like I'd just touched an electric fence or gotten a massive static shock. Either way, rude as hell. "What, now you want to start doing shit?" I demanded of my amulet. Quietly. I was making enough of an impression being the random, pink-haired, tattooed chick with no money and no idea what day of the week it was. I did *not* need to add "talks to inanimate objects" to that list, or I would probably wind up in a mental hospital for real. If I wasn't already.

Carefully, because I wasn't super into pain, I picked the gold disk up between my thumb and forefinger and peered at it.

Nothing happened.

"Hey, cool necklace," the waitress commented, scaring the living shit out of me and making me jump a little in my seat.

I cleared my throat before replying, just in case my voice came out in a scared mouse squeak. "Oh, ah, thanks," I finally said. "Family heirloom."

She smiled, clearing my empty plate away. "Well, it's pretty."

"Thanks," I responded, closing my hand over the amulet a little defensively. I'd had it for years and worn it everyday, but learning it actually contained the power of a god made me a little more paranoid about it.

Just then, the necklace decided to give me a little *push*, and I knew it was time to leave.

"Hey, thank you so much for this," I said to the girl, indicating to the cake and coffee dishes. "I really appreciate it. When I find my, uh, wallet, I'll come back and pay you."

The waitress shook her head. "No need, hun. Just pay it forward somewhere along the line. Karma and all that."

She left for the little kitchen without allowing me any opportunity to argue, so I followed the urging of my possessed necklace and left the store.

Outside, I turned left.

It wanted me to go right.

"For cat's sake," I snapped—under my breath, of course—

when it yanked on my neck to turn me around. "Maybe you should have been more specific in the first place so I don't look like a total nut job."

Yes, I was aware I was speaking to an item of jewelry, and yes, I was aware I already looked like a nut job. But you know. Varying degrees and all that.

For the next... I don't even know how long, I let the necklace guide me. Some might wonder if that was really the smartest course of action, as I had no idea where it was taking me or what its motivations were. Maybe it really liked being wet and it was about to make me jump off a bridge or something. Well, to those people, yeah okay, fair point.

But my question in response would be... do you have a better idea?

Recap: I had no money, no phone, and no way to contact freaking anyone because no one actually memorizes phone numbers anymore. Oh, and I'd somehow just jumped me and Scarface three days into the future. Riddle me that.

The amulet finally stopped tugging on me outside a fancy looking house on a pretty, tree-lined street.

"This one?" I asked the pushy fuck. "You want me to go in here?"

The amulet gave an extra hard tug on the chain in the direction of the front door. Like I hadn't already figured that one out. Asshole.

"Fine," I grumbled, walking up the path. "But if you've brought me to the home of an axe murderer who is going to keep me locked in a cage in his basement for three years before finally cutting me into tiny pieces to feed to his goldfish... well. We will have problems, you and I."

The necklace didn't respond... shocking, I know, given it was a freaking necklace. So instead, I heaved a sigh and pressed the doorbell buzzer.

I waited a few moments, fidgeting with the cuffs of my jacket, before pressing it again. Yes, I'm one of those assholes.

"I'm coming!" Someone yelled from inside the house, and I don't think they meant it in a sexual way. Good thing, too, if they were about to open the door. That would have been super awkward.

Before my mind could wander any further down the path of interrupting someone mid-orgasm—because Hunter was totally right, that was rude—the door flew open.

"Cleo?" Sean gasped. "What the—how—where—Boden!" The last part was yelled—I'm sure you can imagine.

I smiled like a creepy weirdo because this whole situation was freaking me out. "Hey, Sean. You live here? That's... cool." I picked up the necklace and peered at it. "Good work, you."

It could have been my imagination, but I thought the amulet gave a happy little buzz when it came to rest back on my chest.

"So the guys are here?" I peered past him, hopeful. It had only been an hour or so since they'd gone poof—or rather, since I'd gone poof—but I missed those overgrown pussycats. All of them.

Sean was still blinking at me like I was a ghost, so I waited, bouncing on my toes, until my sexy blond friend came into view.

"Cleo!" he exclaimed, shoving Sean aside and sweeping me up in a huge hug—the sort of hug that lifted my feet totally off the ground and left me clinging to his shoulders as he buried his face in my neck.

"Hey, Bo," I said, patting his back and using the nickname I'd heard both Maeve and Sean call him. "Sorry I disappeared on you like that."

"What the hell happened?" he demanded, pulling back far enough that he could see my face but not far enough that my feet could touch the ground again. In fact, he turned and walked with me into the house, just freaking carrying me like I weighed nothing. It was kinda hot. So strong. Mmm.

He finally plunked me down on a barstool at the breakfast bar and placed his hands on his hips. "Where have you been? Where did you go? How did you do it? Where's Axle? How did you get away? How did you find us here? Do you have any idea how worried we've been?" All of his questions came out in what seemed to be one long breath, and I briefly feared for his lung capacity before he paused, presumably for a response.

I opened my mouth, getting ready to answer, like... at least *one* of those questions. But I barely even got a sound out before his lips were on mine, and he was devouring me in a hot, dominant, possessive kiss that sent tingles all the way to my toes.

Fuck the explanations, I was all for *this*.

Gripping the back of his neck, I pulled him closer until my

legs draped loosely around him and his hands roamed my body like he was memorizing me. Our tongues wrestled and teeth nipped, and it took all of my self-control not to climb him like a tree. Curse my better senses, but we *were* in Sean's house and I was pretty sure he was still standing somewhere awkwardly nearby.

I peeled my face away from Boden's and opened my eyes.

Yep, there was Sean, standing in the doorway and trying really hard *not* to look at us while we mauled one another.

Talk about awkward.

I cleared my throat and gently pushed Boden back a little bit. "Are, um, are the other guys here too?"

For a long, heated moment, Boden just stared at me. His gaze was heavy and full of... something I was too emotionally disconnected to really identify. He took his sweet-ass time, pressing one more lingering kiss to my lips before stepping back and running a hand over his face.

"Hunter's in the shower. Raze..." He grimaced. "Hang on, I'll tell Hunter you're back. Wait here."

He disappeared out of the room faster than I could respond—because my brain was slightly fried and my mouth was swollen from kissing him.

Glancing around the beautifully decorated house, I gave Sean a smile. "You have a lovely home."

He smiled back, shaking his head and heading towards the counter. "I was just making coffee when you arrived. Would you like one?"

I beamed. "Love one!"

Sean went about grabbing another cup and pouring the coffee, all the while shooting me sidelong glances. "I won't ask where you've been," he announced, handing over my beverage. "I'm sure you'll tell us in a minute. But the curiosity..."

I nodded my understanding. "Explains that weird look on your face."

A clatter and crash from down the hallway interrupted us, and seconds later Hunter appeared. Dripping wet and totally naked.

"Cleo-babe!" he exclaimed, grabbing me up off my chair and hugging me tight enough to crack my back. My coffee spilled, and as he jostled me, the cup fell from my grip and smashed on the floor. Not that Hunter gave two fucks. "Where have you been? Do you know how worried we were? How—"

"Hunter," I yelled, cutting him off before he repeated all of Boden's questions verbatim. "Can you put me down? You spilled my coffee."

That seemed to snap him out of the panicked frenzy he was in, and he dropped me. I mean, literally dropped me. Luckily he had catlike reflexes and caught me again right before my ass hit the floor.

Unluckily—I guess, depending on how you look at it—the way he caught me landed my face straight in his naked crotch. Yep. I just got slapped in the face by Hunter's wet dick.

Good thing I was sexually attracted to him, or it could have been a whole lot more awkward, that was for sure.

"Hunter, for the love of claws," Boden snapped, picking me up and extracting me from the compromising position I'd just sort of frozen into, like a deer in headlights or some shit. "Put some clothes on. Cleo doesn't need to be mauled by a horny cat the second she walks in the door."

Hunter ducked his head, embarrassed as he hurried back to the bathroom—I assume to find clothing—and I arched a brow at Boden.

"Hypocrite," I murmured quietly.

He gave me a cocky grin. "We all have our faults." He stole another quick kiss before shifting me out of the coffee and broken mug mess to help Sean clean up.

"Sit down, Cleo," Sean suggested. "We all need to debrief a bit, I think."

That sounded like the most sensible course of action, so I sat. All the while I wondered... where the fuck was Raze?

CHAPTER
TWENTY

Part of me had been pretty confident Raze was there in the house, but just really pissy and in such a foul mood that the guys didn't dare bother him with my return. Or maybe another part of me thought he was so cut up and distraught by my disappearance that he was sobbing into his pillow upstairs.

But it was neither of those options.

"Gone?" I repeated, dumbfounded. "What do you mean *gone*? How is that even a thing? Have you seen the freaking size of him?"

Hunter and Boden exchanged a look, and Boden sighed. "Yeah, we know. It's a bit hard for even us to understand. From what we've worked out, you surprised Axle before the rest of his crew were expecting you. After the two of you... uh..."

"Went poof," I supplied, and he nodded.

"Right, after you went *poof*, the other cultists freaked out, and fight started up. We were, as you can imagine, in a bit of a panic. We thought Axle had done something to you, and things got a little, uh, out of hand." Boden cringed, and I suspected he was downplaying the whole event somewhat.

Sean cleared his throat. "What Bo means is that there was some magical clean up to be done afterward. It was during that time that Raze went missing."

I arched a brow that them, urging them to continue. All these dramatic pauses were making me want to strangle someone.

"We're guessing there was another group of Bastites that stayed out of the initial fight, and they somehow managed to overpower Raze and sedate him. We received this by email a few hours later." Boden clicked open a video on Sean's laptop and turned it to face me.

On the screen, Raze was locked in a cage in a dimly lit room, and he was *pissed*. His loose hair just added to the wild ferocity as he snarled and hissed at his captors. All kinds of obscenities flew from his mouth, but the words I latched onto, which he said over and over, were the ones that squeezed my heart until it hurt.

"What did you do with her?" he bellowed. "Where is she? Where's Cleo? If you hurt her, I will skin you alive! Every Bast-damned one of you!"

"Well shit," I breathed as the video cut off. My eyes were damp, and I swiped them with the back of my hand. It wasn't exactly the most romantic declaration I'd ever heard, but from

Raze? It was pretty damn close. Threatening to skin someone alive... for me? Things just didn't get much more serious than that.

"So how do we get him back?" I looked to Boden and Hunter. I mean, yeah, Sean was helpful and stuff, but this was our mission and Raze was our responsibility to save. "How do we find out where they're keeping him?"

Hunter grimaced. "We already know. They took him to Texas. You know those kittens you were on your way to save?" I nodded, confused. "Well, it turns out that 'shelter' was a trap laid to draw you in. The amulet is tied to cat shifters as your guardians, and a side-effect of that is that it'll push you toward all cats. Especially those in need."

"Wait, so the kill shelter in Texas was a front for Bast's cult? And that's where they took Raze?" I blinked at them while processing this information. "How come you're still here? If you know where he is, why haven't you already gone to save him?"

Boden scowled at me. Actually, so did Hunter.

"Because *you* were missing too, Cleo. We knew where Raze is, and he's a big enough kitty to handle himself for a while. We *didn't* know where you were, and that was infinitely more troubling than Raze being locked in a shift-proof cage." Boden sounded almost offended that I would suggest they wouldn't still be here looking for me.

"Well, sure," I said carefully, "but you didn't know when I'd reappear... if ever. So wouldn't it have been a good idea to go rescue Raze? I'm just saying..." I shrugged. I mean, I freaking loved that they'd hung around looking for me, but I hated the idea of Raze in a cage. It was so totally against everything he was... He must be going crazy.

"We knew you were here somewhere," Hunter informed me with a confident nod. "We could sense you were somewhere nearby."

I nodded. "Sort of like how my amulet led me here, I guess. Magic."

There was a short pause during which no one spoke.

"Okay, so we're heading to Texas then?" I looked between Boden and Hunter, waiting for them to do something. What? I had no idea. Call up the private jet and make plans? Respond to the Bastites and be all, "Yo, we're on our way!"

Hunter just dodged my gaze, while Boden looked stubborn. Something told me they weren't on board with my stellar plan.

"What?" I demanded when Boden's jaw tightened to the point of his cheek ticking.

He shook his head firmly. "We're not taking you to Texas."

My brows shot up. "Excuse me?"

"You're not going to Texas, Cleo," he said, his tone brokering no arguments from me. "You're exactly what they want; we're not going to just march in there and hand you over on a silver platter. Raze can handle himself."

I frowned in horror. "You're just going to leave him there? To do what? Free himself? You *just* said he's in a shift-proof cage! Do you know what that means?"

"That he can't shift," Hunter supplied, and I gestured wildly with my hand.

"Exactly!" I bellowed, "That he can't shift! How do you plan on him saving himself when he can't fucking shift, Boden?"

I was getting all kinds of worked up, leaping up out of my seat and gesturing wildly. Something about the way Raze had screamed at the camera, the way he'd threatened bodily harm on them if they hurt me... it brought out that desperate need to protect. The same one I'd felt when I heard about cats in kill-shelters, except way more extreme.

"Cleo," Boden snapped, just as worked up as I was. "You're not going to Texas; it's *not safe.*"

Now, I got where he was coming from. I really did. But here's a crash course in how to handle Cleo.

1. Don't tell me what to do.

2. Don't imply I'm a helpless damsel in distress.

"Where the hell do you get off, telling me what I can and can't do?" I seethed, glaring daggers at him. "You've known me all of one fucking week, and all you do is boss me around. Well, newsflash, sir commander sir, I'm not in your fucking army, and I don't have to do what you say! I've been rescuing cats just fine all on my own before you arrived, and I can do it again."

"Cats," Boden shouted back, "from kill shelters. Not cat *shifters* from crazy ancient goddesses and their cults! Big difference, sweetheart."

Somehow he made "sweetheart" sound like an insult, and my

anger stoked higher. This condescending ass-face had nothing on Raze right now.

I opened my mouth to unleash the wrath of Cleo on him, but Hunter jumped between us. "Guys, cut it out for a minute. Sean has something to say." He indicated to their scientific friend, who had his finger raised in the air—as though either of us were going to notice that over our screaming match.

"What?" Both Boden and I snarled the word in unison, then glared at each other. Our argument was *far* from over.

Sean licked his lips and adjusted those silly, fake glasses of his. "If I might interject, I think I can put an end to this disagreement?"

Boden shot me a smug smile, then nodded to his friend. "By all means, go ahead." He turned back to me, folding his arms over his chest like he'd already fucking won. Arrogant prick.

"Ah, yes," Sean started, shooting me a look, to which I glared death back at him. "So, Cleo is right, and she does need to go to Texas."

"See—" Boden started to say, then it must have clicked what Sean had actually said. "Wait, *what?*"

"Hah!" I jeered at him. "Suck shit, cat-boy. Sean just said I was right, which means you're *wrong*."

"What?" Boden demanded of Sean. "Have you lost your damn mind? Bast herself is in Texas. The goddess *herself*. The one who has been trying to steal the Amulet of Light for three and a half millennia. The one who will kill Cleo without a second glance. That Bast."

Sean sighed and polished his glasses on his cardigan. No joke, he was wearing a cardigan.

"I'm aware which Bast is in Texas, Bo," he replied with an edge of sarcasm, "but unfortunately, you don't have final say on this one."

Boden snorted, and Hunter made a pained groan and muttered something along the lines of, "Oh geez, here we go."

"Oh no? Tell me who has higher jurisdiction than me in this situation, Sean?" Boden challenged his friend, who looked totally unfazed. Maybe Boden's temper tantrums weren't just a byproduct of hanging out with me?

Sean arched a brow and sighed. "The oracles, Bo. The oracles have higher jurisdiction than you in *any* situation, and you know it."

Confused, I shot a look at Boden, whose face drained of color way too quickly for my liking. Shit. That couldn't be good. A quick glance at Hunter showed me a grim expression on his face too.

"This has nothing to do with them," Boden denied, but I could see the truth all over his face. This definitely did have something to do with these "oracles." Whoever they were.

Sean snorted. "It does, and you know it does."

"All right, is anyone going to explain this to me?" I asked, breaking the weird tension in the room. "Who are the oracles, and what do they have to do with me going to Texas?"

Sean turned his attention back to me with a tight, tired-looking smile. "I'm so sorry, Cleo. I forget you know nothing about any of this. Please, sit down, and I'll do my best to explain."

I carefully sat back down in my seat, and Sean flicked a sharp look at Boden. "I think you can go and make us some fresh coffee, don't you?"

Boden scowled at his friend, then gave me a conflicted frown and stalked back into the kitchen to start the coffee brewing.

"Oracles?" I prompted Sean when he looked confused for a moment. Hunter moved from his seat to mine, lifting me up and placing me back down on his lap before wrapping his arms around my waist. Whether it was a show of physical support for whatever Sean was about to tell me or he was just a touchy-feely cat, I wasn't sure. I also didn't care; I loved him touching me.

"Right, the oracles." Sean nodded. "I'll try and keep this as brief and accessible as possible. Sometimes I tend to wander off into academia and confuse my audience."

I bit my tongue to keep from making a sarcastic, "Oh, do you? I never noticed," remark.

"As you're now aware, there is much more to our world than just humans, yes? There are shifters—"

"Right, the Alliance," I interrupted, subtly trying to hurry him along. Okay, not so subtly. Whatever.

Sean nodded. "Yes, but the Alliance is just the governing body for shifters. But as you also know, there are many more magical creatures in our world than just shifters." He nodded pointedly at my amulet, and what he was saying clicked.

"Oh yes. Gods. Gotcha. So these oracles are something

different from the Alliance?" I snuggled back into Hunter's warmth. Damn, he was comfortable to sit on. Soothing, too.

In the back of my mind, I suspected he was letting a little Hunter-magic seep out into me. But it was helping keep me calm, so I wasn't going to argue.

"That's right," Sean confirmed. "The Oracles are technically in charge of all the various species' specific organizations, like the Shifter Alliance. They're in charge because they're quite literally oracles. They see the future." He paused, pursing his lips. "Or they see versions of the future. Unfortunately, they learned a long time ago to keep their visions to themselves because too many people working to prevent too many things just winds up in chaos. Only the strongest visions get recorded for public access. The ones they're confident won't change, no matter how many people know or try to influence them."

A sick feeling pooled in my stomach. "Let me guess, there's something recorded that you think refers to me?"

Sean beamed. "Yes, how did you know?"

I sighed and accepted the mug of coffee that Boden brought over to me. "I read a lot of fantasy novels. So what does the prophecy say, exactly?"

"Well." Sean shifted in his seat and took a sip of his own coffee. "I'd need to see the original to get the exact wording correct. These things can get a bit warped over time and retellings, but I submitted a petition for access the moment I saw your DNA results. Hopefully it won't take them too much longer to grant permission."

Hunter made a sound under me. "On whose time? Humans' or immortals'?"

Sean grimaced. "Good point. It could be months, and they'd still consider it a quick turn around."

"Okay, so what do you remember or know? There must be something specific to me, or you wouldn't all be tripping out right now." I glanced between the three of them, and Sean polished his glasses. Again.

"Right, so—" Sean started, but Hunter interrupted.

"In a nutshell," my Aussie lover said, "the prophecy talks about a half human, half god who was lost in time. It makes some super vague mentions about restoring forgotten gods to their places of power in our world, and then gets super specific that she—or he, maybe it's not you—will need three powerful guardians in order to succeed. Three guardians, and everything works out well. Less than three... doom and gloom." Apparently, they'd already been talking about this.

"None of that specifically mentions going to Texas, though," I commented, wrinkling my nose in confusion. "Other than the fact that..." I trailed off, turning accusing eyes on Boden. "You were going to leave Raze there to die?" Puzzle pieces clicked together in my head, and I jumped out of Hunter's lap, horrified. "What the fuck? I thought he was your friend!"

"Cleo, calm down," Boden started, and a dull ringing of fury built up in my head.

"Oh, you did not just tell me to calm down," I breathed in white-hot anger. "You were just going to leave Raze with the cultists to get, what, sacrificed in some demonic ritual?"

"It's not demonic if it's to Bast," Hunter muttered, and I swung my death glare his way.

"He might have gotten himself out," Boden protested, not sounding anywhere near convincing enough.

I seethed. "Might. Might have. Might *not* have too, and then where would that leave us? Huh? Do you honestly think I would be okay with that course of action?" I threw my hands up in the air at the sheer idiocy of the men in this room.

Except Sean. Sean seemed sane.

"We're going to Texas, and we're saving Raze's ass. End of story!" I stomped my foot as I said that. It was involuntary, I wasn't proud of it, but it happened.

Jesus Christ Supercats, I had never felt more like a petulant troll in my life. Like, even my hair was the same shade as Princess Poppy's. Damn it all to Egyptian Hell.

"Now. How do we get there?" I directed my question at Hunter while Boden glared death and punishment my way. Well, too freaking bad for him that wasn't one of his abilities, so he'd have to just suck it up.

"Um." Hunter flicked a glance at Boden, who gave him a tight, angry nod. "I guess I can arrange a plane, but it'll take a couple of hours."

"Good," I huffed. "Do that." A post-meltdown wake of

exhaustion washed over me, and my eyelids suddenly felt like they were made of pure lead. "Um, Sean, do you have somewhere I can lie down? I'm not feeling so great."

Sean only hesitated a moment before he hopped up and led the way through his house to a guest room. "I'll be back in a second," he told me, ushering me into the room. "You're suffering backlash. Two secs."

I had no idea what he was talking about, so I just sat my butt down on the edge of the bed and wallowed in the total-bag-of-shit feeling that had just consumed me. What the fuck was happening? Had I suddenly caught the flu? Or malaria? Oh my cats, what if it was some weird-ass, freaky time travel disease that I'd picked up wherever I was in between Wednesday and Saturday?

By the time Sean returned, I was almost hyperventilating.

"Am I dying?" I squeaked out as he stepped back into the room holding a fistful of... protein bars? Where were the antibiotics? Surely I needed antibiotics!

Sean gaped, confused, then laughed. "No, oh my goodness, you do have a flair for the dramatic. No, I already told you you're suffering backlash. Here, eat these."

I took one of the bars from him and ripped it open, sniffing it. "What is it? Some kind of magic healing bar?"

"What?" Sean gave me a baffled look. "It's a protein bar. I'm going out on a limb here and guessing that what you did, jumping yourself and Axle three days through time, it's drained your energy. You just need to eat something."

"Oh." I took a big bite of the chocolate-flavored bar, chewed, and swallowed. "So, are you saying I'm just not myself when I'm hungry?"

Sean rolled his eyes at my dumb Snickers joke. "Just eat all of these. They'll help your body restore all the missing energy. Or that's how it works for most magical beings."

My mind wandered back to the truck stop, where Boden had inhaled a whole pile of hot dogs, and to the fact that none of the big cats had anything more than 2% body fat. I guess their shifting and high metabolism were to blame for the lack of dad bods.

"Take a nap if you need to," Sean suggested, heading for the door. "I'll tell those two shit-for-brains to leave you alone a bit."

I chuckled around my mouthful of protein bar. "Thanks."

After he was gone, I dusted off the rest of the bars and really did feel a million times better for it, which was exciting in more ways than one. Firstly, it meant that I actually had used magic, rather than being taken along for the ride. It was me who had time jumped, not Axle and not the amulet. Secondly, this meant I could stop going to pilates to work off my love of food!

Come to think of it, though, a nap didn't sound too bad either.

CHAPTER
TWENTY ONE

The sound of footsteps near my bed woke me, and I sat up with a violent gasp. Was I being attacked again? Was Scarface back to get me? Did I accidentally jump through time in my sleep, and now I'm in medieval times about to be sold into slavery?

"Oh, Boden." I relaxed with a heavy sigh, recognizing the intruder. I rubbed my eyes with the back of my hand, then peered around the room. "How long was I asleep?"

"Couple of hours," he replied, sitting on the side of the bed and looking at his hands. "Hunter organized his jet to take us down to Texas, so we need to leave here in about an hour. Just thought I'd wake you up in case you want to shower and change."

"Oh." I collapsed back into the pillows. "An hour. That's loads of time." Rolling onto my side, I snuggled back into the blankets. "I don't know why I'm so tired. I ate all the chocolate Sean gave me."

Boden gave a small shrug, still not looking at me. "It happens to us too, sometimes. Especially when we first start shifting. Your body's adjusting to the use of magic, and it's sort of like stretching a muscle that hasn't ever been used. Exhausting. Not that we have any other demigods to compare you against; it's just a guess."

I yawned heavily, covering my mouth with the back of my hand. "Makes sense."

He sat there for a moment, not saying anything but also not making a move to leave at all.

"What's up?" I finally asked, after staring at the side of his face way for longer than was socially acceptable. "You look like you have something on your mind."

Boden drew a deep breath and released it in a sigh, still looking at his hands. "I do."

"So?" I prompted, shuffling over and patting the bed beside me. "Come lie down and tell me what's going on. This bed is super comfy, just FYI."

A small smile teased at his lips, but he resisted until I reached out and yanked on his arm. Eventually he kicked off his shoes and lay on his side beside me.

"Cleo, I wanted to come and apologize to you," he said, finally bringing his gaze up to meet mine. We were sharing the same pillow, so it was either make eye contact or be an awkward weirdo by trying to stare at the ceiling.

I shifted more onto my side to face him, tucking one hand under my face. "What for?"

A small frown touched his brow. "Seriously? For earlier... that fight..."

"Oh." I nodded slightly. "Well, I mean other than for being a bit of an overbearing asshole who tried to keep me wrapped in cotton-wool at the risk of his best friend being sliced and diced on a cultist's altar... I don't think you have much to apologize for. Nothing wrong with a little healthy debate."

Boden rolled his eyes at my summary. "Well, yeah. All of that. I just wanted to explain myself a bit. I hate the idea that you think I'm an overbearing asshole, and believe me, I would do almost anything to rescue Raze..." He trailed off, and I understood.

"Anything that didn't put me in danger, you mean."

Boden's face tightened, but he nodded. "If I have to choose between my friend and you, the choice will always be you. Every time. Hunter and Raze will say the same thing. 'Guardian' isn't just a job title that we applied and got selected for. It's a sacred calling, and not one we take lightly."

Reaching out, I stroked a light finger down the side of his face. "I know. Or I'm trying to understand. But me going to Texas does not automatically equate to me being in danger. For all you know, it could be a super easy rescue, and we can go about our lives... whatever that looks like now."

He scowled, catching my hand and pressing a kiss to my fingers. "Or it could end in disaster."

"We won't know until we try," I replied with a cheeky smile. "Besides, I can't just walk away from Raze. There's too much... stuff between us now." My belly fluttered, remembering the way he'd kissed me in the street and the promises of dirty sex the other night in the club.

"Yeah, Hunter told me about that move he pulled with the books. Smooth fucker." Boden released my hand and ran his fingers through his hair. "I don't know what it is about you, Cleo. You've got all three of us panting after you like love-sick puppies."

I gave him a toothy grin. "Must be my shining personality."

He laughed lightly, then sobered up to peer at me with a serious face. "The way we argued earlier, I needed to explain myself. I'm not usually so... volatile."

"Uh-huh, everyone says that." I smiled to let him off the hook, but he shook his head.

"No, I'm serious. You remember how I can sense your emotions?" He raised his brows, and I nodded. "Well, when you start getting really fired up like that, it gets really intense, and I somehow end up just mirroring your emotions. Not to say I don't stand by everything I said, I just usually deliver it with a little less..."

"Passion?" I suggested, understanding what he was saying. He'd flown off the handle because I was already raging. This was going to prove interesting in future disagreements.

"Yes." He smiled back at me. "Passion."

I thought back to that argument and the way his anger had seemed to spike every single time mine had. What a mess.

"Regardless of the way we handled our disagreement, I need to make something really super crystal clear with you, Bo." I peered at him, making sure he understood I was dead serious. "You cannot treat me like a child or a porcelain doll. I know I don't have claws and fangs and shit, but I'm still a person with valid opinions and feelings. If this"—I waved my hand in the air, indicating, uh, stuff—"this thing with the four of us is going to have any longevity, then we all need to be equals. Regardless of our genitals. Understood?"

A small smile pulled at his lips, but he smoothed it out to a serious expression. "Understood. I didn't mean to make you feel like a second-class citizen; I'm really used to dishing out orders and having them followed without question. It's just taking me a bit to adjust to this, uh, combative nature of yours. I promise it's got nothing to do with your vagina and everything to do with your inexperience in magic." He stared back at me for a long moment before that smile peeked back through. "Speaking of your vagina... are you suggesting you're interested in pursuing something less *professional* between the four of us?"

I rolled my eyes. "I think that much is abundantly clear, don't you?

"I don't know; maybe I need some clarification," he teased with mock ignorance. "Maybe I've been misreading your signals. Cats are naturally very affectionate people, you know."

I snickered. "Why don't you get under the covers, and I'll clarify a few things for you."

He only hesitated a fraction of a second—checking if I was serious—before joining me under the thick quilt. His hands snaked around my waist, pulling me close to him, and I hissed when his cold fingers met my waist.

"Damn, Bo," I grumbled, "I thought cats were always warm or something."

He huffed. "Myth. Why do you think we always need snuggles?"

"Ah, good point," I replied, tucking my own hands inside his T-shirt and exploring the hard planes of his back. Damn, he was fit. "You said we had an hour, right?"

"Uh-huh, something like that," he replied, arching into my touch like a, uh, like a big cat. Yeah, I know, my description was on point.

"Awesome," I replied, tilting my head up to kiss his lips. I started small, teasing him with little pecks and nibbles until he growled with frustration and flipped me under him.

"Tease," he accused, kissing me properly and leaving me panting for more.

I was going to come back with another sassy retort, but then, you know what? There were so many better things my mouth could be doing. My lips parted, and I eagerly welcomed Boden's hot, passionate kiss.

Somehow—don't ask me how—my hands found their way down to his waistband. While my lips kept him distracted—hah, yeah right—I made quick work of his belt and fly, and within seconds I had a hand full of cock. Boden groaned against my mouth but didn't leap out of bed in horror when I gripped him firmly and stroked, so I took that as a solid sign to continue.

"Cleo," he sighed, kissing along the line of my neck and biting gently at the bend where my neck met my shoulder. Oh, holy shit. How had I never noticed how fucking hot that was before? My hand tightened on his hard shaft, and he chuckled against my skin. "Interesting."

"Mm-hmm," I agreed because, yeah, it was interesting. But also, "Do it again," I suggested. Not that he needed any encouragement. This time his bite was a little firmer, sending a delicious shiver all the way through me.

"That's going to mark," he commented, tracing his tongue over the same spot. In all honesty, I could barely hear him over the sound of my own heavy breathing. Anyone would think it'd been years since I'd gotten laid, not days. But in my defense, uh, all three of my guardians were walking wet dreams. I had actually done really freaking well to make it almost two weeks without just ripping all my clothes off and demanding a foursome.

"Good," I murmured back, sliding my thumb over the wet tip of his erection. "Payback for scratching your back the other day. Or... last week. I've lost track of time."

Boden gave me a small grin as he pushed my tank top up to tease my nipples through the soft lace of my bra. "Time travel will do that to you."

"Uh-huh," I agreed, way too focused on what he was doing to my body to discuss the finer details of the space-time continuum. Maybe later.

Boden's hand traveled lower, dipping inside my panties and stroking across my aching cunt. Ugh, that reminded me I was totally going to need to work a waxing appointment in somewhere with all this running for our lives bullshit.

His thumb teased at my clit, and I moaned way too loudly before clapping my free hand over my mouth. "Shit," I hissed, shooting a glance at the bedroom door, which stood partly open. Boden hadn't closed it behind him when he'd come in to chat, but I guess he didn't anticipate his apology for being a prick to end up like *this*.

"Shh," he snickered, sliding a finger inside me and making me bite down on my own hand. "Got to be quiet, Cleo." He added a second finger, hooking around to brush over my G-spot and causing me to squirm.

"Asshole," I whispered back but arched into his hand, urging him to keep going.

Two could play at his game, though, and I still had a solid handful of rock hard cock. Giving him a wicked grin, I slid my fist down his length, gripping tight and paying extra attention to the tip when I returned there.

Boden shuddered, but the lazy smile told me he was all on board with our dirty little game of chicken. Who could stay quiet longer? Guess we were going to find out...

His fingers withdrew just long enough to strip my panties off, then he was right back there with three. Ah shit. Fuck. Yep, I was going to lose this one... for freaking sure.

"Guys," Hunter's voice came from farther down the hall, and we both froze. "We need to leave soon; are you all ready?"

Now, I was totally prepared for Boden to sigh, grumble, and move a "safe" distance away before Hunter actually entered the room. I was *not* prepared for him to take it as a challenge and finger fuck me so quickly, with such jaw dropping finesse, that as Hunter pushed the door open and stepped into the bedroom, I was already coming.

But sure enough, that's what he did.

Fucking fireworks exploded in my head, wave upon wave of delicious, orgasmic pleasure shooting straight from my clit all the way through my body and back again. Stars danced across my vision, and I could have sworn I had a little bit of an out-of-body experience. By the time I came back to earth, all I could do was offer Hunter a lazy, satiated smile as he scowled from the doorway.

"You guys are assholes," he muttered, folding his arms and glaring. But I wasn't fooled. There was more than a healthy dose of heat in his gaze, and I was feeling too damn awesome to try and backtrack out of it.

"Hey, Hunter," I panted. I still held Boden's cock in my hand, and just to be a shithead, I gave it another teasing stroke.

Boden snickered a laugh and scooted out of my reach. He adjusted his pants quickly, then slid out of the bed and handed me my underwear from the floor. "To be continued, beautiful," he murmured before kissing me way longer than a peck. "Again."

As he passed Hunter on the way out of the room, I could have sworn I heard him whisper, "Payback, bitch."

After he was gone, Hunter arched a brow at me, and I grinned up at him.

"What?" I asked. "You said it yourself, it's bad manners to interrupt a lady when she's about to come."

A broad grin spread across Hunter's face, despite his obvious efforts to hide it. "Dammit, you're right. Ugh. Okay, hurry up and put pants back on, or I'm going to have to get in there and one-up Boden."

"Tempting offer," I teased, and he gave me a frustrated groan before leaving the room himself.

Left alone with my thoughts, I took a lightning-fast shower and re-dressed. The guys had brought my spare clothes, so at least I had something clean to put on for the trip to Texas. Nothing worse than fighting evil, ancient goddesses with dirty underwear, right?

It did give me a few moments to examine my recent behavior, though. Not that I was the kind of girl who staunchly believed in monogamy, but I'd also never entertained the idea of polyamory. Maybe just because I'd never met the right guy? *Guys*. Plural. Wow, that was going to take a hot second to wrap my brain around.

They seemed okay with it, though, didn't they?

I mean... other than that thing Raze had said about ruining me for everyone else, Hunter and Boden included. But he was just posturing, right?

Sure. Yeah. Let's go with that.

TWENTY TWO

East Texas was hot and humid, but wasn't it always? It was like walking around inside a mouth—not even remotely sexy—and it was wrecking havoc on my heavily bleached and dyed hair. Mother. Fucker.

All the keratin treatments in the world weren't saving me now.

"Now, remember—" Boden started to say as our car pulled up outside the Palm Valley Animal Control Center. PVAC. Just the name made my teeth grind together so hard they hurt. Even knowing it was a front for Bast and her cult didn't help matters. There were so damn many of these kill shelters that were chucking poor, innocent animals in their gas chambers...

I shuddered. There were some seriously fucked up people in the world.

"—stay behind us," Boden was saying, and I forced myself to focus on him again. "I'm not saying that because you have a vagina." He smirked at me, referencing our earlier conversation. "I'm saying that because you don't have claws and fangs. Also, you have no clue how to use your abilities, and I really, really would rather you not do another time jump. My stress levels can't handle another three days of wondering if you're alive."

I gave him a sheepish smile and saluted. "Understood, boss. Stay behind the big kitties."

Hunter grunted an annoyed sound. "Not a cat," he muttered, but followed Boden out of the car anyway.

There had been no point in trying to disguise our arrival; Bast already knew we were coming. We'd seen black-robed weirdos everywhere we'd gone since our plane landed. How the hell they were just wandering around in cultist attire and no one was commenting on the oddity of it, I had no idea. Magic, I guessed?

Outside the car, both guys stripped down and shifted into their feline—ahem, I meant *animal*—forms. We all figured it was best to be fully prepared for whatever we walked in on, especially given how Raze was trapped in an anti-shift cage.

Boden gave me a look that seemed to convey, "Are you ready?" I nodded firmly, gripping my amulet between my fingers and trying *really* hard not to freak out.

But, like, what could go wrong. Right? I had two seriously

badass shifters by my side and the power of a god quite literally at my fingertips. I mean sure, I didn't know how to *use* that power, but lets not nitpick here.

With a snarling yowl, Hunter charged the front doors with his massive shoulder. Once again, not totally sure if cats—or cat-shaped marsupials—had shoulders, but for lack of a better way to describe it, we're rolling with shoulder.

The doors burst open, the chain that had held them closed on the inside snapping like a toothpick and flying across the room ahead of us.

Now *that* was an entrance.

Inside the building was little more than a dirty, damp warehouse with a cage full of pissed off Raze right in the middle of the room.

I wasn't totally sure what I'd been expecting, but this... wasn't it.

Yeah, sure, I knew the animal shelter was a front, but I'd expected more of a dramatic cult headquarters. Where were the open-flame sconces and ancient artifacts? Where was the altar that Bast sacrificed innocent cats on to increase her powers? Where were all the chanting acolytes?

From the shadows, several dozen black-robed cultists appeared.

Oh, there they were. Spoke too soon on that last point, but the rest was still valid!

"What the fuck?" Raze bellowed, his gaze landing on me like a ton of fucking bricks. Uh-oh. "You brought her here? Are you *insane?* Boden, you've completely lost your damn mind!"

I flinched a little at his ire, but the big, tawny lynx in front of me snarled and hissed in response with what I was fairly confident was the cat version of, "Hey, fuck you."

The cultists didn't waste any time fucking around with grand statements and witty banter... In fact, it seemed like most of them had no voice at all. In all the run-ins we'd had, I had only heard maybe three of them speak. They were practically Ninjalinos. You know, from *PJ Masks?* Don't act like I'm the only one who watches kids' cartoons while hungover. We all do it.

They burst into action, running at Boden and Hunter, who fended them off with teeth and claws. Really, these cultists were *not* an army. They weren't even well-trained, and it seemed a bit too easy how fast the guys were dispatching them.

Whatever. My task in all this was to free Raze from the cage so he could shift.

Making myself as small and inconspicuous as possible, I wove between disemboweled Bastites and two aggressive, murderous cats until I reached the barred enclosure in the middle of the room.

"Hey Raze," I greeted the wild man in the cage. "Long time no see, huh?" I gave him an awkward wave and tried not to squirm under the ferocity of his glare. Oh wow, he was *really* mad. "I'm just going to..." I stretched out my hand, passing him the rolled-up leather containing an assortment of lock picks. There was no way in hell the guys would've been able to teach me how to pick locks in those few hours we'd had on the plane, so we all decided

I'd just get the picks *to* Raze, and he could work it out himself.

"This was the plan?" he demanded, giving me a long side eye as he withdrew some picks and carefully reached his arms between the bars to reach the outside of the cage. "You know this is a trap, right? Bast wanted them to bring you here."

"No duh," I snapped back, sarcastic as fuck. "But I also wasn't going to let her drain you of all your blood and then take a bath in it. Jesus Christ Supercats, you must think I'm a real bitch if you thought I'd be cool with that."

Raze quirked a brow at me but didn't stop messing with the lock. "You watch too many true crime documentaries, Maggie," he muttered, grunting as he clicked the tumblers into place and the cage door swung open. "Come on, let's go before she closes her snare."

"Too late," a familiar and totally unwelcome voice sang just moments before Raze went stiff as a board and dropped to the ground unconscious. Behind him stood my old friend Scarface, holding what looked like an electric cattle prod. But like, made for taking down rhinos or... uh... panthers.

"Take her to the portal," he ordered someone behind me. Someones, I soon discovered as several sets of hands grabbed at me and lifted me off the ground.

"Help!" I shrieked before someone clamped a sweaty palm over my mouth. Hunter and Boden were across the room, each surrounded by at least five Bastites. Trained or not, the Bastites were just using sheer numbers to keep my guardians distracted while they took me... where? What had Scarface said? Take me to the *portal?*

I kicked and thrashed against their hold, flopping around like a great white on a fishing line, but it was no good. There were too many of them, and I was too damn small on my own.

Fat load of use the fucking amulet was now! Useless hunk of metal!

The black-robed assholes carried me toward a doorway, but it was no ordinary doorway. This one glowed with a creepy, shimmering green, and the image beyond it was *not* of the next room. Certainly not any warehouse room I'd ever seen before, that was for sure.

I wriggled and thrashed harder, trying desperately to break their hold. All I managed to do was turn myself around, though.

The last thing I saw before they tossed me into the portal was Raze dragging himself back to his feet and shifting.

Then I was gone.

TWENTY THREE

hose pricks must have thrown me harder than I realized because when the spots cleared from my vision, I could feel a painful throbbing at the side of my head. Touching my fingers to that spot, I found blood there.

Ouch. I must have hit my head on...

Oh, right. I hit my head on the edge of an intricately carved block of stone because I *seemed* to be... uh... this could be the head injury, but I was pretty sure I had just relocated to the inside of a pyramid. And not an ancient one... a new one.

It seems like a leap, I know. But I've seen *The Mummy* several times. I know what the inside of a pyramid looks like when it's all new and not crumbling with age.

"What the claws," I muttered, looking around in stunned disbelief. "Hello? Is anyone else here?"

Suddenly, a wash of panic rolled through me. If I really was inside a pyramid, what if I couldn't get out? What if my time-jumping ability had brought me here and I couldn't make it work to take me back, and I had no food or water or...

Holy fuck. Was there enough air? When would it run out? Were there ventilation shafts? Why didn't I have better knowledge of how pyramids were designed?

I was right in the middle of a full-blown panic attack when *poof!*

Just like that, Boden, Hunter, and Raze all appeared in the tomb with me, all in cat form and—

"Raze, is that Scarface in your mouth?" I exclaimed, recognizing the tattooed and bleeding forearm clenched between Raze's teeth. Sadly, that arm was still attached to the rest of Scarface, who was still very much alive.

"Oh good," a woman's voice boomed, echoing through the huge burial chamber, "my guests have arrived."

Looking around, I located the speaker and instantly hated her. I'm aware that it's not nice to judge people based on their appearance, but for starters, this chick was like every stereotype of an Egyptian queen all rolled into one golden, perfectly formed beauty queen. I'm talking the dead straight, silken waterfall hair with blunt cut fringe, heavily black-lined eyes with the cute designs on the outer corners, heavy gold and turquoise jewelry, and sweet fuck-all fabric covering her bits.

For another thing, she was *clearly* Bast. Of course I instantly hated her; her minions had been trying to kill me for close to two weeks!

"Bast, I presume," I responded, propping my hands on my hips and giving her my very best sassy face. "Too good to visit us in the real world? Or just don't have any clothes?"

Yeah, I don't know where I was going with that insult. In my defense I was feeling a bit shaken up and, well, scared. We'd well and truly walked into her trap, and I had no freaking idea what to do next.

The gorgeous goddess-woman grinned a feral sort of grin, and a bigger than average domestic feline circled her ankles as she cat-walked toward me. "So you're the one," she purred. No joke, she purred it. "You're the descendant. The *true* descendant of that whore Hatshepsut." As she said the name of the long-dead queen—my mother, I guess—she spat at the sarcophagus she was walking past.

Was I to assume that *that* was Hatshepsut's coffin?

Ew! Was she in there? Dead?

I shuddered. Dead things creeped me right the fuck out. I could barely even handle walking past cemeteries.

"Uh, yeah," I replied, doing a confident hair flip. "So they tell me."

Bast slunk closer and behind me, and three distinctive growls rumbled from my guardians. I had no idea what Raze had done with Scarface, but I trusted they were watching my back while I faced off with this ancient goddess.

She got within a few feet of me and stopped, stretching out her hand.

"Give me the amulet," she demanded. "You're not worthy of it."

I scoffed. "Um, excuse me? Says who? You're an evil, power-hungry, forgotten goddess. I hardly think that makes you the best judge."

Bast's beautiful face twisted in anger, turning it ugly.

Just kidding, that bitch even made murderous fury look good. The woman was a freaking goddess, for fuck's sake. I still hated her.

"How dare you call me forgotten?" she hissed at me. "I have an entire legion of followers in your world just waiting for my command. It won't be long until I've built enough power to return in my physical form, and then we'll see who's *forgotten*."

From the back of her loincloth situation, she produced a huge, deadly sharp-looking dagger. Where the fuck she had just been storing that, I didn't even want to know.

"If you don't hand it over willingly, I'll simply need to cut it from your neck as you lie dying at my feet." As she spoke, raising her knife, she swayed closer to me, and her eyes seemed to go all creepy. Like, the pupils thinned out to slits, and the gold irises—weirdly, the same color as my own—expanded to cover the whites.

Cat eyes. She had cat eyes.

Oh, shit!

I'd been so caught up in staring into her eyes, I just barely dodged the swing of her blade. What kind of freaky-ass hypnotic bullshit—

"Fuck!" I yelped, scrambling and barely keeping my feet as she advanced on me with seriously impressive skills. It was all I could do to keep backing out of her reach.

Where were the guys? My guardians? Why weren't they leaping into this mess to save me?

I spared a fraction of a second to look around for them and screamed.

Full. On. Screamed.

The three of them were surrounded by... *Oh wow, deep breaths, Cleo. Deep fucking breaths. If you pass out now, you're dead. Finished. Gone.*

With one eye on Bast—because the bitch was trying to kill me—I tried to process what was happening. My guardians, all in big cat form, were surrounded and being attacked by mummies—and I did *not* mean British mothers. I meant legit dead people wrapped all in bandages, yet somehow totally animated and kind of badass fighters.

What. The. Fuck?

This took psychotic breaks to a whole other level. Which sort of made sense given my head injury. But if I died in a hallucination, would I die in real life too?

"Oh, you just spotted my helpers?" the goddess sneered at me, slicing at me with her blade and forcing me back a few more steps. We were moving farther and farther away from my cats, and it was spiking my anxiety. "It was so kind of Hatshepsut to bury her entire army with her, arrogant bitch that she was. A little shot of goddess magic and voilà. Indestructible minions."

Well shit. Did she just say "indestructible"? That... wasn't good.

"Hey!" I shouted, pointing across the room. "What the fuck is that?"

Now, you might be thinking that no one is seriously dumb enough to fall for the oldest trick in the book. And you'd be right. She did not. Instead, I turned and freaking bolted as fast and as far as my legs could carry me.

Which was all of about a hundred feet, until I hit the far wall of the burial chamber and found a grand total of zero exits.

Yep, I was screwed. I wasn't the fittest half human out there, and I was already getting winded. Sooner or later she'd just cut my throat or something.

The evil goddess knew it too. She didn't even hurry to follow me, just wandered casually—sexually—across the space, picking her way through ripped-up, writhing mummies and spinning her pointy dagger around her fingers.

Watching her approach, I clutched my amulet tight inside my fist.

"Okay, now would be a really awesome time to do something magical," I hissed at it. "Anything. Anything at all. You seemed to have no issues dragging me halfway around Boston when I was lost, so a little help right now when I'm about to get skewered by a really pretty, really old chick—that'd be great."

For a hot second... nothing happened.

Nothing.

Useless piece of—

Right when I was considering throwing the damn necklace at Bast because it was clearly defective, it started humming in my grip.

"Yes!" I crowed, jumping up and down with excitement.

My rapid change of mood seemed to startle Bast, and she paused halfway across the room, frowning at me in suspicion. But too freaking bad because my amulet was finally doing *something*.

The humming intensified, and I released the necklace from my grip, gaping as it glowed and floated just above my white tank top. The glow intensified, then abruptly shot out from the gold disc in a laser of light. Straight into the dead center of Hatshepsut's sarcophagus.

"Oh crap," I groaned. "Not more dead people."

The lid of the coffin slid to the side as though from an invisible force and crashed to the ground. So dramatic. Mentally, I cursed the amulet in all the creative ways I could think up while bracing myself for yet another reanimated dead thing.

Shudder. So creepy.

To my immense relief, the physical corpse of Queen Hatshepsut didn't climb out of the sarcophagus like a scene from *Night At The Museum*. Instead, a glowing, see-through woman rose up and floated to the floor.

As her toes touched the stone, she seemed to gain a fraction more substantiality, and her shimmering, gold-painted eyelids flickered open.

"Bast," she croaked, peering at my opponent with a furious glare. "I should have known you couldn't let me rest in peace."

The forgotten goddess's jaw dropped, and she stared at the slightly transparent version—spirit?—of Hatshepsut. Bast almost looked like— Oh wait, that was a good burn.

"Hey Bast," I snickered. "You look like you've seen a ghost."

Yeah, there it was.

"How?" Bast breathed in horror. "How is this possible? I didn't call your spirit forth. Only a goddess can do that, and I didn't—" Her words broke off, and her gaze snapped back to me. "You." She spat the word, then turned back to the dead pharaoh with a bitter laugh. "So the rumors are true, Hatshepsut? You had a bastard baby with Ra? How did you do it? How did you hide her in time?"

The spirit of my ancestor—er, mother—shook her head at Bast, a sly smile crossing her face. "Oh Bast, you fool. Cleo is my blood, but she's not Ra's. I told you when I was alive and I'll tell you again now, our relationship was purely friendship. My heart belongs elsewhere."

Bast scoffed an ugly sound. "Senenmut was infertile. You told me so yourself."

Hatshepsut smiled wider. "That's right. And what did you say when I confessed my most painful secret to you, old friend? When I came crying to you and told you about my heartbreak over never having a child with the man I truly loved? There I was, pharaoh, friend to the gods, powerful beyond belief but cursed to never have a child of my heart. What did you tell me, dear friend?"

My attention shifted back to Bast like I was at a tennis match, watching the ball volley back and forth. This last volley, hit by the spirit of one of Egypt's greatest rulers... this one hit the mark. Bast's beautiful face drained of color, and her golden eyes shot a quick glance at me.

Oh shit, they were talking about me!

"I..." Bast licked her lips, then shook her head in denial. "That night had nothing to do with *this*." She waved a hand in my direction, but the panic all over her face told me that night did indeed have everything to do with *this*. And by this, she meant me.

"Um." I raised my hand slightly. "I'd really like to know what happened that night. If anyone wants to fill in the gaps?"

Both glitteringly gorgeous women shot me a look, but it was Hatshepsut who obliged. Mostly, I think, to lord it over Bast, who was looking more and more uncomfortable.

"You offered me heqet, your very own blend. We were such good friends back then; what better way to forget my problems than to get drunk with good company, right, Bast?" She smirked. "But then Senenmut came looking for me, and what happened next?"

Bast shook her head again, and I ventured out on a limb.

"Uh, did you guys have a threesome? I was sort of getting that vibe from where this story was heading." Neither of the women responded, but neither denied it either. "Ho-ly cats," I breathed. "Am I... are you saying..." I waved my hand between the two of them, then mimed a bit of fucking. Just for good measure.

Hatshepsut shot me a grin, then turned her attention back to Bast. "The daughter of my heart is not the product of Ra. She's the product of *you*, dear friend."

"What. The. Fuck?" I blurted out my exclamation, but my shock had fucking nothing on Bast's right now.

All the blood seemed to have returned to her face, and she was turning an odd shade of outrage. Yeah, that's definitely a color.

"Watch out!" I shouted to the spirit of my mother, just moments before Bast's blade sliced clean through her midsection.

Hatshepsut looked down, peering at her totally unblemished body, then shot Bast a smug smile. "I'm not here in physical form, Bastet. You can't silence me like you did the last time we argued."

"Maybe not," Bast sneered, "but your love child is flesh and blood, and I just bet my blade will do some damage to her."

Oh shit.

Bast suddenly bolted across the room—straight at me. She was no match for the speed of a spirit, though. Hatshepsut smashed into me with the full force of what seemed like a pretty damn physical body, knocking me backward and landing me on my ass with my back to the wall.

"Where did she go?" Bast shrieked, pausing as she stood over me to whip her gaze around the room. "Where is that bitch?"

"Huh?" I replied, blinking at the weird double vision I was experiencing. "What are you..." I trailed off as my hands braced on the floor and pushed me smoothly to my feet. Totally without my guidance. My old English lit professor used to bang on and on about independent body movements, but this? This was the perfect example. My body was no longer in my control, and I was *shit scared*.

"Looking for someone?" I asked, but it wasn't me. I didn't say that! Yet it was my lips that moved and my voice that came out, and *oh my cats, I'm being possessed!*

Bast sneered, looking at me with total contempt. "Sneaky trick, Hatshepsut. But this just means I can kill you both at the same time." She slashed with her knife, and it clashed against mine.

Wait, what? Where the fuck did I get a knife?

In my panic, I somehow regained a flicker of control. Just enough to look down at myself and find my jeans, tank, and denim jacket fading out, being replaced by the linen, gold, and beaded *thing* that Hatshepsut's spirit had been wearing. I guess that explained where the knives had come from? Both my hands—still with the chipped, glitter nail polish—gripped a foot-long, deadly sharp dagger with scary level confidence.

That small moment of inspecting myself gave Bast an opening, and her single blade slashed across my bare upper arm, opening a stinging slice in my flesh.

Holy fucking cats, that *hurt!*

"Stop it," my own voice snapped at me. "You'll get yourself killed like that. Just let me deal with this."

As hard as it was to relinquish control of my own freaking body, she kind of had a point. All I wanted to do was howl in pain at that cut on my arm, so I could only imagine how painful getting shish-kebabbed would be. Yep, let's let the professionals handle this one.

In fact, maybe I should take some notes. One thing was for damn sure, if I made it out alive, then the guys needed to teach me to defend myself. This damsel in distress bullshit was bullshit.

My body dodged out of the way of Bast's weapon, taking my back away from the wall and giving "me" some room to maneuver within.

"Come and get it, kitty," my voice taunted the ancient goddess, and I snorted a mental laugh. Guess I now knew where I got my snark from. Mom was a bad*ass*. Which she then proved over and over and freaking over as her and Bast faced off in what had to be a battle of epic proportions.

I was desperate to know what was going on with the guys, but didn't dare break Hatshepsut's concentration to check on them. Judging by how many mummies I'd seen surrounding them before, they would be busy for a while.

If they were still alive.

Fuck, what if they'd been overpowered? Bast had said those mummies were indestructible!

Without meaning to, my eyes shot across the room, searching out the three cat shifters who'd sworn to protect me. Thankfully, they were all still alive and kicking. Just, several patches of the stone floor showed bright red puddles of blood, and I was pretty confident mummies didn't bleed.

"Fuck!" I screamed as Bast's blade nicked my exposed side, and

I immediately retreated into the back seat of my own mind again.

"*Sorry!*" I mentally apologized to my mother. "*I won't do it again. I was just really worried and—*"

"*It's fine,*" her scratchy voice replied inside my head. "*The guardian bond is powerful. It's nice to see that it's survived all these years.*"

I suspected there was more of a story there, but I wasn't risking my own skin by pressing her while she was in the middle of a high speed knife fight.

It was minutes later that Hatshepsut finally managed to get the upper hand, and Bast's blade skittered across the stone floor out of her reach. Not a second too soon, as well. Despite Hatshepsut's insanely impressive knife-fighting skills, she was still working with my physical body. A physical body that was not even remotely conditioned for this level of activity. All my muscles ached and screamed in pain, and a quiver was building in my arms.

When Hatshepsut tripped Bast in a well-placed leg swing, something in my back popped, and I whimpered silently. So much for never having to visit a gym again... I got the feeling my newfound magic was just the beginning of a long ,hard slog with a personal trainer. Probably a mean, snappy, brutish dickhead of a trainer. Named Raze.

"You can't kill me," Bast sneered, blood flecking her lips from where we had punched her in the mouth moments ago. "Not in your daughter's body. You wouldn't curse the child of your heart like that."

I sensed Hatshepsut's resignation and wondered what the fuck that was all about. Would I be cursed for killing Bast? Like, actually cursed? Or was that a figure of speech in one of those, "This isn't over!" sort of ways?

"You're right," Hatshepsut said in a soft, regret-filled voice, "but I can't leave you free to try this again."

She—we—drew in a deep breath and tapped into something deep inside me. Something warm and comforting and familiar. It glowed bright in my mind and slowly grew to encompass my whole form. Only when every inch of me was bathed in that beautiful light did it reach out and touch my amulet.

When that happened, Hatshepsut slammed one of her knives down into Bast's chest. But it was still *my* hand holding the knife. It was still *my* hand that felt the resistance of flesh, muscle, bone. The spongy tearing of the blade piercing her heart, then coming out the other side and sticking into the stone.

Just how fucking hard Hatshepsut must have driven it in, I couldn't even comprehend, but it was what happened next that prevented me from losing my mind and vomiting everywhere.

Bast's body seemed to drown in that light emanating from me, then that same light slowly began retreating into the amulet... taking her with it.

Moments later, I crouched alone on the floor, clutching a bloody dagger stuck into a floor tile, but Bast was nowhere to be seen.

Nor, it seemed, was my ancient mother's ghost.

"Hello?" I whispered, testing my voice to check that I was

indeed back in control of my own body. Yep. There it was, out loud. "Hatshepsut?" I tried again, releasing the dagger and looking around frantically. "Mom?" I tried again. "Where are you?"

Nothing.

No ghosts popping out from behind anything and yelling "Surprise!"

No crazy, murderous goddesses trying to slice my head off.

No hordes of reanimated mummies trying to eat my brains. Did mummies eat brains? No, that was just zombies.

Down at the other end of the slightly trashed burial chamber, my three guardians looked just as confused as me. Shreds of bandages lay scattered all around them. Chunks of mummy were everywhere, but none of pieces moved. It was like the life had just been yanked out of them all, and suddenly they were just... dead dudes.

Actually, that's exactly what just happened.

"Are you guys okay?" I called out, stumbling as I pushed to my feet, then steadying myself with a hand on a pillar. The gold beads on my skirt brushed over a graze on my thigh as I moved, and I hissed with pain.

Ah shit. Gold beads? Skirt? Fucking Hatshepsut had stolen my denim!

Boden shifted back into human form and met me halfway, grabbing me in a quick hug before pushing me to arm's length and scanning my whole body with his eyes.

"Are you okay, beautiful?" he asked with a cautious frown. "You were... ah..." He waved his hand in the air, like he was totally lost for words. Huh, wasn't that cute? I'd rendered Boden speechless.

"Totally badass?" I grinned, finishing for him. "I wish I could claim credit for that one." His brows shot up, and I shook my head. "I'll explain later over shots. Uh, are they okay?" I indicated to Raze and Hunter, both still in beast form but watching us carefully.

Boden gave them a glance, then nodded. "They're fine. Just took a few injuries that will prevent them from shifting until they replace some energy. Uh, this is an interesting costume change." He tugged on my black, braided, and beaded hair, which showed beneath a heavy, striped headdress.

"Ugh, good point," I muttered, peeling it off my head and wondering how in Egyptian Hell it had stayed put throughout that entire fight scene.

When it was off, Boden heaved a sigh of relief. "Oh good," he murmured, running his fingers through my hair and ruffling it. "That was a wig."

"Huh?" I looked down at the headdress in my hand and noticed it had a wig attached. My own hair—shoulder length, chemically straightened, and obnoxiously hot pink—was still there on my head. "Damn."

Boden grinned. "I like the pink. It's very you."

I scowled at him, then looked around us. "Okay, any bright ideas on how the fuck we get out of here?"

"No, but I know someone who can help." He took me by the hand and led me across the room, behind where Hatshepsut's open sarcophagus sat, and stopped us in front of an ornately carved stone block. Possibly the same one I'd smacked my head on when we arrived.

Using some seriously impressive strength, Boden pushed the top of the block, and it slid open, proving that it was a box, not a block. Inside, though, was a rather pleasant surprise.

"Well hello, Scarface," I said, grinning down at the rather squished cultist. "You said he was a sorcerer, didn't you?" I asked Boden, and he nodded.

"Raze stashed him here when all the madness started with the, uh, the mummies. Wow, I never thought I'd say that." He scrubbed a hand over his face, looking exhausted. "Anyway, silver linings. Axle's specialty is portals."

"Fuck you, I'm not helping you!" the tattooed cultist snarled, but I think deep down he knew he was going to need to. It was either that or starve to death in the bottom of a pyramid with the rest of us.

So, you know, lots of good options there!

CHAPTER
TWENTY FOUR

H unter gave me a stupidly sexy pout, reclining on my huge pile of pillows like a magazine spread with a corner of sheet just barely covering his dick. Damn, I was tempted to yank it off, but then I'd be even later than I already was.

"Come on, Cleo-babe," he coaxed. "Five more minutes? I'll make it worth your while." He waggled his eyebrows suggestively, and I grinned.

"Five minutes my ass, Crocodile Hunter," I snickered.

He gave me a sly smile. "Your ass? No, we need more than five minutes for that. You'll just have to cancel your plans and stay in with me."

I leaned over him, snatching my bra off the lamp and dropping a quick—okay, not so quick—kiss on his lips.

"Nice try," I murmured back when our mouths separated. "But I'm not falling for it. You've already made me too late to wash my hair, but I can't go without a shower."

I evaded his attempt to pull me back into bed and slipped into the adjoining bathroom. I left the door open so we could still chat, though, and heard him laugh as I cranked the shower taps.

"Are you sure?" he called out with an edge of teasing. "I don't think there's anything wrong with having my scent on your skin. It's like a fine perfume."

I rolled my eyes as I jumped under the still cold water, then hurried to soap up with the bar of organic, unscented goat milk soap Boden had gifted me.

"Other shifters would disagree," I shouted back, rinsing the suds from my body and jumping back out. "Besides, weren't you supposed to be at some top secret Alliance meeting about half an hour ago?"

I poked my head back into the bedroom just in time to see him pick up my phone to check the time, then fly out of the bed like his ass was on fire.

"Catch you later, babe," he said, stopping to kiss me with his pants still undone and his shirt only halfway on. "Don't stay out too late; I'll worry."

I rolled my eyes as he ran his fine ass out of *my* house. I'd already given up reminding him that he didn't actually live here with me; it was falling on totally deaf ears. Hunter, it seemed, had a horrific case of selective hearing.

A few moments later I was doing up my bra when Boden poked his head into my room.

"He forgot the meeting, didn't he?"

I snickered a laugh. "Of course. What's the time?"

Boden checked his watch. "A full five minutes after you were supposed to leave. You almost ready?"

"Ugh!" I ran over to my wardrobe and grabbed the first dress my fingers fell on. "Help me zip?" I shimmied into the tight black dress and turned my back to Boden.

His fingers brushed over the freshly inked hieroglyphics down my spine as he zipped me into the garment, then dropped a soft kiss on the side of my neck. "I love that new tattoo," he told me with a small growl under his voice. "Raze can wait a few more minutes, can't he?"

The possessive way his hands gripped my hips left no room for wondering what he wanted to do with that time. Horny cat.

"Yeah, sure. A few minutes." My voice was heavy with sarcasm. "Why do you think I'm so late as it is?"

Boden sighed, but released me to finish getting dressed for my date with Raze.

Yes, that's right, you're not imagining things. I was going on a *date* with Raze. In the month since my showdown with Bast, it'd become pretty clear that Raze was not down with the polyamorous lifestyle. Shit, huh? On the upside, he also wasn't cool with bowing out and letting Hunter and Boden have all my... er... time. So we were just taking things slowly.

Result: date night.

Which I was getting later for by the minute.

"Shoo," I scolded Boden. "Tell Raze I'll be down in seven and a half minutes."

Boden nodded, kissing me on the bare shoulder before clattering down my awesome, old wooden stairs.

When we'd returned from nearly dying inside a freaking pyramid, there had been a whole load of questions waiting for us. Not only had some helpful shifter cleaned up the wreckage of my truck and turned in all our wallets—with IDs—they'd also discovered the burnt-out safe house. Apparently, Boden was supposed to keep them informed of these things and hadn't.

After the Alliance was satisfied with our tale of events, they let us go. But not without a million warnings and ominous threats that I was pretty positive were just posturing. They didn't know what to do with me—and I hadn't told them anything that Hatshepsut had revealed of my origin—so for lack of any better ideas, we'd been released.

As an apology for my poor Candy Jack being wrecked on the side of the road somewhere, Hunter had insisted on buying me a house. The idea that I was essentially homeless was just not working for him, but I couldn't swallow the extravagant mansions he'd kept sending me on real estate websites.

Instead, I'd settled on a crumbling, derelict, old hotel from 1916. The place was insane with all original woodwork and an incredible history. It had needed a huge overhaul to get it livable, but with the help of a few shifter tradespeople, it had all been done in a week.

Now I was the proud owner of a gorgeously restored, possibly haunted, former hotel in my home state of Oregon.

"Shoes and jewelry," I muttered to myself, looking around my room for the items in question. Shoes, tick. There was a pair of killer, black, lace-up stiletto boots poking out from under my bed.

After they were on my feet, I hurried back into my bathroom to put my jewelry on. I was already wearing a necklace—duh—but I hooked some little earrings in and clipped on my favorite bracelets. Okay, technically they weren't *mine*, but what was I supposed to do with all the jewelry Hatshepsut had left me wearing? I guess I could have left it all in her tomb, but at the time I'd been more concerned with getting our asses home.

Anyway, the gorgeously detailed, twisted bronze bracelet was a piece I wore almost every day. Hunter had teased me that it technically made me a graverobber, and now it was known as my graverobber's bracelet. I loved it.

Satisfied, I started to leave the bathroom, then did a doubletake at the mirror.

What the...

I stepped closer, lifted my hand, and wiped the condensation from the glass.

"Fucking claws," I gasped, clapping a hand to my lips and staring in horror at my reflection. Panicked, I turned in a circle just to confirm that there was no one else in the bathroom with me before peering back into the mirror.

Peering back at me... wasn't me. I mean yeah, she had my eyes and the same dark bronze skin, but that? That wasn't me. That was Bast.

"Surprise," my reflection whispered at me, and my heart thundered so hard I worried about cardiac arrest. "We're not even close to done, daughter of my power. Not even close."

The smirk Bast gave me in the mirror sent so much fear rippling through me I lashed out, grabbing my hairdryer from the vanity and smashing the mirror with it.

As the glass shattered and dropped into the sink, my chest heaved and my breath came in short, sharp gasps. Holy shit. Holy fucking shit.

"Margaret?" Raze boomed, his boots clattering through my house and into my bedroom. "What happened?" he demanded, looking from my broken mirror to the hairdryer in my hand to my face, which—I was pretty sure—looked like I'd seen a ghost.

Because I had.

Dropping the hairdryer, I launched myself into his arms, shuddering into his tight hug, and tucked my face into the crook of his neck. My feet were dangling off the ground, and I didn't even care. I was fucking terrified.

"Bast," I sobbed out. "She's back."

STAY IN TOUCH

Facebook page: www.facebook.com/tatejamesfans
Facebook group: www.facebook.com/groups/tatejames.thefoxhole
Website: www.tatejamesauthor.com
Newsletter: https://mailchi.mp/cd2e798d3bbf/subscribe

ALSO BY
TATE JAMES

KIT DAVENPORT SERIES
The Vixen's Lead
The Dragon's Wing
The Tiger's Ambush
The Viper's Nest
The Crow's Murder
The Alpha's Pack
Novella: *The Hellhound's Legion*

THE ROYAL TRIALS
Imposter
Seeker
Heir (2019)

CO-AUTHORED WITH C.M. STUNICH
HIJINKS HAREM
Elements of Mischief
Elements of Ruin
Elements of Desire

THE WILD HUNT MOTORCYCLE CLUB

Dark Glitter

Cruel Glamour (TBD)

Torn Gossamer (TBD)

FOXFIRE BURNING

The Nine

The Tail Game (TBD)

CO-AUTHORED WITH JAYMIN EVE
DARK LEGACY SERIES

Broken Wings

Broken Trust

Broken Legacy

46707840R00174

Printed in Poland
by Amazon Fulfillment
Poland Sp. z o.o., Wrocław